# Lay in Hollywood

Jean Marie Stanberry

This is a work of fiction. Names, characters, businesses, places, events and incidents are either the products of the author's imagination or used in a fictitious manner. Any resemblance to actual persons, living or dead, or actual events is purely coincidental.



ISBN: 1482395096
ISBN-13:9781482395099

# DEDICATION

Dedicated to my wonderful family. My husband Gary and my kids Ryan and Lauren. They are my inspiration for every single moment of my life and I love them with all my heart.

# CHAPTER 1

Only two more miles, I told myself, as I fought exhaustion and struggled to keep my eyes open. I couldn't remember when I had ever been so sleepy. The urge to close my eyes, just for a moment, was almost overpowering. As I struggled with my waning alertness, it became a sincere effort to keep my SUV from sliding off the snow dusted and winding, two lane road.

Darkness was just creeping over the valley, and a light snow was drifting through the tall pines. I could only anticipate how good my bed was going to feel when I finally made it home. I silently reprimanded myself, I should have never attempted the drive down from Denver tonight. I had already been fighting total exhaustion when my plane landed in Denver, it had been ridiculous to believe I could drive all the way home to Colorado Springs on barely any sleep at all.

Call it denial, I guess. I wasn't as young as I used to be and I couldn't burn the candle at both ends like I used to. Now that I was getting older, I had a hard time sleeping on long flights. I had realized, much too late, that I should have found myself a hotel room and resumed my journey in the morning. Unfortunately, my guilt over my long absence was overriding my own common sense. I couldn't help it, I was missing my husband Greg, and my own comfortable bed.

I had just endured more than 30 straight hours of flying and airport transfers, making my way back from Beijing, China to Denver. When I had arrived in Denver finally, I had foolishly thought I could make the more than seventy mile drive back to my home in Colorado Springs without stopping and resting, but I was rueing my decision now.

Seventy miles doesn't seem all that far when a person has just crossed half the globe, though every inch of my thoroughly exhausted body was protesting loudly right now. If I could only make it these last two miles, I would be home, I told myself again, in a last ditch attempt to rally my alertness and end my desperate journey.

The snow was coming down harder now and the wind was picking up, swirling the snow around in little eddies on the blacktop. I tried to ignore the way it mesmerized me, threatening my alertness. I couldn't let my guard down for a single second. I crested a small rise in the highway and was startled when my headlights illuminated a deer, standing there in the middle of the darkened highway. Despite my sleep deprived reflexes, I managed to tromp on the breaks, causing my SUV to careen sideways across the snow covered road.

Luckily, my traction control kicked in and my tires suddenly gripped the pavement, allowing me to steer out of the skid, the deer leapt out of the way at the very last second. I let my breath out in a rush, as my heart beat anxiously in anticipation of the impact, that luckily, never came. I sat there, catching my breath for a few seconds, then I resumed my urgent drive home.

The radio was playing softly, but I turned it all the way down, in an effort to concentrate on my driving in the now, fading daylight. I wondered if Greg was even home. I had called him when I reached the airport in Denver, but he hadn't answered at home, or on his cell.

He sometimes met with clients in the evening, so I hadn't been too worried. Though my close encounter with that deer had renewed a concern in me. Greg was sometimes a distracted driver, he was not good at multitasking. If his cell phone rang or he was distracted for even a second, in this weather, it could be tragic! I could only hope that he hadn't encountered a deer on the way home and slid off the road somewhere.

Night was rapidly engulfing the valley as I finally reached the curve in the road where our driveway met the main road. I smiled in relief when I saw our mailbox, leaning crookedly on it's post, a result of teenagers trying to knock it off with a baseball bat. I was finally home.

I turned into our blacktop drive, which was already completely covered with snow. There were no tire tracks to indicate that Greg had already arrived home. My headlights illuminated the front of our expansive, craftsman style house. The last golden rays of light were filtering through the clouds, mimicking the muted oranges and pinks of watercolor paintings. The light was fading rapidly, as the purple shadows of night enveloped the tall mountain peaks which were already covered in snow. The air was brisk, and a light, powdery, snow was sifting through the tall firs in the front yard. I couldn't help but draw in a deep sigh of contentment. I loved to travel, but coming home to my familiar surroundings was always a joy.

The front yard was shimmering with it's light blanket of snow. I smiled to myself, I loved this time of year. Fall and winter were definitely my favorite time of year. Thanksgiving was coming up next week, then Christmas would be here before I knew it. The valley would be covered in a blanket of snow and there would be all kinds of fun things to do. Snowmobiling, snowshoeing, and of course, skiing. I sighed dreamily, I hoped I would actually have time to go skiing!

I pulled my car into the garage, it was empty, Greg wasn't home yet. I looked at the clock on my dash, it wasn't quite five yet, he wouldn't be home for at least half an hour.

The house was chilly and echoing as I let myself in. I went straight to the thermostat and turned it up to 65. Greg was an avid energy saver, he was always turning the thermostat down to save energy, a noble cause, but I could never tolerate the thermostat set at sixty. I rubbed my hands together, trying to warm them, then I turned the gas fireplace on too, as I shivered at the chill.

I looked around the house in awe, it looked exactly like it had when I left. I glanced around, thoroughly amazed that the kitchen was so clean, everything was put away and there were no dishes in the sink. The wood floors and the leather furniture in the living room were gleaming, there were no newspapers laying around, no soda pop cans sitting on the end tables.

I smiled in amazement as I looked around our tidy house, I couldn't believe it. Maybe Greg was finally growing up. Usually, whenever I came home from an extended trip, the house was a complete mess. In fact, since I had been gone more than two weeks I had been dreading coming home at all. I could barely tolerate the thought of coming home to a house that was completely trashed.

It was weird, for someone who was so immaculate in their grooming and organized at work, Greg was pretty much a pig. For some reason, he never felt the need to pick up after himself. I found it inconceivable that Greg never seemed to be bothered by his underwear laying on the floor in the bedroom or three or four pairs of shoes laying around in the foyer. What Greg really needed was a caretaker, he didn't know what to do on his own, it seemed.

This fall had been a bit of a shock to my system. I was forty two years old and Greg and I had just began our first year as empty nesters when our youngest child, our daughter Baylee, had went away to college at Stanford. Our son Ramsey, who was not quite, two years older, was also away at college, in Boston, and I had still barely adjusted to him being away so much. My busy life as a wife and mother with two kids at home, had suddenly turned around...now it was just Greg and I. I felt completely lost.

For the past ten years our family had been living happily here in Colorado Springs. We had escaped from our high stress lives in Chicago and traded them for the beautiful scenery of the Rocky mountains and a slower paced life. Initially, we had moved for Greg's job, but it turned out that it had been a good move for all of us.

I had produced TV commercials with an Advertising firm when we lived in Chicago, but when we moved to Colorado, I was happy to have the opportunity to do what I really wanted to do, which was be involved in figure skating. Colorado Springs has one of the largest and most renowned ice training facilities in the country, and I found myself lucky enough to secure a position there as a figure skating coach and choreographer.

Since my own retirement from competitive skating, it was the choreography aspect of figure skating that seemed to be my best talent, so now I had the honor to be choreographer to some of the biggest names in figure skating.

Things had started out slow for me, when we moved to Colorado Springs. I wasn't as well known as a lot of the coaches working at the rink in Colorado Springs. My own competitive figure skating career had ended abruptly when I was quite young, and for most of my career, I had traveled in Europe with the European Theater Company's ice show. Before Greg and I married, I had continued to travel with the company as their lead choreographer, as a result, I was well known in Europe, but virtually unknown in the states.

After Ramsey was born, I needed a job with hours that were more predictable. I gave up choreography and settled into my desk job. That had been nearly twenty years ago, so when I arrived in Colorado Springs ten years ago, hoping to step back into the business, I found most people had never even heard of me. Don't get me wrong, in many aspects, that was a good thing. Though in the beginning I wondered if I would ever be as busy and sought after as the rest of the coaches and choreographers.

Luckily, it seemed like it was only a matter of time before I became the busiest choreographer at the rink. Now, I could barely keep up, I was so busy with my big name skaters, not to mention all the up and coming skaters clamoring for me to choreograph a program or two for them.

I felt elated to finally be back in the midst of things. I had been forced to abandon my own career in figure skating after a tragic car accident left me critically injured to the point, most people thought I would never skate again. After an extended recovery, I did manage to return to the ice, though never in the capacity I wished for. My career as a competitive skater had ended forever, but after my kids were born I was happy enough to have my own life put on hold while I kept busy with all their activities.

My husband Greg, an architect, and I had been married for more than twenty years now. With Baylee going away to college, I had been anxious about my now, empty nest at home. I didn't deal well with leisure time, so I had taken on a bit more work than usual this season. Greg had always been understanding of my travel requirements for my career, but this fall, my cram packed schedule had me out of town almost more often than not, it seemed, and it had become a point of contention.

Recently, Greg had been very moody, he was not exactly, happy about my extensive travel requirements. I had gone from being the caretaker of an entire household, to a busy working woman, who was only home a few days a month during the winter months. All the things that Greg and I enjoyed doing together, like skiing, had seemingly fallen to the wayside.

I was enjoying my new found fame as a choreographer, though Greg was not as happy about my new found popularity. He took it personally, he felt like I was abandoning him.

Honestly, I thought he was being a big baby, I had waited a long time to pursue my dreams of being a choreographer. All those years I had given up my own life, to be a mom. I had to turn down work all the time, as I didn't want to take off and leave the kids behind.

I didn't want to subject my children to the same lonely childhood I had. My own mother had been a professional dancer and choreographer for Broadway shows, she had never been around much. I'd pretty much had to fend for myself for as long as I could remember. I didn't want that kind of life for my kids. I wanted to be a real mother to my children.

Greg, on the other hand, was an adult. When we moved here to Colorado Springs, I had been lonely and missing my career and my friends. It was Greg, who suggested that I go back to doing ice choreography. I was overjoyed to be back on the ice, doing what I loved. I was happy that Greg had urged me to do, what seemed to be, in my blood. Lately though, all he ever did was complain about my schedule. He didn't like it, that I was gone a lot during the winter months. He was not good at fending for himself, but I figured there was never a better time for him to learn. I was wrong...

I curled up on the couch in front of the fireplace to wait up for Greg. Unfortunately, I was completely exhausted. I could feel the energy draining out of my body quickly, so after about an hour, I finally dragged my weary body to bed.

After sleeping more than twelve straight hours, I finally woke up and forced myself to drag my aching body out of bed. Even with all the traveling I had done lately, I still didn't deal well with jet lag, though I did seem to be feeling a bit better.

I pulled my robe on, stretched lazily, and wandered into the kitchen to make some coffee. The house was empty and echoing, I realized it was nearly nine a.m. and Greg wasn't home. I wasn't sure if I had slept so soundly I had missed him, or if he had never even came home last night.

As I glanced around the kitchen at the still gleaming countertops and relative lack of clutter, it seemed as if the house hadn't been lived in for days, in fact, it seemed exactly the same as I had left it, more than two weeks ago.

My heart was suddenly pounding with worry, what if something had happened to him while I was away? I had spoke with him before I left China, but that had been more than 48 hours ago now, he could be off an embankment somewhere!

I was suddenly acutely worried about him, so I called his office and his secretary, Jill put me right through to him.

"Greg it's me, are you okay?" I breathed when I heard his voice, I suddenly felt foolish for panicking like that.

"Yeah, I'm fine, why?" he snapped, his voice sounded cold and aloof. I immediately felt as if I was irritating him.

"It's just that I got home from China last night and the house looks like no one has even lived here since I left. I was worried that something had happened to you," I said.

"Lane, we need to talk, can you meet me for lunch?" he asked, I was surprised by the seriousness in his tone. His voice sounded different...distant, emotionless. I was suddenly on edge, something was not right.

"Sure Greg, is something wrong?" I asked. My mouth was dry and I could feel the panic rising in my chest once again, as my 6th sense told me that yes, something was wrong.

"It's kind of complicated to get into over the phone. We'll talk at lunch," said Greg, his voice was cold and dismissive.

I sighed, slightly frustrated. Whatever it was, he wasn't willing to tell me what was up, over the phone. I didn't even press him to tell me, the point was mute. Greg would tell me when he was good and ready, that's just how he was. I was certain that the news he had for me, was not good.

I frowned as I leaned against the kitchen counter and took a sip of my coffee. I had a good idea what was bothering him. Lately, Greg hated it that I traveled so much, he had been fine with it at first, he had even been very proud that I had been following my dreams. Recently though, his attitude had changed. Every time I a planned a trip, it seemed as if Greg took it personally. He whined that I never paid any attention to him, that I was never around for him. This trip to China, had probably put him right over the edge!

I sighed miserably, as I glanced out the kitchen window at the light snow in the yard. The morning sun was illuminating the light dusting of snow and causing it to shimmer like an opal, brilliant and mesmerizing.

My shoulders were almost sagging in defeat already. I assumed the problem was, that Greg wanted me home more. He was old fashioned, he thought it was my job to stay home and take care of him and take care of our house. It wasn't hard for me, in the summer time. I could be outside, working in the flower beds and the vegetable garden. In the winter I felt cooped up. The house always seemed cold and lonely, the few hours I spent at the ice rink weren't enough for me.

My career in Colorado Springs had taken off eight years ago, when I had I agreed to be a coach and choreographer for Kyle and Lucie, a pairs couple who had just teamed up. Now they were twenty and twenty one years old, and I hoped, they would soon be World Champions.

When I first began coaching, there was never much need for me to travel far, I went to a few regional competitions, but I hadn't needed to travel far, or for more than a few days at a time. Now that I worked with World Class skaters I was obligated to accompany them wherever they needed to travel for competitions and exhibitions. It wasn't an issue for me, I loved to travel and I had been enjoying jetting all over the world, seeing all kinds of new and different places.

I was addicted now, I knew I didn't want to give up my new found freedom. It wasn't as if I was abandoning Greg on purpose, I'd invited him to come with me many times, but he refused. Greg really didn't care to fly. It wasn't that he was afraid to fly, but he hated airports and all the recent security fuss. According to Greg, he wasn't about to be harassed by the TSA just to fly to a skating competition he had no interest in.

So I always traveled alone, though now it seemed that Greg had an issue with that too. I wondered if I could ever win. I sighed, I guess if I just stayed home and took care of him, everything would be just fine.

# CHAPTER 2

Greg and I had made plans to meet at our favorite restaurant at 11:30. I was anxious just thinking about it, Greg had planned it early, before the lunch crowd arrived, so I assumed that he was expecting a confrontation. I sighed miserably at the prospect, I was finally happy with my life and my career, I really had no desire to fight with him about it.

When I arrived at the restaurant, Greg was already there, waiting for me. He was seated in a booth in the back corner, it was where we always sat. Everyone knew us there, we had lunch there at least twice a week in the summer time, though I hadn't been there in months, I'd been so busy.

Greg eyed me warily as I approached the table. He was sitting in the corner, with his back to the wall. Of course, I would sit in my usual spot across the table from him. I could already feel my resolve weakening. Greg exuded a presence, a confidence I guess, people rarely argued with him. His manner left no room for argument.

I gave him a slight smile, as I slid into the seat across from him. Even at forty five years old, Greg was very attractive. He was wearing a dark wool suit and a bold patterned yellow tie. His short, dark, hair was peppered with silver and it gave him the look of an aging movie star. His steel blue eyes appraised me cooly as I situated myself in our booth. I looked him over, silently wondering why he seemed so distant.

"Am I late?" I teased, flashing him a sly smile. Greg was always early, and he hated it when others were late, but I knew, I was right on time.

"You look good Lane," he said, not really answering my question. His voice was coarse with emotion.

"Ummm, thanks," I said, a little thrown off by the unexpected compliment. His eyes seemed to be assessing me carefully, I was surprised by his scrutiny, though I hadn't seen him in almost two weeks.

"That dress is nice, you should always wear dresses, you've definitely got the legs for it," he told me, then his eyes darted nervously back to the menu again.

I was wearing a gray sweater dress, and I had spent a great deal of time putting on my makeup and straightening my unruly blonde hair. My daughter Baylee had urged me to start straightening my naturally wavy hair. She told me it would make me look younger. I had been pleased with the results, I really did look younger. Today, my hair was straight and silky and parted to one side. I could almost hide behind it, if I let it fall into my face, which I was thinking would be a good thing, if there was a confrontation coming.

I had just picked up the menu, when our waitress Donna, who I have known for years, approached us to take our drink order.

"Well hey there Lane, I'm kind of surprised to see you here," she cried, flashing me an excited smile.

"Um, I've been out of town a lot, with my skaters," I told her distractedly. I looked up to see that Greg was giving her a bug eyed look and suddenly, I was acutely uncomfortable. Everything was wrong, why was she so surprised to see me, and why was Greg being so rude?

"Iced tea," snapped Greg, narrowing his eyes at her.

"Uhh, white wine," I mumbled, surprised that he was treating Donna so poorly.

Donna didn't seem to even notice that Greg was glaring at her, she was still staring at me as if I were an alien. It was completely unnerving me.

"I'll be right back with your drinks, you look gorgeous Lane, have you lost weight?" asked Donna, smiling at me.

"I don't think so," I told her with a shrug. People rarely saw me dressed up, so I guessed it was the dress. I had picked it on purpose, it was very flattering. It hugged all my curves and I felt very sexy in it. Greg had worked late last night, but I was hoping after seeing me today, he'd be home early tonight.

Greg gave Donna a stern look, she flashed him a fake smile and trotted away to get our drinks. I was glancing distractedly at the menu. I was nervous, I wanted to know what was up, but secretly, I was certain I didn't want to know. I wasn't sure what I would say to Greg, if he asked me to give up my career.

It was what I loved to do, I had traveled extensively before Greg and I were married. I had spent more than three years skating with the European Theater Company's ice show, then when injuries prevented me from continuing in my own professional career, I had worked as their choreographer for another two years.

I had given all that up for nearly twenty years to raise our children. Now I was back on the circuit and I was ecstatic, this was what I had always wanted to do.

I peeked over the top of my menu at Greg. He seemed nervous. That was not like him at all. Greg was always calm, cool and collected, and he always expected everyone to do exactly what he said.

I was anxious, unfortunately, I never fared well in confrontations, especially with Greg. I usually did whatever it was, he asked to me to do. I was pretty much a pushover. I closed my eyes and took a slow deep breath in an attempt to slow the furious beating of my heart. This time, his intimidation techniques, were not going to work on me.

"So, how was China?" he asked, nonchalantly, as he glanced over the menu. I frowned, he was trying to avoid making eye contact with me. I almost rolled my eyes, he didn't need to look at the menu, he always ordered the same thing.

"I wouldn't want to live there, it was much too crowded for me, but I enjoyed it. I love traveling, you know, seeing places I've never seen before and being immersed in another culture temporarily," I told him with a smile.

"Uh, yeah," said Greg, distractedly. I narrowed my eyes at him, he would just grunt, if that were an acceptable response to me, but he knew better.

"And your skaters, how did they do?" he asked, not even looking up from his menu.

"They took the silver, but it was so close, they missed the gold by just a few points. I was so proud of Kyle and Lucie, they did so well. I know they are going to take the gold medal at Worlds this year. They just keep getting better and better together," I told him, swallowing nervously.

I snuck a look at Greg, his jaw was clenched and he appeared to be far away in thought. I was almost trembling in anticipation, this was small talk, Greg was nervous, he was biding his time, whatever it was he wanted to say, was going to upset me. He was waiting for the proper moment. I was nervously waiting for the bomb to be dropped.

Donna returned to the table and set our drinks in front of us. Greg made a big deal of rooting through the sugars and sweeteners in the basket, looking for the raw sugar in a brown packet. Donna rolled her eyes miserably, she was eyeing me warily as she took our orders, which I found to be very odd.

"I'll have the salmon salad, Donna, and can I have the house dressing on the side?" I asked. I was so nervous, I didn't want anything too heavy.

"Certainly Mrs. ummm...Ms. Jensen," said Donna, stumbling over her words, she seemed incredibly nervous as she scratched my order on her pad. She seemed poised for flight and she never even made eye contact with Greg as she waited for him to order. I gave her a curious look, she was acting rather odd. Greg and I had been coming to this restaurant for years now, yet she was treating me as if I were a stranger. I was a bit shaken by it.

Greg ordered a reuben sandwich and fries, pretty much the same thing he always ordered. Donna nodded and gave us a fake smile, then she turned abruptly and headed for the kitchen. I frowned, something was definitely wrong. Donna was acting almost as strangely as Greg was.

I leaned back in my seat and took a sip of my wine, I wouldn't normally have wine with lunch, but my gut was telling me an alcoholic drink was in order. Greg took off his reading glasses and gave me his most serious look, his eyes looked empty and unfriendly. I could feel every fiber in my body constrict with fear.

"I guess you're wondering what is up," he said, staring at me seriously. I was chewing on my lower lip nervously, my heart was suddenly pounding in fear. I hated confrontations, and I knew without a doubt now, that a confrontation was definitely coming.

"Yes," I said. I was numb, my voice seemed to have no emotion in it.

Greg gave me a troubled look. His grayish blue eyes seemed steely and cold, I almost shivered, as they raked over me. Finally, he sighed deeply. "I guess the best thing to do is just spit it out."

I gave him a helpless shrug, for some reason I couldn't speak at all. I had no idea what news I was facing, though whatever it was, I could tell that Greg didn't want to tell me. Whatever the news was, it was going to make me very unhappy! I was suddenly fighting the urge to just chug my glass of wine and order another. Like I said before, I didn't deal well with confrontations!

"I wanted to be delicate about this, so I had to see you in person. I thought it might be a bit harsh to tell you over the phone, but the truth is, I'm moving out Lane." his voice was so distant and matter of fact, it didn't seem like it was coming out of the mouth of someone I had known and loved almost half of my life.

"What?" I mouthed, the shock was rushing over me like a surging tide. That hadn't been what I'd been expecting at all, and my head was suddenly spinning, unable to comprehend the meaning of his words. In the moments it took for my frenzied brain to absorb his words, my lower lip had started trembling and my heart suddenly felt like a rock. I could only hope that I had misunderstood him. I was staring at him blankly, unable to say another word.

"I'm sorry Lane, I'm moving out...I want a divorce," said Greg, his voice was flat and emotionless. I was shaking my head slowly, as if my denial could make his statement go away. I was suddenly struggling to breathe, my mind still couldn't seem to comprehend this. I had been expecting a fight, accusations, tears, but this...this was so final.

"But why?" I managed to breathe, my mind was suddenly going in a million directions. I could feel my chest constricting painfully, his face was completely serious, but I felt like dissolving into maniacal laughter. He was moving out...because I traveled too much?

I struggled to breathe and think, what had happened? Greg and I had been relatively happy, we rarely argued, except recently, about my frequent travel. We'd always had a loving and mature relationship. How could he suddenly want a divorce?

"Why are you doing this? Do you want me to stop traveling? Is that what this is about?" I asked, I couldn't come up with another reason for his unhappiness. My mind was racing, we were happy...I was sure we were happy. We never fought, the sex was great, what was happening?

"I'm sorry Lane, I'm just not happy anymore," said Greg, shrugging nonchalantly.

"Not happy?" the words seemed to stick in my throat. I thought about all the happy times we had together, our wedding, the birth of our children, all our family vacations. How could he possibly be unhappy? Sure our marriage had it's ups and downs, what marriage didn't? Granted, this winter I had been busy, and I had been away a lot, but in May, when all the competitions were over, the kids would come home from college and we would plan a cruise vacation, or a silly road trip of some sort and we would all have a fabulous time. It seemed completely inconceivable to me that he was unhappy.

"Where will you go?" I asked, but suddenly the lightbulb in my head lit up. I was so stupid, I had ignored all the signs, and they had all been right there in front of me! Greg wasn't asking to leave, he was already gone!

I shook my head numbly, I suddenly felt like a complete idiot. It was why the house had been relatively unchanged when I arrived home from China, he hadn't been there to mess it up. This was all planned, he was already living with another woman. I shuddered uncontrollably as it all became perfectly clear to me. I was biting on my lower lip, trying to suppress the tears that were rushing to my eyes.

My frazzled brain was working to process it all. I could see Donna staring at me, as she stood near the window where the food was passed from the kitchen. I shook my head slowly as I suddenly realized, Donna had been surprised to see me here with Greg, because he had been frequenting our favorite restaurant with another woman!

My chest was tight and I was struggling to take in a deep breath. My acute distress was slowly changing to anger, I couldn't believe it. Greg was leaving me because he was having an affair!

"It's kind of complicated Lane," said Greg, rolling his eyes miserably.

"It's not complicated at all! You are having an affair! Who is she Greg, do I know her?" I snapped, I was suddenly certain, he was leaving me for another woman.

Greg looked away, as if it was too painful to tell me. Then he turned to me and looked me in the eye confidently.

"It's Jill," said Greg, he was suddenly glancing at me warily, as if he expected me to jump up from the table and attack him.

Don't get me wrong, I wanted to. I totally wanted to slap the shit out of him. I just had a lot more class than that. My mind was reeling carelessly as it all sank in, it seemed too horrifying to be true. My husband of more than twenty years was having an affair with his secretary!

My heart sank painfully and I was completely bewildered. Jill was maybe twenty five years old, and completely gorgeous. She was dark skinned and exotic looking. She always wore clothes that drew attention to her recently augmented breasts. Of course, he was having an affair with someone I didn't have a snowball's chance in hell against!

"Jill!" I seethed. "You're kidding me, she's a child, she's like twenty five years old!"

"She's twenty seven, and I love her," cried Greg.

"Greg you are forty five years old! You are old enough to be her father! I can't believe you're going to abandon me after more than twenty years of marriage for that little slut!" I cried, I was already in serious danger of hyperventilating.

"She's not a slut, I love her. It was you who abandoned me!" snapped Greg.

"Oh, so being home alone gave you a little too much time on your hands, you couldn't help yourself, you had to have a little fling with your secretary!" I snapped.

"It wasn't a fling, I told you, I love her. We're going to get married," exclaimed Greg. I was rolling my eyes miserably and shaking my head in disgust. I was glad that the restaurant wasn't busy yet, because I was in grave danger of going off the deep end.

"You're pathetic Greg!" I snapped.

"It's your fault Lane, you never have time for me anymore, you're always running off somewhere with your skaters. I need someone who wants to be there for me," cried Greg.

"Greg, that's my job now, remember? I used to make TV commercials. Now I'm a choreographer, travel is part of my job, you were the one who encouraged me to do it in the first place! Remember how lonely I was after leaving all my friends and family behind? Go to the ice arena and get back into skating, that's what you told me Greg!"

"Well now I'm the one who's lonely," he seethed.

"Get a grip Greg, I've been taking care of you for more than twenty years, for the past several years I have finally been doing something for me, something I enjoy. I love skating, I've always loved skating and I pretty much gave it all up for the past nineteen years while our kids were home."

"I have taken care of our family and I've done every crazy thing you asked me to do. I left my job in Chicago, moved here, said goodbye to all my family and friends, all for you...and then you tell me you want a divorce," I cried, I was shaking my head miserably, I just couldn't believe it!

"I didn't do this on purpose, I was just lonely. I didn't plan it, it just happened,"

"Is she pregnant?" I asked, almost sure that she was.

"No, but she does want to start a family, so I guess sometime soon...after our divorce is final,"

I cringed, the words hit me like a knife through my chest. He was going to start a new family with a younger woman. I choked back a sob and put my face in my hands, this was worse than anything I could ever have imagined.

"I'm sorry Lane, Jill loves me, she wants to take care of me, start a family with me," he said.

I was staring at him in shock, that was it! I had always teased him about being a bit of a mama's boy. He still was, only he had switched mamas. He needed someone to take care of him constantly, since I had began traveling extensively, he had found someone else to take care of him. I sighed miserably.

"You're right Greg, we should get divorced. I can't live the rest of my life being your mama. Let Jill do it. Where do I need to sign?" I snapped. I knew I might as well go along with this as gracefully as possible. It was perfectly obvious, Greg had already made up his mind, the decision was already made. He had left no room for working things out with his wife of more than twenty years. What he needed was a caretaker, not a wife. Our kids were grown, I was done with being a caretaker. It was time for me to live my life.

"Lane please, I haven't even talked to a lawyer yet. I wanted to talk to you first. I don't want this to be painful, I didn't want to hurt you. I don't even want anything, you can have the house, the furniture, whatever you want," said Greg.

"You don't want this to be painful?" I mouthed, unable to believe he had even said that. Maybe it wasn't going to be painful for him, he was in love. I was an empty nester, all of a sudden, alone in my nest. I had been completely blindsided, I still couldn't even come up with a single emotion for what I was feeling right now. Maybe homicidal, I wasn't quite sure.

"I just want out, it's over for me. Don't worry Lane, you're beautiful and smart, you'll find someone else," he said, speaking to me like I was a teenager who was breaking up with her high school crush. Did he not realize how ridiculous this was? I was forty two years old! I didn't want to date! How could I ever find someone to grow old with? I was too old to start over again!

"Don't you realize, I don't care about any of that," I snapped. "I loved you, I thought you loved me. I thought we were going to grow old together, I've spent half my life raising our kids, taking care of you, now you're throwing it all away!"

Greg was just staring at me numbly as I ranted, I could feel the distance. I could see it in his eyes, now that he had someone else, he had turned off his feelings for me...he was right, it was over.

"I'm sorry Lane. Hey, maybe you and Justin could..."

"Greg!" I cried. I was staring at him in shock. He totally didn't get it! He thought I was afraid to be alone, that was the furthest thing from my mind right now. I was worried about our family, I had spent the last twenty years of my life nurturing our kids to ensure that they would be well adjusted adults. Granted the kids were grown now, but I still worried what they would think, their dad dumping their mom and moving in with a twenty seven year old. The very idea was preposterous! I rolled my eyes miserably.

"I didn't mean to...it's just that I worry about you being alone. I mean now that the kids are grown, maybe you and Justin..."

I was staring at Greg wide eyed, he was definitely loosing his marbles. I wanted to start screaming like a banshee, but knowing Greg, he would have me committed.

"You can never let it go, can you? After more than twenty years and two kids you still don't get it! I loved you Greg, and of course, I love Justin, he's my best friend. Do you still not realize what my own parents did to me? I was only fifteen years old!"

"He loves you Lane, he loves you more than you know. I could always feel it. He gave you up because he wanted you to be happy, to have the children he could never give you..."

"Stop it Greg!" I cried. My heart was pounding and I was suddenly struggling to breathe. I was biting my lower lip and clenching my fists in an effort to suppress the tears that were threatening to come bursting from my eyes. He was using my past against me again, as if any of that had effected our marriage over the last twenty years.

"Call me selfish if you want, but I want someone who only loves me. Jill adores me, she wants to be with me, and only me. With you, I'm always last. The kids were always first, I was okay with that, but now that they're out of the house, you've changed. You've thrown yourself into your work and you never even have a moment for me anymore," said Greg.

"When we're home together, all you ever do is sleep and watch TV, I hate to watch TV!" I cried.

"See Lane, we're just not compatible any more. Now that the kids are gone, you have all this nervous energy and you can't sit still, it's driving me crazy!" said Greg.

I was staring at him in shock. "You're divorcing me because I won't lounge around on the couch and watch TV with you?"

"It's more than that," snapped Greg.

"I'm listening," I said, trying uselessly to disguise the sarcasm that was sneaking into my voice.

"Regardless, it's over for me. There's really no point in arguing about it, we'll just go on all day placing the blame on each other," said Greg, giving me an arrogant glare. I made a face at him and resisted the urge to roll my eyes.

"Fine, but you're telling the kids." I snapped.

Baylee and Ramsey were both away at college, but I knew it would be a big shock to both of them. I figured it would be the biggest shock to Ramsey, he and Greg were close, they hunted together, they liked a lot of the same things. Greg had never really bonded with Baylee it seemed, the two of them always clashed and I was almost certain that she would not be shedding a tear over the news of our divorce.

My mind was still spinning uncontrollably, it seemed inconceivable to me, that Greg could throw away the last, more than twenty year of our lives, as if it were nothing but a bad dream. He felt like I had abandoned him, he was jealous of my skaters, he wanted a caretaker.

I bit my lower lip trying to suppress the tears that wanted to come rushing to my eyes. I didn't want to believe it was over, there had to be something I could do! I swallowed convulsively as my mind struggled to process my whirlwind of emotions.

Somehow, I managed to finish my awkward lunch with Greg, though the conversation between the two of us had pretty much ceased once I had come to the realization that it was over for him. There was no use making small talk after I realized that Greg no longer wanted me in his life. Greg picked up the check, then we parted ways, without so much as a kiss goodbye.

Greg headed back to his office, and I headed back to our empty house, which he had pretty much already vacated. It seemed surreal that this was probably the last time that Greg and I would have lunch at our favorite restaurant, that Greg wouldn't be coming home to our bed tonight.

Greg promised he would call both the kids and tell them what was going on. My heart felt heavy as I walked quickly against the cold wind in the parking lot. I barely noticed the icy fingers of the cold wind, I was already shaking. I climbed numbly into to my SUV, started the engine, and blasted the heat in a lame attempt to stop my shaking. It was only then, that I finally allowed myself to cry.

# CHAPTER 3

More than two weeks had passed since the day that Greg told me he wanted a divorce. Time seemed to march determinedly on without me. I wanted to climb into bed and let life pass me by, but realistically, that wasn't an option.

I battled sadness and regret, Greg had a new life, with a new love, while I spent Thanksgiving alone. Ramsey and Baylee couldn't get away for the short holiday, but I was happy that the kids would both be coming home for Christmas, at least that, made me feel a little bit better.

For the most part, I felt as if my life had ended and I had been thrust into hell. The sun continued to rise and set, of course, and I had no choice but to haul my butt out of bed every day and keep plugging along. I still couldn't believe this was actually happening to me, it seemed like a horrible nightmare that my body refused to wake up from.

I kept busy enough at the ice rink, luckily, I was able to throw myself into my work. Though later, when I came home, my house was empty. It felt cold and lonely. It seemed so lonely, I wasn't sure if I could keep the house after the divorce was final. I guess I was still holding out hope that somehow, Greg would change his mind.

I hated to sell the house, as a family, we had so many good memories there. I could remember all the Christmases we celebrated with the tall tree in the family room and a fire crackling in the fireplace, both the kid's Graduation celebrations with a barbecue on the patio. It seemed like a cruel slap in the face that Greg wanted to take all of that away from me.

It seemed so selfish, after all I had given him, after I had given so much to our family. Now it seemed, it wasn't good enough. Now Greg wanted to spend his life with someone else. Someone who was younger and sexier, someone who promised to take care of him as if he were a five year child, and actually needed a full time caretaker.

I sighed miserably just thinking about it, how could I possibly compete with a twenty seven year old? Everyone always told me I looked good, young for my age. I was fit and I barely had any lines on my face, most people were amazed when they found out I had two kids in college. Maybe I didn't look forty two, but even I, knew I couldn't compete with someone in their twenties.

Unfortunately, my troubles didn't end with the news of my upcoming divorce. Months had passed and it was late in February, the World Championships were coming up in less than a month. The only thing that had kept me going recently, was my star pairs team, Kyle and Lucie.

They had qualified once again to go to the World Championships and this year, I knew they were going to win! I was excited for them, they seemed to get better every day and the new long program I had designed was going to blow everyone away.

It was just after six a.m., I was standing at the edge of the ice, sipping a cup of coffee when Kyle skated up to me.

"Hey Lane, can I talk to you for a minute?" he asked, as he glided to a stop in front of me.

"Sure," I said, dragging my eyes away from Lucie, who was across the ice, spinning gracefully.

"I wanted you to be the first to know, Callie and I are getting married," said Kyle, giving me a big smile.

"That's fabulous!" I cried, throwing my arms around him and hugging him. I was happy for him, he had met Callie at the end of last season, at the World Championships. She was also a pairs skater who skated with a partner out of L.A. The two of them had hit it off immediately, they began dating and eventually they had fallen in love. Recently, they had been struggling to keep up their long distance relationship!

"Um, the bad news is that I'm leaving," said Kyle, his voice was suddenly breaking uncomfortably.

"You're leaving?" I cried, I was staring at him in shock, as what he was saying began to slowly sink in.

"Callie and I are going to be partners on the ice too, I'm moving to L.A. so we can work with her coach and choreographer," said Kyle, giving me a wry smile.

I was staring at him in shock. I loved Callie, she was a sweet girl, but he and Lucie were pure magic on the ice. Callie and her partner Will, were good skaters, but nowhere near the caliber he and Lucie were. I winced at the thought of him breaking up our team...it was a huge mistake!

"But...you and Lucie...you're going to win the Worlds this year," I was fumbling for the words, my head was spinning. I suddenly felt like I might pass out. This couldn't possibly be happening, I felt as if, my entire life was suddenly falling apart.

"I really wanted to wait until after this season was over, but I can't. Callie and I need to be together, I'm leaving for L.A. next week. I haven't even told Lucie yet," said Kyle, giving me an uncomfortable smile.

"You haven't told Lucie yet?" I whispered. I couldn't believe it! Were all men completely dense? Lucie was going to totally freak out! She had been working her ass off thinking that her and Kyle were going to be top contenders at Worlds this year, suddenly her partner was going to abandon her for someone else. My heart was suddenly aching for her, as I knew exactly how she would feel.

"I couldn't tell her, she's so excited about this season and how well we've been doing. I thought that maybe you could help me...you know, to tell her," said Kyle, looking at me earnestly.

I stared at him as if he were a lunatic, there was no way I could tell Lucie, I was already about to come unglued. My own life was spiraling out of control, there was no way I could be in on it, when Lucie is told that hers is about to do the same!

"Kyle I can't," I told him, tears were already coming to my eyes, I couldn't bare the thought of Kyle and Lucie giving up everything they'd worked so hard for this season.

"Please Lane, I don't know what to say to her," begged Kyle.

"What could you possibly say to her? She's going to be completely crushed!" I cried, I was totally on the verge of hyperventilating. Much like myself, Lucie was being completely blindsided. It was horrible...I could only imagine Lucie's reaction when she heard.

"I know...please Lane.."

"I'm sorry, I can't help you Kyle. When I came home from China, my own husband dropped the bomb on me that he wanted a divorce. Emotionally, I'm a complete wreck, you're going to have to do this without me," I told him. Then I ran into the changing room, so that Lucie wouldn't see my tears.

I secretly hoped that I wasn't around when he told Lucie. It was cowardly of me, but I wasn't strong enough to deal with Lucie's grief and mine. I really didn't feel strong enough to deal with anything right now!

# CHAPTER 4

Just when you think you can't go on in life, the sun keeps rising every morning and, of course, the rest of the world goes on around you. I knew I could succumb to the overwhelming sadness that seemed to be surrounding my heart, or I could buck up, and get on with my life.

It still seemed surreal that the spot next to me in the bed, which Greg had occupied nearly every night for more than twenty years was now cold and empty. I was miserably alone, for the first time in my life!

When I got up in the mornings, I only had to make enough coffee for me. I didn't even have a dog to take care of. Our faithful golden retriever had died last year at the age of fifteen. Neither Greg, nor I had the heart to replace him. I wished I had a dog now, though it really wouldn't be fair to the dog, I was rarely home anymore, it was really just a selfish thought! I wanted unconditional love, a tail that would wag every time I walked in the door.

Kyle had broke the news to Lucie, she had cried and cried and finally decided that she was going to live with her older sister in Connecticut. I had told her that maybe we could find her another partner, even though I knew the chances were slim. Fortunately, she wasn't interested right now. She was going through all the same emotions I was going through. She was too hurt to look for a partner. Her professional partner had left her and was skating with another. It was as emotional as the end of a marriage!

Weeks passed, one like the next. I was going through the motions, but I had fallen into a worthless existence. I felt like everyone I loved had abandoned me. My kids were both really supportive, they told me what a jerk their dad was for walking out on me, but there was really nothing they could do. It was over, there was nothing anyone could do. I just had to deal with it.

I was slowly starting to hate my life, in April I traveled to Paris for an invitational competition with one of my, up and coming pairs. When I came home, my house was echoing and dark, just like my life had become. I was falling into a deep depression and it was not like me at all. I had always been an eternal optimist, but my heart had been painfully broken. I feared at this point in my life, I might never recover.

My best friend Justin was trying to talk me into coming back to Chicago to stay with him for a little while. He hated it when I was sad, and he wanted to cheer me up.

Justin Melbourne had been my skating partner years ago and we'd been best friends since I was twelve. Greg had always been jealous of my close relationship with Justin, so I didn't think it would be a good idea for me to go stay with him just now. It might bring more bang to my divorce proceedings than I was willing to deal with. I wouldn't put it past Greg to accuse the two of us of having an affair.

I tried to throw myself into my work but my two most promising skaters were gone. I had another promising pair, but the female half was turning into quite a princess and I was pretty much done with her. I was sure she would never make it to the top with her attitude. At this point, I didn't have a lot of hope for the future, at least, not with the skaters I was coaching now.

It was a chilly April evening, I was at home, vegging on the couch. I had a fire in the fireplace and I was on the couch wrapped in a fleece throw and I still couldn't get warm. I had the TV remote and was flipping through the channels, restlessly trying to find something to watch.

I rolled my eyes as I scrolled though the titles. I had to admit, I was a bit surprised, I had access to more than 500 channels, and still, there was nothing to watch. Watching TV was not really my cup of tea anyway, it was kind of Greg's thing, he loved the sports channels and the movie channels. I would rather read or surf the net.

I was completely lost, now that I had the house to myself I really didn't know what to do with myself. I didn't even need to clean the house, it didn't really get that messy with just me there, it was kind of amazing. I was startled when the phone started ringing. I figured it was probably one of the kids.

"Hello?"

"Hey Lane, it's me," it was Justin.

"Hey bud, what's up?" I asked, smiling at the sound of his voice. Justin was my one true friend in the whole world.

"Hey I just got the word on a job that would be perfect for you, if you're up for it," said Justin.

"What kind of job?" I asked. I was leery. Justin had his own company. He did ice shows all over the world, he always had some sort of kooky job lined up for me. In the past, I had never really been free to move, when the kids were at home and I was married, now that it was just me, maybe I could finally take him up on one of his kooky job offers.

"Well I think you are going to be intrigued, it's maybe a little bit out of your comfort zone," said Justin.

"What kind of job?" I repeated. At this point in my life, I was game for whatever. Really, what did I have to loose?

"Don't laugh, but it's a reality TV series. Here's the deal..."

"I don't think so Justin, I detest reality TV...it's just so..."

"I know, I know, but this is going to be super cool. I think you're going to like this idea. The network is going to take professional athletes and pair them with professional skaters and try to make pairs skaters out of them," said Justin.

"Sure, kind of like that show they do in Canada, right?" I asked. I was already rolling my eyes miserably. This was definitely not something I was interested in.

"Yeah, sort of like that, though I believe that show uses strictly hockey players. This show is going to use an assortment of athletes, both male and female. I think it will be quite interesting. Anyway, they asked me for my input on a few things and I suggested you as a coach and choreographer.

The producers didn't think you would go for it, I mean you've been so busy. They didn't realize that Kyle and Lucie had split up," said Justin.

I sighed miserably. I hated to be reminded constantly how much my life sucked.

"Anyway, they were excited that you might be free now and they would be thrilled to bring you on," said Justin.

"I don't know Justin. It doesn't really sound like something I would be interested in." I whined.

"I know it doesn't sound like the old you, but this is a huge opportunity to do something different with your life, meet new people, get out of town...you know," pleaded Justin.

"What you're saying is, I need to do something other than wither away here in Colorado Springs," I told him.

"Exactly! I think you should at least talk to the producers," said Justin.

"Okay, what do I need to do?" I asked, I had already resigned myself to at least hear about the opportunity. What could it hurt?

"The executive producer, Jorge Broussard is going to

call you in one hour, seven o'clock their time. They are an hour behind you," said Justin.

"Crap, I'm going to have to go to L.A. for this, aren't I?" I moaned.

"Hollywood baby...step out of your comfort zone and leave the mountains far behind," said Justin.

I frowned, I wasn't a fan of southern California, but I was at least, willing to hear the sales pitch.

# CHAPTER 5

I talked to the executive producer Jorge Broussard, that evening and I have to say that I was intrigued enough, that I took him up on his offer to fly me to Los Angeles so that I could go over the specifics with him. Really, I had nothing to loose, I had decided I might as well do it. What else would I possibly do with my life? My marriage was over, Kyle had already left for L.A., the skating season was essentially over for me.

I flew to L.A. and met with Jorge Broussard and some other network executives, and once I had seen the entire presentation, I was actually very impressed with the whole plan. Believe it or not, I could actually see myself working on this project.

Though the concept was intriguing, I was most anxious to see what athletes they had on the roster and find out who the professional skaters would be. That would tell me if the viewers would be interested or not. I had imagined that the producers were probably recruiting some interesting characters who would be capable of keeping the viewers entertained. Having athletes that were already popular with the viewers, and interesting personalities that kept things stirred up, would ensure that the show topped the ratings each week.

Jorge proudly handed me the tentative list of potential cast members, I looked through the list of skaters, expecting to see some well loved, world class skaters, but my heart sank as I scanned the list. I saw a few names that were vaguely familiar to me, but none of the names stood out to me as well known, world class skaters.

"These are your professional skaters? Where did you get them? I can't say that the average person would have ever heard of any of them," I told him, handing the list back to him. I was a bit put off, and I was suddenly having second thoughts about this project. I was worried that maybe doing this show wasn't such a good idea. I really didn't want to be associated with a show that ended up being a pathetic amateur hour. I couldn't help but have visions of "The Gong Show".

"That's our problem, at the moment, US figure skating has not sanctioned our show, so many of the professionals we approached were afraid they might loose their credentials with the club. Of course, you and our celebrity judges will be immune from the scrutiny, as none of you will actually be skating in this non sanctioned event. But most of the skaters we approached were quite leery. We had to find obscure skaters to whom it didn't seem to matter. Most of them never made it to the top, or they are foreign, of course," said Jorge.

I shook my head distractedly. It did sound maybe, like a disastrous prospect, but I had already made my mind up. Deep down, I knew I should just do it. My life, as I knew it, was over. It was time to start anew, my mental health was dependent on it. "So what will my role be in all of this?" I asked.

"Well, as you see, we have ten skaters, we will also have ten athletes and ten people like yourself, who will serve as the team's coach and choreographer. You will be assigned a team, that has been chosen completely at random. You will be responsible for teaching them all the moves and the best choreography you can come up with.

Since you will be both their coach and choreographer, it will be your job to mold whatever raw talent they have, into a pairs team. Each week you will teach your team a new routine, each week one pair will be eliminated from the competition," said Jorge, giving me a sly smile.

"One routine each week! For ten weeks!" I cried, it seemed impossible.

"Well, the show will run a total of twelve weeks actually, we had to stretch it out a bit to please the network. Don't get your panties in a wad yet. Our first week will merely be an exhibition, and then we will throw in a non elimination week right before the finals, and then basically a recap episode featuring the final two teams, before the final episode," said Jorge.

I was staring at him in shock. I doubted that most trained professionals could perfect one routine a week, let alone a team who had no experience skating together at all.

"How long will will we have to train these athletes, before we jump into this whole thing with the show?" I asked. If it was anything less than six months, I didn't think it would be possible.

"We will bring everyone in to begin their training one month before the first show airs, and that show will just be an intro, so you'll have at least five weeks before you have to come up with a two minute routine with your team," said Jorge.

"Five weeks! Two minutes!" I cried, barely able to absorb the insanity of the very thought. It would be impossible!

"What do you think?" he asked, smiling broadly at me.

I wanted to tell him that he was completely insane, that there was no possible way this could be done, but my panicked brain was still working furiously to process all of this.

"Oh how remiss of me, I forgot to tell you your salary for those couple months you will be employed by the network," said Jorge, then he casually rattled off a number in the six figures. I'm sure my jaw dropped open in shock, since I had no clue that reality TV was going to be so lucrative. I was completely speechless and staring at him in shock, I thought that my heart might stop!

I couldn't speak at all, I was so stunned. Jorge apparently thought that my hesitation meant that I was having second thoughts about taking on this ambitious task, so he promptly added another fifty thousand dollars to my already excessive salary. To say that I was stunned, would have been a serious understatement.

"Ummm, okay," I finally managed to mumble quickly, before the offer expired into thin air.

"Excellent!" cried Jorge, standing and shaking my hand. "Oh, I forgot to tell you, if your team wins, you get a bonus!" he said, smiling at me.

I gave him a weak smile in return. I couldn't get too excited about a bonus yet. Especially, when I had no idea what my "team" would be like. I truly had no idea who any of these people were.

Jorge and I went to work signing contracts and working out details. I would fly home to Colorado Springs to tie up loose ends there, then I would return to Los Angeles in five weeks to begin my new project. As exciting as all this seemed, I was scared. Justin had been right. This **was** something out of my comfort zone.

# CHAPTER 6

In the weeks before I arrived, I had been worrying about my upcoming move to Los Angeles. For the next, more than four months of my life, I would be stuck in Los Angeles, where I essentially knew no one, with the exception of Jorge, and the few other network executives I had met.

I was worried about lots of things, where I would stay, how I would get around. Luckily my worries had been for nothing, the network had taken care of everything. They had provided me with a very nice condo not far from the studio, and a rental car, a stunning red convertible. I had to pinch myself to make sure I wasn't dreaming. I was quite pleased that I was being so spoiled.

It wasn't until I was introduced to my "team", that I began to have second thoughts about this entire fiasco. When I met my "team" it was obvious that I would have my work cut out for me. I realized that every show had an angle, and unfortunately, I was feeling like I was the butt of a huge joke that the network had constructed at my expense. As soon as I met my team, I was convinced that the angle for this reality series would be that, my couple was pretty much a hopeless cause!

The couple I had been assigned to work with, who had supposedly been assigned to me completely at random, seemed more like fodder for a situation comedy than an athletic competition! I suddenly had my doubts that this pair had truly been assigned to me randomly, and I was feeling a bit set up. I feared the network executives were all secretly snickering at me, as I met my team. It just seemed to me, that my team was destined to be the long shot of the entire competition.

My athlete was retired football star, Ron Brannon. I didn't really follow football at all, but Jorge told me that Ron had been a star quarterback, a fan favorite, and Jorge was quite pleased to have recruited him. I, on the other hand, wasn't as excited about his presence as

Jorge was. Just looking at this man, I had serious doubts that I could ever teach him to skate. I couldn't get that old saying out of my head. "The bigger they are, the harder they fall".

Ron Brannon definitely looked like a football player, he was huge! He was tall, probably six foot three or six foot four, and he was a broad shouldered, mass of muscle. I wasn't sure how old he was, but I was guessing that he was probably close to forty, and he walked with a bit of a limp, apparently, from an old hip injury, he had sustained on the football field.

I was grimacing at the very thought of this man getting on the ice, I worried that he would most likely finish off his hip the first time out on the ice. I was looking around the room at the rest of the producers, biting my lower lip anxiously, waiting for someone to tell me that this was a huge joke.

Regrettably, the punch line never came. No one burst into laughter and told me this was a joke, like I had hoped. Jorge was gushing on and on about how fabulous Ron Brannon was, and how he was going to grab spectacular ratings for the show.

I sighed miserably, of course, it was all about the ratings. Jorge didn't care that teaching Ron Brannon to skate, would be a lot like teaching a dog to whistle, it just wasn't happening! Jorge did not share any of my reservations, in fact, I was realizing that all Jorge really cared about, was having Ron Brannon's name in the credits. I tried to conceal my troubled frown, I was totally screwed!

I was more of a baseball fan, than a football fan, so I really couldn't get all that excited about having Ron Brannon on my team. Of course, I wasn't completely naive, I knew the value Jorge placed on a celebrity like Brannon. I hadn't just crawled from beneath a rock, I'd heard his name before and seen him on TV commercials, but I really knew nothing about him personally. Jorge told me that Ron Brannon was one of the greatest quarterbacks ever! Now he was retired from football and he worked as a sports commentator in New York.

Jorge told me all I had to do was dress Ron Brannon up in a sexy outfit and the ratings would soar. Apparently Mr. Brannon was quite popular with the ladies, and of course, as far as the network was concerned, it was all about the ratings.

I sighed in resignation, it was, what it was, there was nothing I could do about it. I could only hope that Ron Brannon would be able to pull in the ratings for the show based on this good looks alone, because I seriously doubted that I was going to be able to make him into a professional pairs skater.

I could only chuckle when I thought about it. All I could think about was the fact that Ron Brannon was built for football. He was a huge, black man, who paired with my skater, who was petite and blonde, was going to look completely ridiculous!

Unfortunately, my luck in the professional skater draw hadn't been any better. My skater was Elena Denkova, a tiny Russian skater who was about ten years past her prime. I didn't remember her from the height of her career, so I assumed she had never been to the World Championships. Elena was twenty nine years old and she apparently had retired from competitive skating because of a bad knee.

I shook my head disgustedly, this wasn't fair! I didn't have a snowball's chance in hell of making it past the first week in this competition! I had already resigned myself to working with Ron, but geeze, at least give me a decent professional to work with. Elena had never done any pairs skating or ice dance and she spoke only limited English. She was just a tiny thing, barely 5 feet tall, and approximately ninety pounds. About the size of one of Ron's legs!

Of course, our first day on the ice was a complete disaster! Ron didn't even know how to put the skates on. After I helped him lace them up correctly and helped him to get them tight enough around the ankles, he landed flat on his back on the ice, with his very first step out of the gate!

I sighed miserably as I watched him floundering around on the ice, like a fish out of water. I was trying to avoid getting discouraged, but I already had a pretty good idea which team would be the first one going home. I had expected that the network would have chosen people who could, at the very least, stand on skates.

I was happy that Elena seemed to be able to skate good enough, even with her knee bandaged, she could skate circles around Ron. Her downfall was going to be her stubbornness, she wanted everything her way, and communicating with her at times was a challenge, she spoke English, but not well. If you told her something she didn't like, she would just pretend she didn't understand you.

As I watched Ron struggling to get back to his feet, I sighed miserably. Why did I take this job? What the heck was I thinking? Then I remembered what Justin had told me. I needed to do something different, something out of my comfort zone.

This definitely qualified. I reprimanded myself and resolved to make this work. Life as I had known it, was officially over. I was destined to spend the next four months of my life in Hollywood. I vowed to make the best of it. I skated over and offered my hand to Ron, I hauled him up off the ice, then I struggled to help him over to the wall.

The poor guy, I felt bad for him, he seemed so embarrassed. He was very apologetic, but I couldn't really blame him for his lack of grace on the ice. Ron had been asked to come on this show, and I was guessing he had no idea as to what he was getting himself into.

As far as I was concerned, this was all Jorge's fault! In my opinion, the contestants should have some sort of skating ability before they were asked to come on the show.

There was not much I could do about it at this point, I was committed. All I could really do was smile for the cameras. Of course, the show had assigned our team it's very own cameraman who was there to film all of our practices, all of our interviews, and all of our thoughts about how this little fiasco was going.

I guess in a way, that was good, all of America at least, would know it wasn't completely my fault that my team totally sucked. I had nothing to work with! My grandpa always said, "You can't make a silk purse out of a sow's ear." Amen to that!

So it seemed that I was going to have to teach Ron to skate from scratch. Luckily, the very first show was going to be an introduction, of sorts. It would be mostly a bunch of interviews, fluff pieces, clips from our practices and then a short, 30 second "preview" skate. I wouldn't have to come up with a real two minute program for my team, until the second week on the air.

I only hoped that by the time week one was shot, I would have enough to work with, to present a 30 second intro skate to the American viewers. Right now, even that, didn't seem possible. At this point, I would be lucky if Mr. Brannon could complete one lap around the rink.

That first day, I had no choice but to start out by teaching Ron the basics of skating. I felt like I was back in Colorado Springs teaching a basic skills course to five year olds. Arms out, glide, step, glide.

I was pleasantly surprised, Ron was actually a very good student and quite anxious to learn. It wasn't long before he had the basic steps down and he was slowly gliding around the rink some, without me holding on to him.

I chewed nervously on my bottom lip as I watched him skate around the rink, his arms outstretched as he toddled around the ice, always on the verge of falling. I felt bad for him, it was embarrassing, and he seemed like a nice enough guy.

I was impressed because he was enthusiastic and he seemed to be so driven to make this work. Unfortunately, all the drive in the world was probably not enough to get him to the level I needed him skating at. I was still certain that my team would be the first one going home.

I had been so absorbed in trying to help Ron learn to skate, that I had been completely ignoring Elena. She had been skating by herself the entire time, she was obviously completely bored. I glanced across the rink at Ron, picking himself up off the ice, for like, the millionth time, and I could tell that he was wearing down. I decided, it was time for me to end practice for one day.

"Okay Ron, that's good," I called, waving him back over to me. I didn't want to overdo him on the first day.

"That's it, we're done?" he asked. He was disappointed, like a kid who'd been told that playtime was over.

"It's your first day, I think that's enough," I told him.

"But we didn't do any jumps or lifts," he said, his face falling in defeat.

"Well, let's just concentrate on the basics for now, we'll get to that eventually," I told him with a smile, though secretly, I doubted I would ever get to jumps and lifts with this team. If we made it through the first elimination, it would be a freaking miracle.

"I'm glad to see you're finally smiling. You've got a beautiful smile," said Ron, flashing me a stunning smile of his own. I'm sure I blushed. I had to admit, Jorge had been right, Ron Brannon was very attractive, and a little bit of a flirt, it seemed.

"Thank you," I told him, I looked away, suddenly embarrassed. My heart was faltering at the unexpected compliment. I was suddenly fighting tears, it was what Greg had always told me, back when Greg still thought that I was attractive. Greg had always loved my smile and my eyes, somehow it hadn't been enough, though.

"I guess you don't have much to smile about, getting me as your athlete. I guess if you were lucky you would have gotten a hockey star, then at least the guy knows how to skate," said Ron, flashing me a sly smile.

"I'm sorry if I seem moody, really, it's not your fault. I guess I haven't had much to smile about lately," I told him ruefully.

"I probably wouldn't be smiling either, if I had just been informed that I had to teach a guy with my abilities to ice skate. I mean hell, I never even put on skates before," he told me with a little laugh.

"Actually, getting you as my athlete was the luckiest thing to happen to me in a long time," I told him.

"How do you figure?" he asked, giving me a quizzical look.

"Well, when the show airs and everyone sees the clips of all our practices and you falling down on your butt today, they are going to be completely amazed with my coaching talent when you and Elena actually win the competition!" I told him, giving him a coy smile.

"Well at least you have big ambitions. Either that or you're completely delusional," said Ron, laughing.

"Everyone has a dream right? It's not any different than when you played football, just keep looking ahead to the Super Bowl," I told him with a smile. I was smiling because he was attractive and for some reason, I couldn't wipe the sappy smile off my face, not because I actually thought we had a chance to win this competition.

He laughed and smiled back me. I struggled, almost uselessly to focus, I had to admit, I was completely mesmerized by his charm. I could definitely see why Jorge thought that Ron Brannon would grab female viewers for the network, he was completely adorable!

I had almost completely forgotten about Elena. In a few moments, Elena skated over to us and looked at me expectantly. Of course, she was bored. She had essentially been skating by herself the entire time, while I struggled to keep Ron upright on his skates. I gave her a wry smile, as I was feeling bad for ignoring her.

"I can go? We are done?" she asked, peering at me expectantly.

"We are done, go on," I told her, waving her away.

"Okay, bye bye," she said, stepping off the ice and putting her skate guards on. Before I realized it, she was gone.

"So what now?" asked Ron, looking at me expectantly.

"Well, I guess I'll see you back here tomorrow," I told him with a little shrug. I wasn't sure what to tell him. I thought it was best if I got him off the ice now, before he got hurt. Besides, the network was supposed to get us access to a gym with mats and weights, but as of yet, that hadn't happened. Not that it would do my team any good at the moment anyway.

"So that's it, we're not going to skate any more today?" he asked, he seemed to be completely perplexed by the fact that I was ending practice for the day.

"No, it's your first day. It would be easy for you to overdo it, that would be completely counterproductive," I told him, with a little shrug.

"What can I do? You know, to help learn to skate?" he asked, he seemed lost.

"Well, since you have no previous experience, it's just going to take time. It's not as easy as it might seem, professionals work for years to learn the moves you see on TV. It doesn't all happen overnight. You need to strengthen your ankles I guess, and in time, with practice, you will learn," I told him with a little shrug.

"If I need practice, then why are we quitting for the day?" he cried in exasperation.

"Ron, you've never even been on skates before, your body needs to adjust to being on these thin little blades, there's a risk of overdoing it. Besides, your skates aren't broken in, that in itself, can take weeks. If your feet get all blistered up, you're going to be feeling some serious pain. There is only so much abuse your body can take, your muscles need a break, and your feet need a break from the skates," I told him.

"Listen here. You don't know what I can endure. I was a football player, you think I don't know pain? I'm used to working through the pain, I've played with broken ribs, and a broken hand. I'm not a sissy little girl and I'm not ready to give it up yet today," he snapped, eyeing me seriously. I bit my lip and resisted the urge to roll my eyes.

"Ron please, I'm not trying to insult your masculinity. I'm sure you have enough testosterone for yourself and everyone in this arena. But this is not football. I'm just afraid you might overdo it and injure yourself. You need to take it slow, go home and rest tonight, tomorrow is another day. If we try to do too much today, you might end up being worthless tomorrow," I said, giving him a little shrug.

"You let me worry about that. I'm not done. I want you to teach me more. Are you too tired to help me?" he asked, eyeing me arrogantly.

"No I'm not too tired to help you. Ron, I'm simply trying to protect you. Your body is not used to being on skates for long periods of time. I'm just worried that..."

"Are you going to help me, or not?" he cried, staring me down angrily.

I rolled my eyes, then I skated over to where I was standing just a foot in front of him. I stared him down arrogantly. If nothing else, he had determination, but I was not going to surrender to him simply because he was a muscle bound, testosterone loaded, god.

"I will help you, but I will listen to no whining tomorrow, if your feet hurt," I snapped.

"I promise, no whining!" he said, giving me that smile again, my heart seemed to accelerate almost automatically.

"Okay, let's do this," I said, taking his right arm and placing it around my waist, then I linked my left hand with his and soon we were gliding around the rink together.

We were far from graceful and he stumbled often, a result of leaning too far forward and having his toe picks suddenly grab the ice. He was good natured about it all, if he fell, he would get up and go right back to work. I was pleased for the most part, we had actually spent more time on our skates, than we had on our butts!

Ron and I skated together for another hour and soon I was feeling like he wasn't totally a lost cause. If nothing else, he had the drive to make this work. I was actually very proud of him!

We were laughing as we sat side by side on a bench in the lobby and took our skates off. I had to admit, he was a very funny guy and I was enjoying my time with him. I was a little self conscious about our developing friendship, it seemed that the cameras were always there to catch our every move.

"I will see you tomorrow," I told him, as I finished packing my skates in my bag.

"Okay boss," he said, giving me a mock salute as he stood up to leave. "Oh crap, I can't walk," he cried, almost falling over, then comically hobbling around the bench a couple of times.

I shot him a worried look, then I realized he was mugging for the cameras. I giggled as I watched him hamming it up. I had to admit, Jorge was definitely a genius. I had no doubt now, that Ron Brannon was destined to bring in big ratings for the network, he was obviously quite a character!

I shook my head in amusement, I was sure he was going to be pretty sore tonight. It was later, when your body relaxed, that you started to feel the pain. I still felt that way sometimes after long sessions, and I skated all the time. Those first few minutes you actually have to walk after getting off the ice are always tricky, you kind of have to learn how to walk all over again.

Our cameraman began packing up his things and Ron walked out of the ice rink with me. I had showed him some exercises he could do to help strengthen his ankles. As we walked across the parking lot, I expected him to head straight to his car, instead he followed me to mine.

"Hey Lane, I'm sorry I was a bit of an ass earlier. Can I make it up to you? Do you want to go get some lunch or something?" he asked. I turned to look at him, I wasn't really sure if he was pulling my leg, or what.

I knew that he was close to my age, but I wasn't really sure how old he was. He was completely gorgeous, but I was almost certain that he must be married. Guys like Ron just didn't stay single for long.

"Ummm, I don't know..."

"I just thought we could talk, you know, get to know each other better. We're going to be working together for the next four months," he said, giving me a smile.

"Uh...well, okay," I finally stammered.

In a matter of minutes I found myself seated at a table for two with him, in one of Hollywood's most exclusive restaurants. I was a little self conscious, he was attractive and famous, and I was...well...me. He was apparently quite recognizable, because from the time we arrived at the restaurant, everyone was looking in our direction pointing and whispering.

"So tell me, how is it that the most incredible figure skating choreographer of all time, ends up doing a reality TV series?" he asked, looking into my eyes with a smile. I had to stifle a little giggle, my heart was suddenly pounding nervously and I wasn't sure why.

It was probably because Ron was so attractive and he was a little bit of a charmer. I hadn't been alone in restaurant with a man that wasn't my husband for more than twenty years! I felt like a teenager who was out on her first date, even though I knew this wasn't really a date.

"I don't believe for one minute that you know the first thing about figure skating. I'll bet you've never even heard of me," I exclaimed, staring him down haughtily.

He started laughing, then he shook his head in amusement and smiled at me.

"Okay, you got me there. I never even heard of you. It was Jorge who told me you were the greatest choreographer of all time. But really, if you are the greatest choreographer of all time, which I totally believe that you are, what are you doing on this lame show?"

I sighed miserably. I hated to admit defeat, but my life had been falling apart as of late. I hated to talk about it.

"It's a long story, I recently had a few unpleasant surprises in my life. I guess I just needed a change. I was depressed, not really myself, and my partner Justin told me I needed to do something outside my comfort zone, so I did!" I told him with a laugh.

"Your partner?" asked Ron, looking at me puzzled.

"Okay, ex-partner, best friend, whatever you want to call him. Justin was my skating partner years ago when I skated professionally. The two of us were paired when we were basically just kids, we have been best friends since I was twelve and he was sixteen. He still lives in Chicago. I really miss not having him around," I told him.

"When did you skate professionally? Were you like an Olympic Gold medalist? Sorry, I never really followed figure skating," said Ron, giving me another smile, my heart seemed to melt. I took a deep breath and struggled to focus.

"It was years ago, Justin and I went to the Olympics, but it was a bit of a disaster, so we didn't medal. We did get the bronze medal at the world championships the following year, then we skated with the European Theater Company for three years and toured all over Europe," I told him.

"That sounds like a blast," said Ron.

"It was, those were great times," I told him, smiling at the memories.

"Did you know you have a beautiful smile?" said Ron, once again flashing me a stunning smile of his own.

My heart accelerated crazily. I could feel the heat of my cheeks blushing. "Thank you," I said, I was too embarrassed to even look at him. I felt like a silly school girl.

"So tell me about yourself, are you married? Do you have kids?" asked Ron, taking a sip of his drink.

"I am currently going through a divorce after more than twenty years of marriage to my husband Greg, and I have two children, a son Ramsey, and a daughter Baylee. They are both away at college," I told him with a sigh.

"I'm sorry, that's pretty rough," he said, giving me a wry smile.

"It's okay," I told him with a sigh. "That's why I'm

doing something new, moving on. How about you, are you married?" I asked.

"Yep, I have two beautiful daughters, eight and ten years old. I guess that's how they were able to coerce me into doing this show. I guess you could say, I'm really in it for the money," he said, taking another sip of his drink.

"Oh?" I wasn't really sure what to say.

"My wife hasn't been very happy since I retired from football. I was ready to retire, I wasn't sure how long my body could take the abuse, playing football. Now that I'm a commentator, the paychecks aren't as big, yet my wife just keeps spending money, like I'm still pulling in the big bucks. She rides me all the time about my retirement, if it were up to her, I guess I'd be back on the football field," he said, shaking his head ruefully.

"She doesn't care that you might be hurt?" I asked, incredulously.

"She was the one that pushed me to do this show. I wasn't so sure when Jorge approached me. I thought I was too old to learn to skate, besides, I have a bit of a bad hip. Jorge really didn't care if I could skate or not, he just wanted my name in the credits. Jenae didn't care if I felt comfortable doing it or not, think of the money, she said."

frowned when he said that. I hated to be judgmental, I didn't know her at all, but she sounded incredibly shallow to me.

"I guess she doesn't care that you could hurt yourself skating, since you've never done this before," I was frowning, I had never met the woman, but I didn't like her at all.

"She cares I guess, she just worries about the girls, she wants them to have a good life," he said, shrugging.

I nodded at him half heartedly. He loved her, he

obviously couldn't see her for the gold digger that she was.

"What about your soon to be ex-husband? What does he think about you jetting off to L.A. to be in some silly reality TV show?" asked Ron.

"He really doesn't care what I do. When I came home from the Cup of China months ago, he was already gone. He was already shacking up with his twenty seven year old secretary," I told him with a little shrug.

"Holy crap! That totally blows!" he exclaimed, staring at me in shock.

"It was a shock, I thought that Greg and I would be together forever, like my grandparents, but I guess it just wasn't meant to be. That's why I'm trying something different, moving on with my life," I told him.

"Here's to your new life," he said, raising his glass to me and flashing me another stunning smile. I tried to ignore the way it seemed to make my heart race nervously.

"To my new life, and your new career," I said, raising my glass to him.

Ron and I had a nice lunch, we spent a lot of time talking and laughing. We had a lot in common, so we ended up spending more than three hours there at the restaurant, having lunch. I really hadn't given it a second thought. Ron was a nice guy and the two of us seemed to get along well enough. We had mostly talked about skating and the show, I thought I might as well get to know him. The two of us were going to be working quite closely together over the next several months. How was I to know that having what appeared to be an intimate lunch with Ron, would be a serious error in judgement that would change Hollywood's view of me forever?

# CHAPTER 7

I returned to my fully furnished luxury condo on North Vista street that afternoon, completely unaware of how ridiculously naive I was. I had already stirred up a huge scandal and I didn't even know it!

At quarter after five the next morning, I stepped out of the shower to the sound of my cell phone ringing urgently from the bedroom. It was Jorge. He told me that I needed to meet with him urgently, but he wouldn't elaborate as to why. I made coffee, poured it into a to-go cup and drove to his office, so I could meet with him before my seven a.m. ice time with Ron and Elena. When I walked into Jorge's office I was slightly taken aback by the icy glare he flashed at me. He was obviously furious with me, and I had no idea why.

"Would you like to explain this to me?" he asked, slapping a newspaper down on the desk in front of me.

I picked up the paper and stared at it blankly. The front page had a large color picture of Ron and I at the restaurant, our glasses raised, mid toast. The headlines shouted out the nasty rumor, like unexpected kick in the gut. Sports commentator Ron Brannon runs wild in Hollywood with reality TV Co Star Lane Jensen, the headline screamed out.

I cringed in shock, I felt incredibly stupid that I had so quickly forgotten everything I had learned about Hollywood from my own mother. Someone was always watching...I knew that. I dropped the newspaper back on his desk, distastefully. I wasn't sure if I even wanted to read the accompanying article, it was obviously nothing but speculation.

"Jorge, this is nothing but horse shit! Ron and I just went out to lunch...it was nothing," I cried, though my heart was already pounding, guiltily.

"Hmmm. It doesn't look like nothing. In fact, it looks rather intimate. It couldn't have possibly been a team lunch, where was Elena?" asked Jorge, raising his eyebrows at me.

"It was a spur of the moment thing. Elena had already left, she was bored, she couldn't wait to get out of there!" I cried, rolling my eyes miserably.

"Ron Brannon is married! I will not have my new show at the center of some adulterous scandal. Whatever the two of you have, I want you to end it now. I'm completely serious!" boomed Jorge, the anger seemed to be oozing from every pore of his body. I was actually frightened that I had already lost my lucrative new position.

"Jorge, I'm sorry about how this looks, I guess I forgot how it is in Hollywood. I promise, I won't make the same mistake again."

"Listen Lane, perhaps this is nothing, but the press is always looking for something. We cannot give them the tiniest bit of fuel for their fire," said Jorge, I sighed and shook my head miserably.

"Think about it Lane, you are essentially single, he, on the other hand, is not. As far as the media is concerned you are a hot divorcee on the prowl, though I am not sure that the media is aware that you are going through a divorce yet. But I am quite sure it is only a matter of time before they figure it out, when they do, these kind of intimate little lunches are only going to look that much more suspicious."

"It wasn't like that at all. It was just lunch, we were just trying to get to know each other. I realize he's married Jorge...I just forgot about the media." I was rolling my eyes.

Jorge gave me a sly smile. "What do you expect? I mean, you are gorgeous, of course, he's attractive. What usually happens when two attractive people have to work very closely together? It happens all the time in Hollywood. You know, co stars hooking up in real life, when they have been filming a movie together. Think about it, the two of you are going to be working closely together for the next four months. It only stands to reason that the press is going to try to link the two of you, they are going to monitor every moment the two of you spend together and dissect it," said Jorge.

I rolled my eyes. "It was nothing," I snapped. I was tired of talking about this, I may have been a tiny bit attracted to Ron, but I was sure he didn't feel the same way about me, the man was obviously happily married!

"Lane my darling, don't be angry with me. I'm not the enemy here. I realize that this little lunch date was nothing, but we've only just begun here, comprende?

I want you to be strong and make sure it stays nothing. You and Mr. gorgeous muscular body, are going to be spending a lot of time together, he is going to be lonely, you're going to be lonely. Shit happens Lane. I realize that Ron is very attractive and charming, but the only reason he is even doing this show, is because his wife is a freaking spending machine.

He does well enough, but obviously he needed more money to keep her supported in the lifestyle she thinks she deserves. If she, for one moment, even suspects that he's screwing around on her, she'll divorce his ass and freakin clean him out!" said Jorge, eyeing me seriously.

"I realize that Jorge! I'm not a home wrecker, I promise, it's nothing." I told him, looking away guiltily and shaking my head.

"I mean it Lane, if Brannon gets caught screwing around on this broad, I don't want it to be with you. Brannon can get laid anywhere, I realize he's loaded with testosterone and..."

"Jorge, really..." I snapped.

"Okay, okay. So, how's the skating coming?" he asked, flashing me a sly smile. My mouth suddenly dropped open in shock. One look at his amused smile and I was suddenly angry. I was getting the sneaky feeling that my team, who was supposedly assigned to me randomly, was a huge set up. The network was making a huge joke at my expense, I was suddenly sure of it!

"You set me up!" I cried, staring at him in shock.

"No I did not! Honestly Lane, you truly got the luck of the draw, but all the other contestants did claim to be able to skate some. Poor Ron had never even put on skates before," said Jorge, with a satisfied giggle.

"You better get your jollies now Jorge, by the time I get done with Ron, you won't be able to tell he was a mere novice when we began the season," I told him, indignantly.

"I certainly did get my jollies watching the most recent clips of your practice, though several of Ron's falls were so bad, they jarred me to the core," said Jorge, with a grimace.

"Well I'm sure he's feeling the pain today," I told him, with a little smile. I had to giggle when I thought about it, poor Ron, he had spent so much time sprawled on the ice, his butt was probably one big bruise!

"If anyone can teach him to skate, it's you. I have full confidence in you," said Jorge, smiling at me.

"Thanks, that really inspires me," I told him, shaking my head miserably.

# CHAPTER 8

When I finally arrived at the ice rink, I was excited to see that Ron and Elena were already on the ice, working on their stroking together. I stood back and watched them for a few minutes, just so I could see how they interacted when they thought that no one else was watching. It was almost a comical sight, Ron was so huge and clumsy, yet Elena was so small, she was struggling to keep him upright and shouting at him, what I could only hope, were helpful hints...in Russian.

They were actually gliding pretty naturally, as long as they traveled in a relatively straight line. Ron hadn't mastered crossovers yet, so when they hit the corners the two of them seemed to flounder around the curve, completely out of control, Elena's tiny body trying to steer Ron's large, completely out of control body.

After they had completed the turn at the opposite end of the rink and lived to tell about it, I started to head to the edge of the ice. I paused when I saw that Elena had turned and was skating backwards in front of Ron now. She was shouting commands to him in Russian. He was definitely skating a bit better, though it seemed as if his skates were still hell bent on traveling in opposite directions. He reminded me a bit, of the scarecrow in The Wizard of Oz.

Elena continued to call out commands in Russian, even though I was pretty sure that Ron didn't speak a word of Russian. Even I, had no idea what she was about to have him try.

As they clumsily rounded the next corner, Elena did a little spin, then she attempted to get back into step with Ron. Like I said, Ron hadn't mastered crossovers and unfortunately, he really didn't have much of a rhythm, so he caught the back of Elena's blade with his skate, and both Elena and Ron went down hard on the ice.

Elena jumped up from the ice and glared down at Ron angrily. "Nyet!" she cried, shaking her head furiously at him.

I skated over to them, shaking my head in amusement. I was trying hard to suppress my laughter, I didn't want them to think I was making fun of them. I just thought the entire scene was unbelievably cute!

Elena spun around to face me, with her hands on her hips. She glared at me angrily, upset that Ron had brought her down on her bum. I offered a hand to Ron and hauled him up off the ice. He was giving me an embarrassed smile. I gave him a wry smile and a little shrug, I had no expectations of him, at this point. My team could only give me, what they could give me.

"Theese ees eensane!" Elena cried angrily, stomping over to stand in front of me.

"Elena, please have patience, it is only our second day," I pleaded with her.

"Heee eezz beeg and clumzeee...like ox. Heee eeez bad. We never ween," she snapped, folding her arms over her chest and assessing me haughtily.

"He will get better, in fact, he's already gotten better. We just need to practice," I told her.

"Nyet, I weel queet!" she pouted, with a shake of her blonde ponytail toward the cameraman, who was filming us, from just steps away.

I frowned, she was providing drama for the cameraman, either on her own, or prompted, I wasn't sure which. I rolled my eyes miserably and went with it.

"Please don't quit Elena, I need you on my team. Things will get better, I promise," I pleaded earnestly.

"You skate weeth heem. I skate alone," snapped Elena, and with that, she turned and skated away from us.

I stood there numbly with my mouth gaping open as

she skated away. I was shocked and infuriated! She was acting like the spoiled little princess I had left behind in Colorado Springs. The big difference between Elena and the spoiled little princess I had left behind in Colorado Springs, was that the spoiled little princess was just fourteen, so there was, at least, a tiny bit of hope that she, might outgrow it!

I skated slowly over to Ron, who was eyeing me warily.

"Well, I thought that my days of working with adolescents were behind me, obviously I was wrong. Mr. Brannon, will you skate with me?" I asked, raising my eyebrows at him playfully.

"Okay, but people are going to talk," he said, giving me a slightly seductive smile.

I bit my lower lip in a sincere effort to concentrate. I was suddenly single after more than twenty years of marriage, and Ron Brannon was way too good looking for his own good. I could only hope that he wouldn't be flirting with me a lot. I was only human.

"Umm...I'm sorry about that Ron. When we went out to lunch, well...I should have realized...we're in Hollywood..."

"I'm kidding, it's not your fault, it was I, who asked you to lunch. I had forgotten how sneaky the media can be, I've been on the dark side for so long. I completely forgot what it's like to be the scrutinee," he told me with a smile.

"The scrutinee?" I asked, staring at him blankly. It was a sincere effort for me to focus on the conversation and not just stare at him like a complete idiot. His smile seemed to light up the entire arena. I was completely mesmerized by it, besides, he was flirting with me!

"Sure, if your not the scrutinizer, you're the scrutinee. Take it from me, it's much better to be the scrutinizer," he said, with a little shrug.

"I can only imagine, I guess I've been mostly the scrutinizer myself, with my students," I told him with a little smile.

"I guess that's what we both do for a living, huh?" he said, smiling back at me. My heart was suddenly pounding crazily and I was struggling to fight off a feeling of giddiness that was overtaking my body. I silently reprimanded myself. I was a grown woman for God's sake, not a teenager. Ron Brannon is married, I told myself, no matter how charming he is.

"Let's get to work," I told him, taking his right arm and wrapping it around my waist and taking his left hand in mine.

"All right, head up, back straight. Keep your knees slightly bent at all times. Imagine that your knees are shock absorbers, absorbing all the impact as you skate," I told him, as we took a tentative glide forward.

We began to skate slowly down the length of the ice. I was showing him how to match his strides to mine, which wasn't all that hard for us, I was tall and I had long legs. It would be much harder for him to shorten his stride to Elena's.

When we approached the corner I tried to help him with his crossovers.

"Okay Ron, we're going to make the turn now, shift your weight to your left and lean a bit, bring your right skate up off the ice, we're going to place it slightly in front of our left foot and across, slowly now," I told him.

We both shifted our weight to our left foot and began to lean into the turn, Ron picked up his right skate to do the crossover, but he didn't have a lot of control yet, the front of his blade caught the back of mine and suddenly we were both laying in a pile on the ice.

He had flipped over completely and was laying on top of me. I was laughing as I struggled to push him off of me, he was heavy! He floundered around on the ice for a few moments, then he finally managed to scramble to his feet. It was so hilarious, I could only lay there on the ice and laugh. Maurice had skated over with his camera and was panning in close, capturing our embarrassment for all of America to see. I was still laughing hysterically.

"Oh my God, are you okay? Did I hurt you?" cried Ron. He started to skate toward me, I scrambled to my feet quickly. I knew he hadn't mastered stopping yet, and I really didn't want him on top of me again!

"I'm thinking that crossovers are maybe something you should work on alone," I told him with a sly smile.

"Really are you okay?" he asked, anxiously. I felt bad, he looked worried.

"Didn't your football coach teach you anything?" I asked.

"Huh?"

"Rule number one, never tackle your coach. Rule number two, no cooler full of Gatorade on my head when we win," I told him with a little laugh.

He laughed. "Seriously, are you sure you're okay? I fell right on top of you," he said, his voice was filled with concern.

"I was a professional skater Ron, this is not the first time I've fallen on the ice," I told him with a smile. Ron smiled back at me, then he gave me a serious look.

"What were you like, back when you were a professional skater?" he asked, looking into my eyes, mesmerizing me once again.

I shook my head in an effort to shake off the spell he was casting over me. No moment was ever private, I could see Maurice filming us out of the corner of my eye. I sighed miserably.

"I was pretty much the same person I am now, except

I was younger and prettier...probably stupider too," I told him with a little smile.

"I can't imagine you being any prettier. Did you have to fend off the guys with a stick?" he asked, giving me a sly smile.

My heart was suddenly pounding again as he looked down into my eyes, and that smile...well, it was too bad that Mr. Brannon was married, because if he wasn't, I just might have to flirt with him. I took a deep breath and tried to focus.

"That's what I had a partner for," I told him with a little wink. I silently berated myself, okay, so I slipped up a little bit. No more flirting, from here on out.

He smiled at me and I slowly started to skate backwards away from him.

"All right, back to work. We need to work on your crossovers Mr. Brannon, you're going to follow me, and you are going to do them all on your own, come on, skate this way!" I called to him as I skated away.

Soon he was following me as I attempted to help him with his crossovers at each corner. I skated backwards in front of him, telling him what to do, he followed and attempted to do as I said.

The first three turns resulted in serious wipe outs. I felt bad for him, but I was glad that he wasn't taking me down with him each time. I had old injuries too and I really didn't want to get hurt.

By the fourth turn, he had actually started to get it. He was very shaky, but his skates were under control and he didn't fall. After about half an hour of him following me around the rink, I actually felt brave enough to skate with him and help him with his stroking.

I was actually enjoying skating with him, as we glided around the rink. It was the first time in quite a while, I had skated with a man who was anywhere near my age. I was used to working with up and coming skaters, most of them were just nearing adulthood.

Ron was very strong, which was going to help me immensely with his training. I could feel the strength in his body as we skated around the rink together. His muscular strength was the one thing, I hoped would be in my favor.

"You're doing much better today, I'm quite impressed," I told him, as we made another pass around the ice.

"I've been practicing," he told me proudly.

"When did you practice?" I asked, completely surprised.

"I came back to the rink last night and practiced for three hours," he told me proudly.

"Don't your feet hurt?" I exclaimed, three hours was way too much, especially, on skates that hadn't been broken in yet.

"Like I said, I can work through the pain," he told me.

I stopped skating and turned to look him in the eye. He was so stunned with my abrupt halt, he stumbled, then he did a desperate little dance, to avoid falling. He was able to avert disaster this time, but just barely. I bit my lip to hide the smile that almost automatically came to my lips. This big, intimidating looking guy, was completely lost on skates. It took all the concentration he had, just to remain upright.

I folded my arms across my chest and gave him my most serious glare. I didn't want him skating without me, at least, not this early in the game. It would be too easy for him to get hurt, he didn't know what he was doing, he needed guidance. I didn't want to be eliminated from the competition before it even began!

"Don't you ever do that again! I am your coach and I

will tell you how much you practice," I snapped, angrily.

"I'm fine," he told me, shaking his head nonchalantly. I narrowed my eyes at him, his male athlete ego was sneaking out, and it was totally pissing me off. I had thirty years of skating experience and he was acting like he knew more than I did.

"You arrogant jerk! You have no idea what you are doing, you could hurt yourself. I didn't come all the way to stinking Los Angeles, to have one of my team members overdo themselves and possibly get hurt and have to quit!" I ranted angrily.

"I'm a grown man, I will not have you berating me, like I'm one of your adolescent skating students!" snapped Ron, angrily.

"Then stop acting like one of them!" I shouted, I was nearly stomping my feet I was so angry with him. Ron had stepped closer to me and I could suddenly feel him towering over me. I was suddenly rueing my decision to pick a fight with a retired football player, who could obviously kick my ass without much effort on his part.

I could feel our cameraman Maurice hovering nearby, capturing every second of my dramatic little meltdown. I was suddenly feeling very uncomfortable.

I kept forgetting where I was and who I was dealing with. I was in Hollywood, every moment of my day, it seemed, was being recorded for the show. I was no longer working with children who worshipped me, and hung on my every word. I was working with a professional who was a legend in his own sport, who probably had a huge ego to go along with that huge persona.

I was stunned when I realized that Ron was suddenly laughing uncontrollably. I stared at him numbly, but soon I was fighting laughter as well, this whole scenario seemed completely ridiculous!

In moments, I was a laughing uncontrollably. It was

a bit comical, I was reprimanding Ron as if he were a fourteen year old boy who'd stayed up too late or something. He gave me a smile and folded me into a huge bear hug. My body stiffened in surprise, I hadn't expected that. His strong arms felt heavenly around me. It took every ounce of will power I had in my body to wiggle myself out of his arms before I melted into them blissfully.

I stepped back and gave him my most business-like glare. "Okay then," it was the only thing I could think of to say, my brain had been reduced to a mass of goo, the consistency of mashed potatoes.

"You're pretty damn cute when you get angry," whispered Ron, giving me a sly smile.

Once again, that smile had my heart pounding completely out of control. Luckily, I realized that Maurice was still standing there with his camera trained on us, otherwise I might have done, what I really wanted to do, which was just kiss him and get it over with.

I wasn't sure what was wrong with me, I had been fighting the urge to just kiss him all morning. There was just something about him that I couldn't put my finger on, it had been years since I had these kind of feelings for anyone. I wasn't sure why Ron had suddenly stirred up these feelings in me. I glanced up at him smiling at me, I sighed in resignation, it was impossible for me to stay mad at him!

"Do you have blisters?" I snapped, still trying to sound sufficiently angry at him.

"A few," he said, shrugging nonchalantly.

"Listen to me Ron, if you mess your feet up, you'll be totally out of this competition! You will skate when I tell you to skate, not a minute more!" I snapped.

"I'm sorry."

Maurice was still hovering nearby, of course the drama

was irresistible to a reality show cameraman. This was exactly what they lived for. It was only our second day and I had already grown tired of having every single second of my day recorded, just so the show's editors could go through the hours and hours of video and pick out only the juiciest morsels to air on the show.

I was cooling down some, but I was still angry, this competition could be over before it even began if Ron messed his feet up. I had decided it was time for me to take a little break.

"Go away Maurice!" I snapped, skating away from Ron and the annoying camera man.

"Oh, this is some good stuff," said Maurice, flashing me a little smile as he skated away with his camera. I retreated into the changing room so I could have a moment of solitude. The changing room was one of the only places the cameras weren't allowed.

When I had finally cooled down some, I returned to the ice. Ron was skating at one end of the rink, Elena was skating at the other. I sighed miserably, getting this pair to work together was going to be quite a challenge.

I wasn't sure what either of their true intentions were. I had competed all my life, so obviously I wanted to win, but I wasn't so sure about my little team.

I had my theories about Elena. I was under the impression that she was here because she thought that this show might lead her to some sort of acting career. I still wasn't sure what Ron's real intentions were. What would motivate a legendary football star like Ron, to come on a reality TV show where he was going to stick out like a sore thumb?

I knew that his wife had her heart set on the money, but what about Ron? He was the one that was going to be embarrassing himself on a weekly basis. Even if he skated a clean program during the show every week, I was sure that all this footage that was being shot during our practice was going to be exploited during the shows.

Besides, I could only imagine what all his football player buddies were saying about this. They probably thought that "Fire on Ice" was the gayest show on television!

"Okay you two, come over here," I called. They both began skating toward me. Elena glided into a hockey stop right in front of me, essentially showering me in ice, while Ron crashed into the wall clumsily. He hadn't really mastered stopping yet.

"All right, we are going to have the two of you do some stroking and then we are going to work on some dance steps," I told them.

"I not skate weeth heem, he eez a klutz," said Elena, folding her arms over her chest arrogantly.

"You wish to quit? You don't want to do the show?" I asked. I had already decided I was not going to tolerate Elena's piss poor attitude any more. If she refused to skate with Ron, she was going home. I wasn't going to play games with her anymore.

"I weel not have heem treeping over me!" cried Elena.

"If you want to quit, tell me now and I will let Jorge know. I'm sure he has other skaters that will be most happy to have this opportunity, to be on television," I told her with a slight shrug.

Elena assessed me carefully, with her arms folded across her chest. When she finally realized I was completely serious, she sighed miserably.

"I weel skate," said Elena, with a slight frown.

"Good, because Ron needs to skate with his partner, not me. The more he skates with me, the more comfortable he gets with a stride that does not belong to his partner...right?"

"Yes," snapped Elena.

I urged them both out on the ice. Elena wrapped Ron's arm around her waist and they were off. I was happy to finally have Ron and Elena skating around the ice together. I had to snicker a little bit as I watched them, Ron was so huge and she was so tiny, poor Ron was hunched over trying to listen to Elena's instructions in her choppy, broken English. Ron was quickly able to adjust to Elena's stride and soon they were looking like a matched pair.

Towards the end of the session we worked on some steps and I was finally feeling like we were making a bit of progress.

I told Elena and Ron goodbye and headed back to my condo. I wanted to take a nap, we had a big publicity party to go to tonight and I knew I wouldn't be back in bed before 2 a.m.

I had a beautiful sequined blue dress that the network had picked out for me to wear to the event tonight. Our practices had been closed, so it would be the first I had seen of any of the other teams, and it would be the first time they would be getting a look at our team as well. I was excited to finally get to meet our competition in person and see what we were up against.

I guess I shouldn't have been so surprised, Hollywood was a completely different world than I was accustomed to. I was always stunned by how everything was so carefully arranged. The network had sent my dress directly to the salon and I was to go there to get my hair and makeup done, then the limo would pick me up there. The network didn't really leave much to chance, they planned to have each team arrive together.

I wasn't looking forward to that. The press had already linked me with Ron once. I was worried about more speculation! I wondered, miserably, if there was any way possible I could make it through the next, nearly four months with my sanity intact. The way things were starting off, it didn't seem possible.

# CHAPTER 9

I sat there in the salon, completely lost in my own thoughts as the hair and makeup artists worked their magic on me. I couldn't help it, but I let out a little gasp of surprise when the hair stylist turned my chair around and I finally got a glimpse of my reflection in the mirror. I was so stunned, I almost didn't recognize myself. I wasn't used to wearing a lot of makeup, so when I saw the gorgeous blonde staring back at me in the mirror, I couldn't believe it was really me.

My hair was curled and twisted into an up do that allowed a mass of curls to fall over my right shoulder. The eyeshadow, eye liner and mascara made my already large eyes, look huge. It was the only facial feature I had inherited from my gorgeous mother, her beautiful blue eyes.

Elena was also at the salon having her hair and makeup done. When I finally got to see her, I had to smile, she looked every inch the movie star she longed to be. Wardrobe had dressed her in a shimmering white beaded and sequin encrusted dress and her long blonde hair had been curled and sprayed into an elegant mass of waves, reminiscent of a classic Hollywood beauty.

When it was time for us to depart, they ushered Elena and I into our limo, that was when I realized Ron was already in there waiting for us. He smiled at me as I slid across the leather seat. I tried to hide the fact that the very sight of him had rendered me completely speechless, but it was impossible. He looked incredibly handsome in his tuxedo, with that now familiar smile, lighting up his entire face.

"Good evening ladies, you both look lovely," he said, as Elena and I situated ourselves in the limo. I smiled at him in response, I was so filled with emotion, I couldn't trust my voice to speak as I slid up next to him, our legs almost touching. I would have preferred it, if Elena would have sat next to him, but she refused, for some reason.

Unfortunately, she didn't really like Ron at all and I wasn't sure why. I was pretty sure she was only doing this show as a chance to be discovered as an actress. I hated to tell her...fat chance of that happening.

Elena was rolling her eyes and giving us both a fake smile, I resisted the urge to say something snide to her. Her decided lack of class annoyed me, but I was sure her attitude would turn around as soon as the cameras were rolling, Elena was as fake as they came.

We arrived at the party, as a team. Of course, as we stepped out of the limo there were photographers and videographers there recording our every move from the moment we arrived.

Elena had snapped out of her sullen mood and mugged for the cameras with Ron and I. She had her arms around Ron, smiling coyly, as if the two of them were the best of friends. I resisted the urge to roll my eyes at her and instead, I gave everyone a fake smile as I waved to the crowd that had gathered there, outside the restaurant.

Jorge was waiting at the entrance of the restaurant and as soon as he saw me, he strolled over to me and took my arm to escort me into the restaurant. I could tell immediately that this had been a very deliberate action. He wanted me to walk into this event on his arm, not Ron's.

I had to admit, Jorge was very clever. Like the network, Jorge never left anything to chance, he was trying to dispel all the rumors that were circulating about Ron and I by making it appear to everyone that he was my date.

Despite the fact that I had no desire to have my name linked romantically to Jorge, it made sense to me. Ron was happily married, and hooking up with a co star would be scandalous. A scandal, especially this early in the game, would equate to bad publicity. Bad publicity was something our fledgling show didn't need at the moment.

I couldn't really fault Jorge for his concern, this new show was his baby. He felt the need to protect it, like a dog with a bone. I knew from our earlier conversation, that Jorge had already decided that he would do whatever it took, to make sure that Ron and I didn't look like a couple. He was hell bent on presenting a new image of me to the viewers. Jorge had a plan to show viewers that whatever those photos had implied, it was all a hoax.

I gave Jorge a stunning smile as I took his arm. The dozens of cameras clicked away as I walked into the restaurant on Jorge's arm and despite my outward smile, I felt like a fake, just like Elena.

When we arrived inside the restaurant, I could see that the network had taken over the entire place. There were cameras everywhere recording this historic event as the competitors were finally introduced to each other. Of course, I didn't recognize most of these people, but it was good to finally see what we were up against.

Two of the professional athletes were hockey players, which hardly seemed fair to me, they would have lots of skating experience. But what could I do? I was merely a character in this little cast that the producers had arranged.

In the mix of professional athletes, there were two football players, two hockey players, two baseball players, two volleyball players and two women's tennis stars. That made six guys, four girls on the professional athlete side.

There were six female professional skaters, and four males, most of them I really didn't know, they were either washed up, foreign, or so obscure, no one remembered them.

There was also an international mix of coaches and choreographers, there were four of us from the US, a French choreographer, a Swiss coach, a German coach, a Japanese choreographer, a British choreographer and a Canadian coach.

I figured it would be hard on a lot of these international coaches and choreographers, I knew that some of them weren't used to having to do both coaching and choreography. I was sure that some of the coaches would be struggling with the choreography. I almost giggled, I could only hope so, there had to be something to level the playing field a little bit!

As I assessed the other teams, I decided the biggest threat in the entire competition would be team Muramsatsu. Emi Muramsatsu had been a popular Japanese skater years ago and she now made her career as a very skilled choreographer. Emi was quite sought after in her own country and here in the states, she had created many an award winning program. I was almost pouting in disgust when I realized that she had been blessed with the dream team of Mick Santos, a professional hockey player and Annicka Vogl, a professional skater from Austria.

Annicka was not a world famous skater by any means, but I had, at least, heard of her. She had been an Austrian favorite. As talented as she was, Annicka had never made it to the world ranks, but I had seen her skate before, she was good!

I sighed as I watched team Muramsatsu in their interview, it wasn't fair at all. Not only were they talented, but they were bound to be a crowd favorite as well.

What could I say? They had the look. Annicka was young, maybe twenty three, and gorgeous. She looked like a model, all auburn curls and curves, and of course, the network had played up her ample cleavage, it threatened to spill out of the ruby red, sequined dress they had selected for her.

Of course, Mick was young too, and he was the picture of rugged handsomeness. His dark hair fell rakishly over one eye. Every pore of his body seemed to ooze pure sex appeal. Emi was a character, a powerhouse in a small package, is how I had heard her described one time. That had certainly been true in her skating days. I couldn't help but like Emi, her smile was infectious and she always kept everyone laughing. I had no doubt that after tonight, team Muramsatsu would be America's favorite team, and the show hadn't even started yet.

The party seemed to drag on and on, it was mainly set after set of publicity photos, interviews and a bit of socializing between the teams, of course, it was all being captured on camera. I had armed myself with my best fake smile and was forced to pull out my best poker face whenever I was interviewed with Ron or Jorge. I was determined that my outward appearance would give the viewers no reason to suspect that I was hopelessly smitten with Ron.

It was late in the evening and I was standing back from the crowd, watching a slightly hilarious interview with team Maricelle. French Canadian coach Andre' Maricelle, was saddled with a gorgeous, but ditzy, female tennis star and an arrogant Russian, for his pro skater. They were all jockeying for position in the interview, as each of them thought that they were the most important person on the team. The coach was so full of himself, I doubted this team would last the first week, it was almost comical.

I was smiling as I watched the interview. As luck would have it, my amusement was short-lived, a female reporter had approached me.

"Good evening Ms. Jensen, what do you have to say to the rumors that you and Ron Brannon are a bit of an item?" asked the woman, as she rudely stuffed her microphone into my face.

"I find it very flattering that the media would believe that Ron Brannon and I are lovers, since he is very attractive, but the truth is, Ron and I are just friends," I snapped, my voice raising slightly in distress. I was clenching my jaw uneasily, looking around for anyone who could save me from this unwanted interrogation. I totally sucked at lying, my voice would betray me every single time.

"I saw the photos, it seemed like a very intimate lunch for two people who claim to be just friends," said the woman, staring me down intently. My heart was racing anxiously, I wasn't sure what I could tell this woman without giving myself away. I never dealt well with confrontations. Besides, I already felt guilty enough about the feelings I had for Ron.

"Don't be ridiculous darling. Lane is all mine," said Jorge arriving at my side, and draping his arm possessively around my shoulders.

"Really?" said the woman, eyeing me quizzically. I smiled at her serenely. She seemed completely unconvinced, of course, it did seem like a bit of jest. Jorge was hardly my type. He was probably about ten years older than me, and he spoke effusively, with a thick, French accent. He was just barely taller than me, and he was almost completely bald. I was also quite sure that he was gay, but if this was what rumors Jorge wanted flying about Hollywood, then so be it. I wasn't about to contradict anything he said, on the record.

"Oh darling, I had so hoped to keep it a secret a little bit longer. Now the press will never leave the two of us alone," I told him, with a bit of a pout.

"I know my sweet, but it was going to come out sooner or later," crooned Jorge, taking me by the hand and leading me away from the annoying reporter.

Jorge led me over to the bar and handed me a glass of wine. I took it from him and took a small sip, relieved to be away from the scrutinizing eyes of the reporter.

"Thank you for following my lead. I appreciate your discretion, it is better this way. Believe me," said Jorge, giving me a little smile.

"If you say so," I told him, giving him a bland smile.

"I usually trust that these things will just blow over, but this time, I am not certain I can count on that," said Jorge, staring me down seriously.

"Really Jorge, why is that?" I asked, he laughed in delight.

"I imagine I must place half of the blame on your somewhat, colorful past," he said, raising his eyebrows at me seductively.

"And the other half of the blame?" I asked, tilting my head to the side a little. I gave him a cool smile.

"My keen observation skills. I could not help but notice that there is a bit of a spark between you and Brannon. I think he is finding himself quite charmed by you," said Jorge, flashing me a sly smile.

"I guess I'm finding myself charmed by him as well. For some reason I can't seem to help myself," I said.

Jorge gave me a gentle smile. "I imagine it's partially my fault, I had let my guard down. Since you are now over forty, I find it quite ironic that nearly twenty five years later, you can still turn on the charm and seduce any man you want," said Jorge, giving me a little wink.

"Mr. Broussard, what do you know of my life, twenty five years ago?" I asked, I was assessing him haughtily. I did have a somewhat colorful past, but thankfully, most people didn't seem to remember that anymore.

"Perhaps you do not remember me, but I was Tom Singleton's assistant in France, when you skated with the Theater Company. I guess I remember you best as Justin Melbourne's wife," said Jorge, flashing me a sly smile.

I gasped and stared at him in shock.

"Oh, I am sorry, have I hit a bit of a raw nerve?" asked Jorge, smiling at me coyly.

"That was a long time ago," I managed to whisper. I was suddenly shaking, my voice had faded away to nothing.

"The point I am hoping to make, Ms. Jensen, is the

show must go on. I know the position you were put in, back in Paris. You did what you had to do for the show once before. Now I am asking you to go along with this little scam for the good of my show," said Jorge, eyeing me seriously.

"The scam is, the two of us are lovers, am I right?" I asked, looking him in the eye.

"That is correct my love," said Jorge, raising his glass to me in a silent toast.

"Well, since you traveled with the show in France, undoubtedly, you've heard all the rumors about me. I only hope that you can handle me," I told him, flashing him a seductive smile.

"I will certainly give it my best effort," he said, smiling back at me. I almost cracked up, he was flirting with me, but I was almost certain that he was gay. I felt like this was some sort of contest...he was trying to shock me. I hated to tell him, but he was about to loose at his own little game.

"I find your offer to be quite intriguing, if a lover is what you want, a lover is what you get! I can't wait to get you home so I can rip all your clothes off," I told him, giving him a little wink and a sly smile.

"I believe that might be construed as sexual harassment Ms. Jensen. I am your boss," said Jorge, eyeing me casually.

"I was merely following your lead Mr. Broussard," I told him, anxiously stifling a giggle. "I mean, why pretend when we can just do it. I mean, who's stopping us?"

"Am I to believe that you think that I wish to have an affair with you?" asked Jorge, his face was suddenly shocked. I was biting my lip to avoid laughing hysterically.

"Well Jorge, I am a woman, and I do have needs..." I

was smiling seductively at him.

"Lane I..." Jorge mumbled, his face suddenly looked panicked.

I couldn't help it, I dissolved into laughter, I couldn't keep a straight face any longer. Jorge was staring at me in shock.

"You were messing with me!" he cried, unable to hide his shock.

"I'm sorry, I couldn't help myself. Besides, it was you who started it. I'm not stupid Jorge, I get what's going on, I'm willing to go along with it and take the heat off of Ron," I told him, rolling my eyes.

"Good, for a minute there, I thought you might have gotten the wrong idea about me," said Jorge, giving me a smile.

"Don't worry Jorge, I won't tell your partner that you made the moves on me," I giggled.

"Partner...I do not believe I told you I have a partner," said Jorge, assessing me carefully.

"But you do, don't you?" I asked, raising my eyebrows at him, daring him to deny it.

"Yes, but..."

"Shhh, here comes Maurice," I whispered, flirtatiously straightening Jorge's tie. "I'll see you later my little stud muffin," I crooned as I turned toward Maurice, who's camera was rolling, of course. I acted surprised to see him and I gave him an innocent little wave. "Uh oh, you weren't supposed to see that."

Maurice panned his camera in on Jorge's embarrassed face. "Go away Maurice," he snapped.

# CHAPTER 10

That first week I was in Hollywood flew by, and as the weeks turned into a full month, I have to say, I was beginning to see a tiny glimmer of hope in my terribly mismatched team.

As green as Ron was, he had more determination than anyone I had ever met. Elena had also become quite inspired as Ron improved and they were actually starting to impress me with the way they skated together. Soon, I was comfortable enough to introduce them to a few easy dance steps for opening night.

I was still a bit aggravated with Ron's arrogance, he had nearly ruined his feet by pushing himself with his extra skating. Those first few weeks I spent at least 20 minutes before each practice, covering all his blisters with moleskin before he could even get his skates on.

Our whirlwind month of training was drawing to an end, and we would now fall into a new routine as the actual competition began. We were to have practices on Mondays and Tuesdays, then we would tape the first show of the season on Wednesday and it would air on Thursday night. Then on Fridays we would begin working on the next week's program, and start the whole process over again.

I was dreading our first taping, as I sat in the conference room with the network executives as they went over the story line for the upcoming season premier. The actual skating part of the show was going to be filmed in front of a live audience and the show itself, was going to feature clips of our interviews and, of course, clips of all the drama during our practices.

The skating portion of this first show was merely going to feature a 30 second intro skate for each team, which would simply introduce the audience to each team and highlight a bit of what they had learned thus far.

For my team's intro, I had picked a 30 second clip

from the song "Smooth" by Santana, for Ron and Elena to skate to. I was teaching them a few dance steps that had a bit of a tango influence. I didn't want them to do anything too fancy, lest Ron might be laying on the ice.

I was a bit frustrated, even with the tango steps, the whole thing seemed a little lame. I wanted something memorable, this was their intro for the entire season, I wanted my team to make a stunning impression on the judges and the viewers. What could I have them do, that no other team would even try? I wanted my team to stand out, but Ron could barely skate, let alone wow the audience with some technically difficult stunt.

Suddenly, I had a brilliant idea! If I could teach Ron and Elena a death spiral for their intro, it would completely blow everyone away. I wasn't sure if they could master it by Wednesday or not. It should be easy enough for Ron, if he could plant his skate in the ice and maintain his footing enough to allow Elena to glide around him on the ice.

The hard part, was that Elena had never been a pairs skater, so she had no experience doing a death spiral. Trusting your partner was an integral part of this move. Elena seemed to barely tolerate Ron!

Ron was staring at me blankly when I announced excitedly what I wanted them to do. Of course, the name does sound rather daunting, though Ron was not the one who's life was in danger. Elena, at least, knew what I was talking about, and she downright refused to even try it.

"Are you crazeee? He weel keel me!" cried Elena, glaring at me as if I were a complete idiot.

I was frowning and rolling my eyes. Why did Elena even come on this show? Maybe since I had virtually grown up doing these things, they didn't seem all that scary to me. Personally, I thought she was being a big baby. I had already decided, if we were going to stand out during our intro on Wednesday night, we needed to do it, unfortunately, my team was not convinced. I frowned with the realization that if we were going to try this, I would just have to be the guinea pig. I would try it with Ron first, if things went well, I would work on coercing Elena to try it.

I explained to Ron what he needed to do, he basically just needed to skate in a small circle, holding my arm, and keep my head from hitting the ice. It seemed easy enough, but I was suddenly nervous. What was I thinking? Ron was, by no means, a skater and I hadn't done a death spiral in years. I had just recently turned forty three years old! Luckily, my life meant little to nothing to me anymore, all I had left were my children, and they were both far away at college. Really, what did I have to loose?

Elena was staring at me in shock, as I gave Ron a few last minute instructions before we actually tried the stunt. Elena was watching wide eyed as we skated around and gained speed for our first try. I felt a twinge of fear as I grasped Ron's hand tightly and I slowly leaned into the spin, my back parallel to the surface of the ice. I'm sure Elena thought that I had completely lost my mind!

On that first try, I hadn't quite got my edge, so my foot slid out from under me, and I skidded across the ice on my back. Ron was horrified, but it really wasn't his fault. Like I said, I hadn't attempted this in years. I was beside myself with excitement that we had come so close to nailing it!

I was anxious to try the move again, but Ron was not so enthusiastic. He wanted me to give it up, he was afraid I would get hurt. I was finally able to coerce him to try it one more time. Our second attempt was much better. We made two nice rotations, then Rob pulled me up so hard, I almost fell on top of him. As I struggled to right myself, I looked up to see that he was gazing down at me, admiringly. I almost fell right on my butt, I was caught more than a little bit off guard.

"Wow, that was completely incredible," said Ron, smiling down at me. He was beaming at me proudly.

"Well, if you pull Elena up that hard, we might have to retrieve her from across the rink," I told him with a smile.

I had to look away. I was very uncomfortable, he was still smiling at me, and for some reason, my heart was pounding with an adrenaline rush. I wasn't sure if it was because I had just pulled off the craziest move of my middle aged life, or if I was just charmed by his dazzling smile.

It seemed as if I was paralyzed, I was standing there staring up at him, suddenly completely mesmerized by his smile. Abruptly, I was snapped back to reality by Jorge's voice booming across the ice.

"Lane Jensen, you are completely amazing!" cried Jorge. I was completely stunned to see Jorge standing there, near the entrance of the ice.

I whipped around quickly and tried to conceal the look of pure guilt that was washing across my face. Jorge was standing there at the edge of the ice waving at me, I couldn't read his face at all. Elena was smiling sweetly at him. Of course she was, he was a producer, and her ticket to stardom, or so she thought.

I tried to hide my embarrassment, I'd been caught in the act of ogling. Of course, Maurice was right there, with his camera trained on our every move. I grimaced painfully, I couldn't get away with anything, I'd totally forgotten about Maurice.

I gave Jorge a guilty smile, hopefully, he hadn't noticed that I had been gazing up into Ron's eyes like a school girl with a massive crush.

"That was amazing, obviously, I picked the wrong woman to do the actual skating," said Jorge, giving Elena a meaningful glance as he waved her away distastefully. "Lane darling, may I have a brief word with you?"

My heart sank guiltily. The jig was up, Jorge had seen everything. He had trusted me, now, I was about to get a lecture. I hesitated briefly, then I skated toward the gate, Maurice started to follow me with his camera.

"No, I do not think so, Mr. Dubois, please take your little toy elsewhere," said Jorge, waving him away like a child.

Maurice rolled his eyes, then he turned abruptly and trained his camera on Ron, who shook his head miserably, then calmly skated away.

"What?" I snapped, as I skated up to Jorge.

"What, exactly, do you think you are doing?" he cried.

"I thought a death spiral would spice up our 30 second intro. I wanted to do something no other team would even attempt this early in the game. Elena refused to even try it, she's afraid because Ron is so big and clumsy. I knew he would be fine. I thought that if Ron could do it with me, she would see it was okay, then she would try it," I told him shrugging nonchalantly.

"Listen Lane, I may be gay, but I am not completely blind as to what is going on here. If you would let him, Ron would do it with you, then where would we be?" cried Jorge.

"What are you talking about? I was only skating with him, isn't that what you hired me for?" I cried indignantly.

"I know what I did not hire you for! I do not know what kind of crazy, middle age, chemistry you and Ron Brannon have together, but you need to put a lid on it! There is a spark there, I can see it. I imagine it is only a matter of time before everyone can see it! I realize you're divorced and it's probably been months since you got laid, but you can't do this, he's married Lane!" cried Jorge, he was waving his arms excitedly as if he were on the edge of a breakdown.

"Jorge!" I cried, my face suddenly turning red with embarrassment, my life totally sucked, I didn't need Jorge to point that out to me.

"I understand...you have needs...there are plenty of single men in Hollywood..."

"Jorge, for God's sake! I didn't do anything!" I cried, struggling to keep my voice at a reasonable tone. It wanted to creep up an entire octave in hysteria. My heart was pounding nervously in my chest. I wasn't sure why I was feeling a strange attraction to Ron, but I couldn't help it. No matter what I felt, I already knew I couldn't act on those feelings, the fact that Jorge kept bringing it up, was making me crazy!

"Lane, I was so excited when I walked into the rink today and saw that you were teaching him the death spiral. With your talent and drive, you could take that hopeless team all the way to the finals, that is how much confidence I have in you. I mean, if the two of you could just work together as coach and student, I would be fine."

"Jorge!"

"Lane, I believed you, when you told me there was nothing between the two of you, I trusted your judgement. Now that I have seen it first hand, I am very worried. He has feelings for you Lane, I saw it on his face. I seriously doubt that the two of you can work together closely, and not act on those feelings for nearly twelve weeks."

"Jorge please, I'm trying to make this work, we're just friends for God's sake!" I cried, trying to keep my voice low, so only Jorge could hear me.

"Lane, you are essentially single now. If he made the moves on you, do you really think you could resist him? I mean look at him, he's yummy," said Jorge, flashing me a sly smile.

"Jorge really...he's married. Of course, I'm attracted to him, I guess I just can't help it. But believe me when I tell you, you have nothing to worry about, we're just friends."

"I trust you to keep it that way, do you understand?" he asked, staring into my eyes determinedly.

"Yes Jorge," I told him, rolling my eyes miserably.

"You can wait twelve weeks, right? When the show is over you can screw his brains out if you wish, but not before," said Jorge, giving me a coy smile.

"Jorge, you know you're the only one for me," I crooned, then I turned to skate back out on the ice. I had work to do, I didn't really want, or need a lecture. Ron was off limits, I realized that. Jorge grabbed my arm, before I could skate away.

"I mean it Lane, I will not have the negative publicity, it would ruin everything. I know you, of all people, are well aware of the power of negative publicity," he crooned, giving me a meaningful glance.

I snatched my arm from his grasp and glared into his eyes. It was true, I knew all too well the power of negative publicity. It was a destructive force that seemed to have a life of it's own. Once it gained a foothold, it would leave reality in the dust, leaving it's victims completely powerless to stop it.

Jorge had done his research on me, he knew that the media had destroyed my life years ago. I wasn't about to let that happen again. "I know Jorge, trust me, just let it go," I snapped, then I gave him a dazzling smile and skated away.

When I arrived back with my group, Elena and Ron were both staring at me blankly, not really sure why Jorge seemed to be so angry with me. Maurice was eyeing me with a smug smile on his face, it was as if he knew exactly what had upset Jorge. I narrowed my eyes at him, I was sure my face was red with embarrassment. Hopefully, the rest of the group hadn't heard any of my annoying exchange with Jorge.

"Okay, are you two ready to try this?" I asked, trying to sound enthusiastic, even though I was feeling a bit like a whipped dog at the moment.

Luckily, Elena had been so impressed with Ron's effort, she was actually excited to try the death spiral. Elena had never actually done one, so it took quite a bit of coaching to get her through it. By the end of our practice session they nearly had it down and I knew, it was going to be the highlight of our 30 second intro.

When our practice was over, I was sitting on the bench unlacing my skates, Ron came over and sat next to me. He was only being friendly, but given my earlier encounter with Jorge, I was nervous. I didn't want Jorge freaking out again.

Besides, Jorge was right, if Ron and I were publicly linked it would be bad publicity for the show. Not to mention the fact that I had no intention of becoming involved with a happily married man.

"I'm pretty excited about the death spiral. Do you think any of the other teams have anything that cool planned for their intro?" he asked, flashing me a stunning smile.

"From what I've seen, I seriously doubt it, but we can't get too cocky. This is just an intro, it's not worth any points, next week we will need to focus on our first program. There's a lot more to learn if you want to fill up a full two minutes," I told him.

"I know whatever you come up with will be spectacular," he said, unlacing his skates while he talked.

"Thanks Ron," I told him, unable to conceal the smile that seemed to automatically come to my lips.

"There's that smile I love," he said, gazing into my eyes for a moment or two, then looking away shyly. I drew in a deep breath, warning bells were suddenly going off in my brain. Hopefully, it was nothing more than a friendly compliment, but I was worried, I couldn't have him flirting with me. I was almost sure I wasn't strong enough to deal with that for twelve weeks!

"Ron, I..." I wasn't sure what I wanted to say, but whatever it was, it wouldn't come out anyway. My mouth was dry and my heart was pounding nervously.

"Yeah, I know. You and Jorge, you have some kind of thing going on. I realize that, I just don't understand it. I don't really see that the two of you have anything in common," said Ron, giving me a little shrug.

"Jorge and I have plenty in common," I snapped, trying to force my voice to sound convincing. I realized that trying to convince anyone that Jorge and I were lovers, would be a bit of an uphill battle.

Jorge was not what I would consider attractive, he had been born into money, that was obvious from his demeanor, and in the way that he dressed. I was guessing that he was fifty four or fifty five. He worked out, so he was pretty fit, but he was not really what I would consider to be drop dead gorgeous. I had developed a sincere affection for Jorge, he was driven, but deep down he was a kind and caring person.

"It's just that he's like fifty or something, and you're how old? Like thirty eight?" asked Ron.

"I just turned forty three, and why should you even care? You're married!" I cried.

"You're forty three? Wow, I had guessed that you were younger than me. I just turned forty," he said, with a little laugh.

"Listen Ron, Jorge and I have a history together, we both toured Europe with the European Theater Company. He knew me years ago, back when I was the professional skater," I told him with a shrug. I wasn't sure how else to explain my strange relationship with Jorge.

"Actually, now that you've brought all that up, this is what I had been wondering about. I was curious, I knew you must have been one hell of a skater, I mean you still are. I'm just a bit confused, because I Googled you and I couldn't find much about you at all. What I found was a detail of your choreography experience in Colorado Springs, but it seems like before that, you didn't even exist," said Ron.

"You Googled me!" I cried, trying to sound appropriately exasperated.

"Sure, I have the right to to know who I'm working with, and what your experience is. I even looked under your maiden name. I really only found a few news clips, before 1980, nothing too spectacular. I was a bit confused though, Jorge had told me that you were a pairs skater, but the news articles I found didn't say anything about pairs skating," said Ron, eyeing me carefully.

I sighed miserably, maybe coming here had been a mistake. Maybe my scandalous past was finally coming back to haunt me. I guess I'd been so heartbroken by my divorce, I hadn't even considered the consequences of putting my life back in the limelight.

"I wasn't a pairs skater at first, try Googling the name Lane Melbourne and see what you come up with, you may find out a little bit more than you really want to know about me," I told him, rolling my eyes.

I was cringing inwardly, over the years the scandal had faded away. I had forgotten that in this day and age people could easily revisit the past with a few clicks of a computer's mouse. I should have known better than to come on this show and put my past back on display for further scrutiny.

As far as I was concerned, Lane Melbourne was a completely different person than I was now. A person created out of necessity, when I was barely old enough to know better. Who would have known that my own parents would sell me out when I was just fifteen years old?

"Really Lane, I don't care about your past, I wasn't trying to dig up dirt on you or anything. I just wanted to know what you were like, when you were younger," said

Ron, looking into my eyes very earnestly.

"All I can say is that Lane Melbourne was a person I left behind a long time ago. You may be shocked, when you figure out who I used to be," I told him with a wry smile.

"I really can't imagine what Lane Jensen would have to hide," said Ron, smiling at me.

"I'm not hiding anything, do your research if you must. I don't begrudge you your right to know. I'm just saying, some stones are best left unturned," I told him with a shrug. Jorge had been right, I did have a colorful past, some people might not realize that I did what I had to do, just to survive.

My seemingly perfect childhood had been nothing but an illusion and my transition into adulthood had been a crazy drama, made even more public by the ever present media. Growing up is always difficult, unfortunately growing up in the spotlight is a nightmare!

"Lane, I realize that everyone thinks I'm just here for the money. Maybe it started out that way, but the truth is, I really don't even know who I am anymore. I loved playing football, but everyone knew I couldn't do that forever. I took the job with the sports show in New York because it was decent money and it seemed like a good fit for me."

"I was happy, but Jenae is convinced I did it to punish her. She's constantly riding me about doing something that makes more money. I feel like my life is never my own. I keep doing what I think is right for everybody else, but I never do what is right for me. For just once in my life I wanted to do something strange and unexpected, something no one would think I was capable of. This is it," he said, looking into my eyes.

I nodded at him, I couldn't find the words to speak. We were a lot alike. Jorge was right, there was some strange chemistry between the two of us, a chemistry I was forced to ignore.

"Remember what you said to me that first day we met Lane? You said that you were starting over, you were doing something outside your comfort zone. That's what I want. I want to live my life. I feel like I've been a pawn on a chess board for too long, everyone else was making the moves, but it was my life. First my father, then my coaches, now my wife."

"I feel like I haven't been happy since I was just a small child. I've been successful, but I haven't really been happy. How pathetic is that?" he asked, giving me a rueful smile.

"If you want to be happy, you need to follow your heart," I said, mindlessly repeating an old saying my grandmother had told me years ago.

"What if my heart leads me to you?" he asked, looking into my eyes, earnestly.

"Ron...I need to go," I snapped, standing up and turning away from him quickly.

"Did I do something wrong?" he asked, standing up and taking my hand. I wanted to pull my hand away, but suddenly, my heart was pounding and I felt as if I could barely breathe.

I scanned the arena quickly, to see if Maurice was lurking nearby, secretly filming our intimate conversation.

"Ron, it's Jorge, it's just that..."

"Lane, I realize that Jorge is your boss and the two of you are having some sort of a thing..."

"No Ron, there's no thing! Jorge is my boss, and he has forbid me to have any contact with you except on the ice, even on the ice we have to be careful. You're married, and if people suspected that we were attracted to each other, then that would only make for bad publicity for the show!" I cried, finally feeling free, now that all that was out in the open.

"So you are attracted to me," said Ron, as he flashed me a sly smile.

"Ron I'm sorry, I shouldn't have said anything. If Jorge suspects anything, he'll break our team up. I don't want that, I really think we may have a chance in this competition."

"What if I told you I feel the same way? "asked Ron, looking into my eyes, making my heart pound completely out of control.

"Ron please don't do this, you're married," I breathed, still looking around the ice rink nervously.

"What if I told you my marriage was on the rocks anyway?" he whispered, his body seemed to be drifting closer to me.

"Ron, your marriage is not on the rocks. You love Jenae, you love your girls," I told him, as heartbreaking as it was to say the words. I wanted to tell him that Jenae was using him, that she didn't deserve him, but really, it was none of my business. Besides, even though I had feelings for Ron, I had meant what I said to Jorge that day. I wasn't a home wrecker.

"No, I've been in denial. Jenae wants out, I can feel it. She used to love me, the man. Now she loves Ron Brannon, the legend, now that I'm not playing football anymore...things are different. I can't help but feel like she's out there looking..."

"Ron don't be ridiculous! Maybe she pushed you to do this show for reasons other than money. Maybe she just wanted you to prove to yourself that you can do whatever it is you set out to do. Maybe..."

"Lane, you don't know her like I do. You're different, you care about me, the man. You care about my feelings, my dreams. I was drawn to you right away," said Ron, laying his hand gently on my cheek. He was looking down into my eyes, casting a spell over me. I couldn't move, in fact, I felt as if I could barely breathe.

He was going to kiss me, and I wasn't sure I had it in me, to stop him.

"Ron, don't do this," I whispered, as I felt his arms sliding around my waist.

"I have to do this," his voice was deep and velvety, it felt heavenly to be in his arms. I was so swept away, I forgot where I was, maybe even who I was.

"Ron, we can't...I managed to whisper, I barely realized I was drifting even closer to him, in anticipation of the kiss.

"What Jenae and I have is over," said Ron, drifting even closer to me. My own conscious was crying out to me. Someone was always watching, he was married, we couldn't do this.

"It's bad publicity either way, just let it go Ron," I said, finally managing to pull myself from his embrace. I was almost panting as I turned away from him, unable to look him in the eye.

I cursed myself, what was wrong with me? I had almost made a huge mistake! I wanted a man who wasn't mine for the taking. I could not submit to my body's insane longing for him.

Ron was standing there, just a few feet away staring at me in shock. His breathing was labored and he looked so hurt, you would have thought that I had slapped him.

"Lane why do you push me away, when I know you want me too? I can feel it, you can't deny it," he whispered, his voice was heavy with emotion.

"Goodbye Ron," I snapped, picking up my bag and leaving him standing there in the lobby. I wasn't strong enough to face my feelings for Ron. Maybe I was just weak because Greg had hurt me so badly. I wasn't really sure. What I was sure of was that Jorge Broussard was a very powerful man, and I had no intention, whatsoever, of pissing him off.

# CHAPTER 11

Somehow, I managed to make it till Wednesday, and the taping of our first show in front of a live audience. The network had made it into a big tadoo and was billing the season opener as an exclusive event, as the entire audience was there by invitation only.

I was excited because I had choreographed our team's little 30 second teaser into a steamy tango, with the death spiral as the grand finale! I was almost certain that none of the other teams would try something so risky, right at the very beginning.

Ron and Elena had been practicing faithfully all week and I had actually been a little bit surprised myself, as our little teaser looked completely incredible! Putting an advanced move into our intro was a bold move, and all our practices had been closed, so I hoped that the other teams would all pee in their pants when they saw that my team actually had a death spiral!

Since all the performances this week were just intros, there were no required elements and the teams could pretty much do whatever they felt comfortable doing. I was giggling to myself, I was sure no other team would try anything even remotely risky.

The premier was going to be a huge deal! The network had been promoting the show shamelessly with 30 second teasers all week. They had invited some of the biggest names in figure skating to come to tonight's performance and make comments on the talent. To be included among the invited guests were family members of the cast, including Ron's wife Jenae and his daughters Arianna and McKenna.

The morning of the premier was crazy busy. My team had our final practice and I was scheduled to accompany the skaters to their final costume fitting. The costumes I had picked out for them were red and black Spanish style outfits, suitable for a tango. Elena squealed with delight when she tried her sexy dress on.

"Look at me, I am a flamingo dancer," she giggled, the seamstress tugged on her sleeve and gave her an odd look.

"It's flamenco dancer Elena," I told her with a giggle. Elena didn't care, she was too busy fussing with her long ruffled skirt to pay me any mind.

I was doing my best to avoid looking at Ron, he looked so handsome. I kept myself busy by pretending to fuss with the ruffles at the neckline of Elena's dress.

Since my recent lapse of good judgement, Ron and I had tried to keep our time together completely professional, though Jorge was right, there was some sort of crazy chemistry between the two of us. I just hoped that it wasn't completely obvious to everyone else, especially his wife, who was in town for the taping of the first episode of the show. I was already anxious about meeting her. Hopefully, she wouldn't notice the undeniable chemistry Ron and I had together.

That evening the taping of the show went well. Ron and Elena performed like true professionals. The tango steps even appeared to be appropriately passionate, despite the fact that the passion that Elena and Ron felt for each other was extreme dislike, not love.

Watching the other teams perform was a bit comical. None of the other routines were technically difficult at all, we were the only team to try anything a bit tricky. I was now secretly glad that I had not been assigned one of the hockey players. They may have experience skating, but not in figure skates, and it was the figure skates that they were required to wear, that were tripping them up. They were used to zipping around the rink in hockey skates, not skates with toe picks.

Team Muramsatsu had a bit of a rough performance due to the toe picks. I pretended to concerned and shocked when Mick stumbled, but I was secretly pleased.

After the performance, we mingled with everyone in the lobby. I was trapped there between Jorge, who was still desperately trying to pass me off as his girlfriend and Ron, who I was hopelessly attracted to.

I had tuned out most of the din, but soon I realized Ron was speaking to me.

"What?" I mumbled, suddenly returning to reality.

"This is my wife Jenae. Jenae, this is our coach and choreographer Lane Jensen," said Ron.

Hello," said Jenae, flashing me a condescending smile and offering me a limp handshake.

"So nice to meet you," I told her as I pulled my hand away, slightly disturbed. There was something about a limp handshake that always set me on edge. I was looking her over carefully and she seemed to be assessing me as well.

Jenae Brannon was perfectly gorgeous. She was tall, but still slightly shorter than me. Her hair was swept up in an elegant chignon and she was wearing a dazzling designer dress with a plunging neckline that dipped so deep, she threatened to spill right out of the front of her dress. I tried to remain expressionless, but I caught Jorge in the act of checking her out.

He gave me an embarrassed smile and whispered. "They're fake."

I rolled my eyes, but Jenae didn't even notice, she was glancing ambitiously around the room. She was obviously ready to mingle with people who were much more important than me. I was finding Mrs. Brannon to be haughty and detached. Her children were standing there beside her, but they might as well have been miles away, as she barely acknowledged them.

"These are your girls?" I asked, smiling at them.

"Yes," said Ron, beaming proudly. "Arianna and McKenna."

"Such beautiful and well mannered young ladies. How did you like your daddy's skating?" I asked them, with a smile.

"It was funny!" said McKenna, with a little giggle.

"Yeah, I didn't know he could skate at all. I thought he was going to mess up bad," said Arianna.

"How do you girls like it in Hollywood?" I asked them.

"It's fun!" cried McKenna, excitedly.

"Yeah, we got to go shopping on Rodeo drive," said Arianna.

"Mr. Broussard tells me you're the best choreographer on the cast," said Jenae, eyeing me with barely concealed disdain. I was still clinging to Jorge's arm, hopelessly trying to convince Jenae, and everyone else, that Jorge and I were lovers.

"Oh Jorge, you're such a bragger," I said, kissing him on the cheek affectionately.

"Darling, why would I lie? Nobody's better than you," he growled, spanking me on the behind, familiarly. I gave Jorge a stern glare, but I didn't slap him, like I really wanted to. I kind of thought he was taking this girlfriend thing, a little too far.

I was hoping, Jenae didn't notice that Ron had given Jorge a stern glare as well, and he was now rolling his eyes miserably over the entire, ridiculous charade.

"Hopefully you're good enough to ensure that Ron makes it to the finals. We could use the extra money. You've no idea what a pay cut he had to endure when he retired from football," said Jenae, shaking her head miserably.

"Oh, that's so sad," I mused. "Rest assured, I will do my best Mrs. Brannon." I had to bite my lower lip, I almost burst into maniacal laughter. Poor Jenae, she thought she was suffering, she probably had no idea how the rest of the world was struggling in these hard times. Even with his enormous pay cut, Ron still made probably five times what I made back in Colorado Springs. The Brannon family was hardly anywhere near the poverty level. Though I must admit that my own fortunes had improved since I arrived in Hollywood.

I was happy that the taping was over for the night. We were scheduled to go to the gala send off party, yet another publicity ploy, that the network had cooked up to promote the show. I was expected to attend, as part of my contract. I wasn't looking forward to it, big Hollywood parties were not really my style, I planned to show up for a few hours then go back to the condo and straight to bed. For some reason, I was completely exhausted.

At the gala, I had no choice, but to spend the entire evening on Jorge's arm. He was determined for everyone to believe that the two of us were a couple, and it was working, though it was getting a little nauseating for me.

I may have been on Jorge's arm, but I couldn't keep my eyes off of Ron. Now that I had met his wife, I realized she was just as awful as I had imagined she was. They had been married for fifteen years, he told me that things had been different in the beginning, the money had changed who she really was, now the need for it, consumed her.

Every time I caught his eye, he would give me a little smile, it was the only time he smiled all night. He was obviously miserable, I was obviously miserable. Jenae had sent their girls back to her hotel with a babysitter and she was busy working the crowd, and dragging Ron along with her.

I was completely bored with the entire affair. I was not a Hollywood socialite, and I had no desire to stay there and work the crowd. I had no acting ambitions, I had taken this job just to try something different, now that I was here, I realized that Hollywood was not the place for me. As soon as the show finished taping, I planned to go back to Colorado Springs. Hollywood was not really my style.

Unfortunately, it seemed as if I wouldn't be escaping the party any time soon. Jorge was obviously afraid I was going to sneak off with Ron if he took his eyes off me for a single second. I was stuck there, as Jorge ambitiously tried to convince everyone that the two of us were sleeping together. I was growing quite tired of his annoying sexual innuendo and his new found need to spank me or grope me, just to prove his point.

After an especially annoying encounter, Jorge and I were finally standing in a corner alone, just watching the crowd in front of us. "Are we going to have sex later?" I whispered. I was messing with him, I wanted to giggle, I'd had a few glasses of wine, everything was starting to seem completely hilarious to me.

"Oooh, why would you ask me that?" asked Jorge, eyeing me disgustedly.

"It's the foreplay darling. That's the second time tonight that you've spanked me. It's making me totally hot," I told him, raising my eyebrows at him playfully.

"Good God, if you want to get laid so badly maybe you should hook up with Mick Santos. Look at the man, he's nothing but a raw piece of male meat, and very single," said Jorge looking me over, disgustedly.

"Maybe I just want your meat," I told him, flashing him a seductive smile. I was trying hard not to giggle. I was being very naughty, but I had decided I was ready to leave, and Jorge was about to send me home without an argument.

"You're drunk!" he cried, glaring at me in shock.

"Just a little bit," I crooned, giving him a seductive smile and pressing a wet kiss on his cheek.

"Bloody hell, we must get you out of here," he snapped, glancing around the room nervously. I had to conceal my satisfied smile, he thought I was totally wasted. Of course, loose lips sink ships, and Jorge had no desire for me to drunkenly spill any secrets. He was suddenly quite ready for me to go home. I had draped myself on him, feigning inebriation, Jorge was completely horrified.

"Maurice!" called Jorge, waving down our camera man. Maurice trotted over to us quickly. "Can you do me a favor and get Lane a taxi and make sure she gets back to her condo safely. I fear she's had a bit too much to drink," said Jorge, pressing a hundred dollar bill into Maurice's hand. Jorge watched him like a concerned parent, as Maurice took me by the arm and walked me toward the front lobby.

I walked out clinging to Maurice's arm, as the concierge got me my taxi. I was quite pleased with my new found acting skills. I was ecstatic to be leaving the party, until Maurice got into the cab with me, and I realized he planned to accompany me home, for some unknown reason.

I was leery as the cab pulled away from the curb, I didn't like this one bit. I had never really trusted Maurice anyway, he came off as a bit of a sleeze ball, so needless to say, I was not happy to realize he planned to accompany me back to the condo. I could only hope that he would see me in, and then go on his way.

Within moments, my worst fears were realized. Maurice gave me a creepy smile and slid closer to me.

"Well Ms. Jensen, we are finally alone," he said, leering at me.

"Whatever you have on your mind the answer is no!" I snapped. "Sir, can you please turn around and take this man back to the party, we're not together."

"Oh come on Lane, don't be that way," said Maurice, looking into my eyes and sliding even closer to me, sliding his hand up my thigh.

I grabbed his hand and removed it from my thigh. "I mean it Maurice, back off..."

Without warning, Maurice pounced on me. In seconds the slime bucket was on top of me, ambitiously trying to cram his tongue down my throat.

"Maurice, what are you doing?" I cried, trying to push him off of me.

"Did you want to go back to your place or mine?" asked Maurice, raising his eyebrows at me seductively.
"Get off of me now Maurice, or I will..."

"Or you will what? I don't believe you can make me any hotter than you already have. Come on Lane, I can give you what you need," breathed Maurice, pressing his body seductively against mine. I was struggling to push him off of me.

"Mr. Dubois, I advise you to keep your hands to yourself. I am very sorry to inform you that I am not drunk at all. My drunkenness was simply a little act. I was merely hoping to get out of the party early. My boyfriend, your boss, I might point out, will not be very happy to learn that you have been hitting on me," I told him, playing the only card that I had.

Maurice rolled his eyes and gave me an arrogant smile.

"Lane darling, you may have everyone else around here fooled, but you cannot fool me, Jorge is not your boyfriend, he is gay...I am not an idiot. Besides, I have been there on the ice with you every day, I can see what is going on. Ron Brannon is the one that you want. I've been going over the practice footage, and I must say, I have some very interesting footage of the two of you together, when you think that no one else is around."

"You have nothing, Ron and I are friends, that's all," I snapped angrily.

"Most people would believe that, but being there

every day, I guess you could say, I see more. I see the smiles, the glances, the longing..." he whispered seductively.

I glared at him angrily. I couldn't say anything, I was guilty.

"You want him," said Maurice, as he reached out and traced his finger across my cheek. I snatched his hand away quickly.

"I mean it Maurice, don't touch me!" I seethed.

"Come on Lane, you want me to keep your little secret, don't you? You and me, one night, I promise you'll have a good time."

"If you so much as lay a finger on me again I will make sure that you loose your job," I snapped. My voice was strong, but I felt like I was on the verge of tears. I didn't deal well with intimidation. Maurice obviously thought that he had the advantage over me somehow.

"I'm the one holding all the cards here. I have incriminating video footage, video clips that could sneak off to another show that would pay handsomely for it. I could be a rich man, just by ratting you out," he said, smiling at me seductively.

I grimaced, I found Maurice to be completely repulsive. I narrowed my eyes and glared at him, there was no way I would ever give in to someone who was trying to blackmail me.

"You have nothing...I'm his coach..."

"Brannon is married, but the two of you are very close. In fact, I get the feeling that you and Mr. Brannon have done a little bit more than just skate together," said Maurice, leering at me.

"There is nothing between us. I'm his coach and choreographer, so of course, we spend a lot of time together..." I was trying to sound indignant, but my voice was laced with guilt.

"Think about your career Lane. Let's just say, I know exactly how Jorge feels about negative publicity, he's pretending to be your boyfriend, to keep the heat off of you and Brannon. I think Mr. Broussard might be a bit shocked if he saw some of my footage, and saw the way you have been throwing yourself at Brannon," said Maurice, flashing me a sly smile.

"I have not been throwing myself at Ron!" I cried indignantly. I was acutely aware that the cab driver was assessing us casually in his rear view mirror. I wondered if perhaps, there was a reason Maurice was throwing names around so freely.

"I'm sorry, but you haven't exactly been playing it cool and aloof either," said Maurice, staring me down arrogantly.

"What, exactly, are you planning, Maurice?" I seethed, the man was a snake.

"Let's just say that my good discretion comes at a bit of a price. A price that no amount of money can satisfy," Maurice was flashing me a smug smile.

"Let me out," I cried, I was suddenly panicking. My own cameraman meant to blackmail me.

"Wait a minute darling. It's so easy, all you have to do is give me what I want and my lips are sealed. No one needs to know that you and Ron Brannon have been getting it on," said Maurice.

"Keep your voice down Maurice," I seethed, the cab driver's eyes darted back to the road when I caught him looking at me in the rear view mirror. "Ron and I haven't been getting it on!"

"The footage I have is pretty steamy," said Maurice, fanning himself and raising his eyebrows at me. "What did you think of my video clips Tamir? They are like lovers, are they not?" asked Maurice, now addressing the cabbie, who had obviously heard everything.

"One could hardly deny the passion," said the cabbie in a thick middle eastern accent. I frowned, Maurice had totally set me up.

"Too bad he's married. The whole thing...it would be nothing but bad publicity, especially if the press were to get ahold of some of my steamy practice footage." said Maurice, flashing me a sly smile. I was furious.

"Jorge will kill you himself," I seethed, silently fearing that he might kill me also. I wondered if Maurice had caught my barely aborted kiss several days ago. Of course, that would put Jorge right over the edge!

"I'm not stupid Lane, your little affair with Jorge...it's nothing but a scam. Jorge can't give you what you need. Jorge don't want you baby, he likes the men." Maurice was leaning over me, his body was on top of mine and he was now sliding the straps of my dress over my shoulders.

"Get off of me Maurice. I swear to God," I snapped.

"Come on Lane baby. I want you, and you want me to keep my mouth shut, that's just how things work in Hollywood," said Maurice, his voice was taunting as he whispered in my ear.

"Jorge will rip your balls off with his teeth, if you cause any bad publicity," I seethed.

"I would much rather have you rip my balls off with your teeth. You're much sexier than Jorge," taunted Maurice, his hot breath was in my ear as he rubbed his body against mine.

"Don't tempt me. I might actually do it," I told him dryly.

The cab had pulled up in front of my condo and the driver was waiting patiently for me to get out.

"What's the matter? Aren't you going to ask me in? You might be sorry if you don't," said Maurice, his voice was dripping with sarcasm.

"I'm sorry Maurice, I'm afraid you're not up to it tonight," I told him, flashing him a coy smile.

Maurice was suddenly towering over me again, pressing his body against mine.

"I beg to differ with you. Would you like to feel how up, I am for it?"

I was angry and I'd had enough of his games. I grabbed his crotch and began squeezing as hard as I possibly could. Soon, Maurice was begging me to let go, but I kept squeezing. His pleas became more and more desperate and high pitched. Finally I let go and he flopped down on the seat in relief. I slipped the hundred dollar bill out of his shirt pocket and handed it to the cabbie.

"Keep the change," I told him, then I stomped away angrily.

# CHAPTER 12

I paced back and forth across the floor of my condo. I was worried. Unfortunately, I didn't doubt that Maurice had convincing footage of me with Ron. I was attracted to Ron and there were times when I felt like I didn't do a very good job of hiding my barely concealed lust.

I finally stopped my pacing and went down to my car. I had decided I was going to Jorge's house, surely he would be home by now. I thought it was important that I speak to Jorge before Maurice did, I had the feeling that Jorge's house would be Maurice's second stop of the evening.

I was feeling guilty, I had no doubt that Maurice had caught some rather "special" moments on tape, but I refused to be blackmailed. I figured the best thing to do would be go straight to Jorge and fess up. If he wanted to fire me, then so be it.

I would never succumb to Maurice's threats, anyway. How could I be certain that he would have destroyed the tapes, even if I slept with him? I cursed myself for being so naive.

I pulled into the driveway of Jorge's gorgeous Hollywood Hills home. The house was still aglow with dozens of lights so I assumed that someone was still awake. I marched right up to the front door and hit the buzzer. I was startled when the front door opened and it was Jorge's partner, Jean Luc, that answered the door. I was completely astounded when I got my first look at Jean Luc. I knew that Jorge had a partner, but Jean Luc, was not what I had expected.

Jean Luc looked more like a male Italian supermodel, than the French lover of an aging Hollywood producer. Jean Luc was tan, muscular, and not a day over thirty five. I now knew why Jorge had found Ron so "yummy". His own lover was a stunning mix of dark skin, six pack abs and rippling muscles. I could barely stop staring, Jean Luc did have a certain "drool factor" about him.

"Bonjour?" said the man, eyeing me curiously. I gave him an embarrassed smile, once again I was ogling, I couldn't help it. I hadn't paid much attention to things like this when I had been happily married, suddenly, here I was, thrown head first into a buffet of gorgeous men here in Hollywood. I was anxiously trying to compose myself as I stood face to face with Jorge's lover. Even his voice had "drool factor". It was deep and velvety, with a smooth French accent.

"May I come in?" I asked, I hesitated a bit. I didn't want to frighten Jean Luc with my boldness, but what I really wanted to do was barge in anxiously. I felt a certain urgency in my need to speak with Jorge. "Actually, it is imperative that I come in...forgive me for my brashness, you must be Jean Luc. My name is Lane Jensen, I..."

"Who is it?" I could hear Jorge's voice as he came around the corner. He stopped short when he saw me standing there in the foyer. He was standing there in a navy silk bathrobe, staring at me in shock.

"Lane? What are you doing here? It is late, we were getting ready to go to bed," he cried, staring at me in shock.

"Jorge, I'm sorry to barge in on you at home like this, but I wanted to talk to you before Maurice did. He's trying to to blackmail me. He told me he had incriminating footage of me with Ron, I'm afraid he might try something underhanded."

"What have you done with Brannon, that Maurice has incriminating footage of? I told you to stay away from him," boomed Jorge, who was suddenly enraged.

"I haven't done anything with him, but Maurice seems to think that I want him and..."

"Listen to me Lane, Maurice Dubois has been working for me for ten years. I hardly believe that..."

"Please Jorge, just hear me out. I never saw any of

the footage but I'm afraid I haven't been hiding my attraction to Ron very well, and the other day when he almost kissed me..."

"You almost kissed him?" cried Jorge, his face was devoid of any color he was so shocked.

"It was a weak moment, I'm sorry, but Maurice has no right to try to force himself on me, and I think the cabbie was in on it too, and..." I felt as if I was ranting on, I was so nervous and shook up.

"Wait a minute...Maurice tried to force himself on you?" cried Jorge, staring at me intently.

"Yes! I wasn't as inebriated as I let on to both of you, thank God for that. I might not have been able to defend myself against him, had I been as drunk as I let on," I cried.

"Oh my God, I cannot believe it!" cried Jorge, thoroughly upset.

"Really Jorge, nothing has ever happened between Ron and I, Maurice was trying to make it seem like..."

"Yes, I understand...what did you have to do to get him to back off?" asked Jorge, he appeared to be thinking now.

"I had no choice but to use force," I said, shrugging slightly.

"What kind of force?" asked Jorge.

"The man disgusts me, I tried to twist his nuts off," I told Jorge, hiding my amusement as much as I could.

"Oh," said Jorge, cringing distastefully. Jean Luc, let out a shout of laughter.

We were all startled when the doorbell rang. Jean Luc checked the security camera and announced that it was Maurice.

"What now?" whispered Jorge.

"I have an idea," I told him.

In moments, Jorge was opening the front door for Maurice.

"Maurice, what are you doing here?" cried Jorge, when he saw him.

"I have some information for you, it's something very important, I thought you should know. It's about one of your cast members, Lane Jensen," said Maurice, his tone was conspiratorial.

"Really? Does this information have anything to do with the fact that you tried to force yourself on my girlfriend when I simply asked you to get her a taxi cab home?" asked Jorge, eyeing him seriously.

"Wherever would you hear such a tale? The very idea is ludicrous!" cried Maurice.

"Oh, I don't know Maurice. Maybe Lane told me herself tonight, when we were in bed. Didn't you darling?" asked Jorge, as I walked around the corner into the foyer, wearing nothing but Jorge's silk robe. I gave Maurice a coy wave as he stared at me in shock.

"This is crazy! I'm not buying this for a moment. I know you and Lane aren't a couple, you're gay, you have a partner!" cried Maurice.

"I'm sorry Mr. Dubois, but I have no idea what you are talking about," said Jorge, taking Maurice by the arm and walking him toward the door.

"This is some sort of a scam, Lane is doing Brannon...I know it!" cried Maurice.

"By the way Maurice...you're fired," said Jorge, as he escorted him out the front door. I let out a sigh of relief when Jorge had finally closed the door behind Maurice. I couldn't believe the nerve of that slime bucket, trying to blackmail me like that.

The next morning I was back on the ice with my team, minus one cameraman. It was actually pretty nice to be free and not have a camera in my face constantly. We were actually able to get a lot accomplished.

Neither Elena nor Ron seemed inclined to ask about Maurice's absence, and I had no intention on telling them what had went down last night.

Jorge would have another camera man lined up soon enough. We were already working on our first two minute program. The program that we taped next Wednesday would be the first elimination round. I would be happy enough if my team wasn't the first to be eliminated.

For this first round the only requirements for our program was that we incorporate one lift, and the costumes and the moves must interpret the music. The music theme for the week was "popular music of the 70's".

I'd had a hard time selecting this week's music. I wanted something we could have fun with, yet I didn't want it to be too fast, or too slow, like a ballad. After listening to, what seemed like, thousands of music clips, I had finally decided on the song "Gypsies, Tramps and Thieves", by Cher.

Since my team was new to ice dance and pairs skating, I thought that giving them a song with a clear theme would make it much easier for them to interpret the music. Besides, the costumes and the music would be fun, or at least, I thought so. Elena was excited when she heard the music, and my ideas that went along with it. Ron, on the other hand, wasn't quite as enthusiastic.

I frowned when he voiced his displeasure. "What don't you like about it?" I asked. I was willing to compromise in any way possible, so that he wouldn't feel uncomfortable.

"I don't know, the whole thing just sounds kind of gay, that's all I'm saying," said Ron, shaking his head miserably.

"Well if I were a big strong football player like yourself, this whole show would sound gay to me, but it was you who signed up for this gig. Like it or not, you are now a figure skater. Now, do you want to do something outside of your comfort zone, or not?" I asked, staring him down determinedly.

He gave me a surprised look, then he started laughing.

"You're pretty damn cute when you're pissed," he said, laughing.

"I'm not pissed, I'm just saying..."

"Yeah, yeah, I know. I'm all yours, make me into a freakin gypsy," he sighed, pirouetting around with one arm over his head.

The hardest part about this week's program was that I needed to incorporate a lift of some sort into the program. It was the required element for this week in the competition, so we needed to include it in our program, or risk loosing points.

The issue was, Ron was not a strong skater, and he would have to support not only his own body weight, but Elena's too, on his somewhat shaky skates and hold the position for several seconds.

Even if he could manage it, Elena had never done any kind of pairs skating, so trust was an issue. At some point she was going to have to be confident enough in Ron, to take both of her skates off the ice and allow Ron to completely support her body above the ice. At this point, Elena had no confidence in Ron's skating ability, so getting her to try any type of a lift was going to be a hard sell on my part.

We spent quite a while working on other moves for

our program, paired turns and other easy things that would help to build up Ron's confidence, and Elena's. Then I decided it would be a good idea to work with Ron exclusively for a while. Since Ron basically had no skating experience prior to this competition, I would have to make sure that his basic skating skills were strong before moving on to the harder things.

To make Ron a strong base for the lift, I needed to know what position he was most comfortable in. The male, as the base of the lift could assume many different positions, I just needed to find out what position would make Ron the strongest base for Elena.

I had Elena go to the other end of the rink to work on some spins. She had an extensive repertoire of spins and she was quite talented, I felt if we could capitalize on some of those spins in the future, it would be a gold mine!

I worked with Ron for quite a while, showing him all the different positions we could work on for the lift. The other good thing about this competition was the rules. Since we were working with inexperienced skaters it was silly to try and use official figure skating rules, so basically, the show's rules were based on official rules, but really much more relaxed. In this competition we could choose to use actual pairs lifts which were more difficult or we could use ice dancing lifts.

Since ice dancing lifts were easier and there was a huge variety of them, I chose to use an ice dance lift for our first program. The best part about ice dancing lifts, was that not all of them were exactly lifts, as long as one skater suspended the other off the ice, it was considered a lift, that opened up a lot of possibilities, as far as I was concerned.

After working with Ron extensively that morning, he seemed to be quite stable doing a lunge in a straight line. I had been a pairs skater, so I was not well versed in lifts used in ice dance, but suddenly I had a fabulous idea. I called Elena over and told her what I wanted her to do, she just glared at me as if I were a moron and told me, "Nyet!"

"Elena, it will be so easy for you, Ron will be fine, he's very stable in the lunge position," I told her, but she just kept shaking her head determinedly. I sighed miserably, this was much harder than working with children. Children were always eager to please and usually, they didn't even care if they fell occasionally.

I was aggravated, I knew they could do it! I guessed I would have to show her that Ron was going to be fine. My idea was to have Ron skating in a lunge position and have Elena skate facing him, place her left blade on top of his right skate then Elena would lean forward, Ron would support her waist with his arm, while she pulled her right leg up behind her head, in a full Beilman position.

I took them off the ice, so we could try it on the rubber mats that were right next to the ice. I got Ron into position, then I did it myself, to show her that it could be done. She was still shaking her head empathetically.

"He weel fall on me and keel me," said Elena.

"He can do it," I told her as I ushered them both back to the ice.

"Fine...you first," said Elena, gesturing for me to try it on the ice with Ron.

I rolled my eyes, I was supposed to be the coach and choreographer, this was getting ridiculous!

I gave Ron a few, last minute instructions. Then the two of us began skating around to gain some speed. Ron had to have enough momentum to support his weight and mine without falling.

I spun around in front of Ron, so that I was skating backwards, he cautiously began to slide down into position, I carefully placed my left blade, on top of his right skate, then leaning forward onto his right arm, I slowly pulled my right leg up behind my head, holding it for 3 seconds, then I carefully came back down onto the ice. We were both a little bit shaky, but we did it! I was stunned when I heard a solitary person applauding us from the edge of the ice. Of course, it was Jorge.

"Once again I tell you, I picked the wrong person to do the actual skating. Would you and Elena like to switch roles?" asked Jorge, his voice was dripping with sarcasm.

"Maybe next time you should only hire skaters who have pairs experience," I told him, raising my eyebrows at him.

"Step to it Miss Denkova, it's your turn to try it," said Jorge, clapping his hands to make his point. Elena frowned, then she took Ron by the hand and began skating with him.

Ron was very cautious and Elena seemed to be moving in slow motion, but they actually did it! Elena was too nervous to completely extend herself, but they did it well enough that I felt like it was a definite possibility.

I was bursting with pride as they skated back over to u s, with a little bit of work the move was going to be stunning! I was excited.

"I can't wait to see the entire program. I had my doubts at first, but I think this team may actually be a top contender. I'm very impressed," said Jorge.

"Thank you," I said, giving him a smile.

"I came to invite you all to a private screening of the show's debut tonight at Spago," said Jorge.

"Spago, like Wolfgang Puck's Spago?" cried Ron, excitedly.

"The very one," said Jorge, giving us a little nod.

"Yeah!" cried Elena, clapping her hands excitedly.

"Once again you'll be arriving as a team, the media will all be there, so be on your best behavior. Check with wardrobe and Carmelita when you are done here, she'll set you up for hair and makeup," said Jorge.

I resisted rolling my eyes. I hated these big Hollywood events, I just wanted to put my jammies on and watch it at the condo, instead we had to make a big Hollywood night of it. Of course, it was part of my contract that I had to go to all these silly parties, but that didn't mean that I had to like them.

# CHAPTER 13

Early that evening I was back at the salon, having my hair and makeup done. Then I would be dressed in the black designer dress that the stylist had picked out for me and I would be off to yet another party.

I arrived at Spago with my team, completely overwhelmed to be amongst Hollywood's "in crowd". Elena and Ron both looked completely gorgeous and I had pretty much forced them to sit next to each other in the limo. The three of us posed for photos on the red carpet together, then, when we reached the door of the restaurant, Jorge took my arm possessively.

The whole affair wasn't as bad as I had anticipated. In fact, I actually enjoyed myself. We had a wonderful dinner prepared by Wolfgang Puck and his staff, then we all got to watch the season premier there on the big screen. I had to giggle as I watched it, my team definitely looked the worst in their practice videos, and of course, Maurice had been capturing all my deep sighs and eye rolling as I tried, often without much success, to make a figure skating pair out of my seriously mismatched raw talent.

All ten teams did their 30 second intros, but ours was definitely the most stunning. After watching my team's sorry practice clips, you'd almost swear they weren't even the same team out there on the ice performing! At the end of the show, we finally got to hear the comments made by the panel of judges and guest skaters who had been brought in.

I was happy, most of the comments were pretty positive. The judges and the guest skaters all thought that team Muramsatsu had the most raw talent, though several had commented that despite my team's rocky start, they had definitely seen a glimmer of potential.

I was content enough, it was good that the judges had recognized us as actual contenders in this competition, without putting the idea into people's heads that we would be the team to beat. I really preferred to fly under the radar a little bit. I didn't want to be everyone's enemy right off the bat.

The rest of the week went by very quickly. My team had finally settled into a routine of sorts and they seemed to be working quite hard, and surprisingly, without a lot of complaints.

The days seemed to be racing by, on Wednesday we would be taping yet another show, it seemed surreal to me, that our first elimination would be this week. I was pretty stoked about our "Gypsies" routine. I knew we were going to blow everyone away!

Our last run through on Wednesday went perfectly and I knew my team was ready for their performance in front of the studio audience that night. Our team would be second in the lineup to perform, right after team Maricelle.

After the director briefed us, we were brought into the arena as a group. There was an entire section of seats designated for the skaters and their coaches. Across the ice was judges box with the studio audience seated directly behind them. Of course, this was our first real taping, so things didn't go real smoothly, we weren't really into a routine yet. The viewers would never know of our difficulties working through the first episode, all that would be edited out.

Team Maricelle was first up. I smiled to myself as I watched their program. The concept was cute, they were skating to "Don't stop till you get enough," by Michael Jackson, their steps were good, but their lift never really got off the ground, both skaters stumbled clumsily, then they went back to their lame dance moves.

I suppressed a little giggle, if my team performed as good tonight as we'd been doing all week, we definitely wouldn't be the first team eliminated.

Finally, team Maricelle had finished, and they were taking their bows at the center of the ice, the three judges each gave them fives, giving them a score of fifteen out of thirty.

I smiled as Ron and Elena were introduced. They skated confidently out onto the ice, they looked so cute, all done up in their gypsy costumes. I tried to ignore the cameraman who was hovering nearby, ready to record my reactions as I watched excitedly. I smiled serenely as my team pulled off a nearly perfect performance. The crowd seemed to enjoy the performance too, as the applause seemed to be deafeningly loud as they both skated back over to me.

I hugged them both as they returned to me at the edge of the ice. I had hold of both their hands as the three of us sat in the judging area, dubbed the "Kiss and Cry" just like a real skating competition, while we waited for the scores.

I was actually pretty happy with the producer's choices for the judges. They were all accomplished skaters who were well known and creditable and it was actually kind of entertaining to listen to their comic banter.

The first judge was Natasha Webber. She had been a legend in her own time and an Olympic gold medalist. She had retired from skating years ago but she was still well known, and quite witty.

The second judge was Jack Montrose, he had been a men's world champion several times and was now a popular coach and sports commentator.

The last judge was Hal Luther, he was the oldest of the judges and probably the best known figure skater of all time! As a judge, Hall Luther was proving himself to be quite a hard ass, he craved perfection, though at this point in the competition, perfection was hardly attainable. I was enjoying his sometimes, awkward comments. If he had something to say, he didn't hold back, and it was cracking me up.

Finally, my team received their scores, eight, eight and a seven, from Hal Luther, of course. I was beside myself with excitement! That was even better than I could have imagined for our first week doing a full program. In fact, I had originally imagined that my team would be eliminated tonight, now I was certain that we would be able to stay, at least, one more week! I could have went home right then and there, I was so excited over my team's performance. Most of the teams did well, though no one really stood out to me, and so far, no other team, had beaten our score. All the teams, including ours, were still a bit shaky. I was a bit worried about the next team that was preparing to skate, Jorge had seen them in action and he told me they looked really promising.

The team consisted of retired Canadian figure skater, Ed Costello, and his partner, volleyball star Valerie Vasquez. The team was skating to the song "Stairway to Heaven", by Led Zeppelin, which seemed perfect, because Valerie looked like an angel in her white dress, she was so beautiful.

I watched their program in awe, the program was beautiful and mesmerizing. It was hard to believe that in such a short time period they had pulled together such a technically perfect program. Even I had to admit, the choreography was stunning, and the program was well practiced, even to my trained eye, I hadn't noticed one tiny flaw. I was waiting to see the required element, their lift, I was sure it was planned to be the grand finale.

I was almost holding my breath as I watched couple skating rapidly around the rink, obviously to gain speed for their lift. I gasped as Ed lifted his partner up into a star lift, which was very difficult. Too difficult, I thought, for a pair that were not seasoned professionals and had only just begun working together.

I could feel my heart beating nervously in my chest. I guess maybe it was the mother in me, but I was a stickler for safety. The last thing I wanted was for one of my students to get hurt. I was almost panicking as I watched them, the scary part, for me, was that Ed was spinning across the ice, almost too fast, as far as I could tell. I was cringing nervously, these pairs were way too inexperienced to be attempting stunts like this.

I had a sick feeling of dread when Valerie changed her position to come down from the lift. My worst fears were realized as Ed lost his footing somehow and fell, I cringed as they both crashed full speed into the wall.

I had already jumped up from my seat and was heading that direction. It seems as if everyone else had the same idea, their coach was already on the ice with them and a crowd had gathered around Valerie, who was laying on the ice perfectly still and had not gotten up from the fall. I was almost sick to my stomach, seeing her laying there, it was heartbreaking to see someone get hurt like that.

Finally, I let out a sigh of relief as they helped Valerie to her feet and she waved self consciously to the cheering crowd. The ice was now covered with her blood and her coach was holding pressure with a bandage to a large gash on her chin.

The ice was resurfaced and the host was forced to do multiple takes when he finally announced the last few teams. Valerie's crash had shaken everyone. I can't really say that either of those last two teams stood out to me in their performances. Maybe it had nothing to do with either of the actual performances, I was still numb over poor Valerie's crash.

Soon the host had returned to the ice and was announcing that the judges had made their decision and they would be announcing which team would be eliminated tonight. I figured it would be team Maricelle, they'd had the lowest score of anyone.

I was surprised when Ed and Valerie's coach stepped up to the microphone to announce that their team was withdrawing from the competition. Apparently, Valerie had injured her shoulder badly and would be unable to continue in the competition.

So that was it, the judges chose not to eliminate a team this week, based on the fact that Ed and Valerie had withdrawn due to injuries. It was sad, they had truly been a beautiful team, but I was happy that Ron and

Elena would be back for another week. We had even earned the high scores for the week, which was very exciting.

I went back to my condo that night, very pleased with myself. Tomorrow night this episode would air and my team would be in first place. I wasn't planning to watch the show on TV tomorrow night though. I wasn't sure I could watch Valerie plow into that wall again. It had been much too painful to watch the first time.

Tomorrow my team would begin working on a brand new program, new music, new costumes, and a new required element. It seemed like an awful lot to get done in one short week.

# CHAPTER 14

I sat in my condo that night planning our program for the following week. Our theme this week was 50's music, which was okay, though I couldn't really find myself all that inspired by letterman sweaters and poodle skirts. As far as I was concerned, that era had been done and overdone.

But of course, the network was concerned with ratings, not creativity, and as their employee, I was bound to follow their guidelines. Still, I wanted to think outside the box a little bit and come up with some music that was a little different than your normal sock hop music, which I assumed, is what everyone else would be picking for their programs.

After doing quite a bit of research on the internet, I finally decided on the song, "That's Amore'" by Dean Martin. I liked it! It was kind of quirky and more mature than some of the other songs I had been considering.

I spent the rest of the evening playing the music over and over and dancing around the living room, trying to come up with a plan for my choreography. Each week the producers would tell us what required element they were adding to our programs, that element would be added to the element from the previous week and that would give them an entire list of required elements by the end of the season. This week we were required to add a pairs spin to our program. So this week, our program would have to include a lift and a pairs spin, no problem.

I was thinking about teaching Elena and Ron a simple cartwheel lift and a pretty fool proof version of a pairs spin. I was pretty excited about the choreography I'd come up with so far, I thought that this was going to be a fun week for us.

The next morning in practice I told Ron and Elena our plan for 50's week. Ron was game, but Elena was pouting, she wanted to skate to "Good Golly Miss Molly".

Oh well, I guess you can't make everyone happy.

We got right to work, luckily Elena was not adverse to learning the pairs spin, I was hoping that meant that she was trusting Ron a little bit more, but I seriously doubted it. Our new cameraman was on the ice with us this morning. His name was Javier and he was very polite. The best part was that he was a lot less obtrusive than Maurice had been.

We worked hard all week and our program seemed to be coming together nicely. Elena was even enjoying playing up the quirkiness of our song, I was happy she was finally enjoying herself. We had a pair spin, though it was still quite shaky. The size difference between Elena and Ron was quite substantial, if Ron didn't bend over far enough, Elena would just crash into his chest, it was kind of comical.

Tuesday morning I poured my coffee into a to go cup and headed for the rink. I grabbed my mail out of my mailbox on the way out. I had quite a stack, I'd forgotten to get it for a couple of days. I immediately noticed a thick envelope right on top. I pulled it out and looked at the return address.

It was from Greg's lawyer in Colorado Springs. I ripped the envelope open and stared numbly at the contents. I let out a distressed sigh, it was all over...my divorce was final.

It had taken months, but it barely seemed like any time at all. It seemed crazy that a union that had lasted more than twenty years, could end, in just a matter of months. Just reading the words that made it all final seemed to tear a hole right in my chest. I bit my lower lip and fought the tears that seemed to come to my eyes almost automatically.

I shook my head angrily and gave myself a silent reprimand, I wasn't going to cry any more. I had cried enough about this. I tried to tell myself that Greg wasn't worth my tears, but I had put my heart and soul into our relationship, and our family. I had thought that we were happy. How was I to know he would throw it all away for another woman who was almost young enough to be my own daughter?

I tossed the letter and the rest of the mail into the passenger seat and drove to the ice rink. I blasted the stereo in the car and sang along as loudly as I could, I was trying to turn my morose mood around. It really wasn't working, but I was attracting quite a bit of attention whenever I stopped at a stoplight. Unfortunately, I just couldn't shake the feeling of overwhelming sadness that was engulfing me.

When I got to the rink, Elena was there, sitting on the bench waiting for me, but Ron was nowhere to be found. I was a little worried, it was not like him at all! Ron was never late. I put my skates on and checked my e-mails on my phone, but he hadn't called or e-mailed me.

"Elena, have you heard from Ron? Did he tell you he was going to be late?" I asked, I was getting more and more worried.

"No, he not call me," said Elena, shaking her head.

I tried his cell phone, but there was no answer. More than twenty minutes had passed and my heart was pounding nervously. Finally, I broke down and called Jorge.

"Jorge, have you heard from Ron? He's not here at practice, he's never late, I'm worried that something has happened to him," I cried, no matter how much I tried to disguise it, my voice was raising in fear.

"Did you happen to see the news last night?" asked Jorge, his voice was flat and calm, in contrast to my own voice, that was rising in hysteria.

"No, why?" I asked, not sure what the evening news would have to do with Ron.

"There is a bit of trouble in paradise. Have Javier show you the news clip. I'm going to run over to his condo to check on him now, I'll call you back," said Jorge.

I stared at my phone in confusion after he ended the call. News clip? What, exactly, was going on?

"Javier," I called, waving him over to me. He skated over, eyeing me with concern.

"Yes, Ms. Jensen?"

"Jorge said that you could show me some sort of a news clip, I'm not quite sure what he was talking about," I said.

"Yes, I have it here, on my phone," said Javier, pulling out his I-phone and pulling up the video clip for me.

I stared at the clip on the small screen. It was hard to tell, but it looked like the woman in the clip was Jenae Brannon, but I couldn't really tell who the man was. I still wasn't really sure what I was looking at.

"I'm sorry Javier, I don't know what this is about. Why does Jorge want me to see this news clip?" I cried in frustration, I had no idea what I was looking at, or what this had to do with Ron not showing up for practice.

"This clip was on the news last night, it's secret footage taken in Hawaii. It is Ron's wife, she's out with Roman Fleming, a professional football player," said Javier.

"Oh shit!" I exclaimed, as I finally realized what the news clip meant. The woman in the video was not acting like a woman who was currently married to someone else. She was sitting on Roman Fleming's lap, whispering in his ear. I shook my head disgustedly. As angry as I was about Jenae's indiscretions, I was not all that surprised. I had suspected that she was a gold digger, unfortunately, this was not a good way for Ron to find out.

Poor Ron, everything he did was for his wife and his

daughters, this was like a sobering slap in the face. He was busting his ass trying to learn how to figure skate for a reality TV show and Jenae was stepping out on him while he was gone!

I jumped anxiously, startled by my phone, which was playing music in my pocket and vibrating annoyingly, I pulled it out nervously and nearly dropped it in my haste.

"Hello?"

"Mr. Brannon won't be there for practice this morning," said Jorge, I almost cringed at his tone. His voice was sharp with anger on the other end of the line.

"Is he okay?" I asked, I realized I was pretty much holding my breath.

"He will be, he's suffering from an incapacitating hangover at the moment," said Jorge, his voice was laced with sarcasm.

"I'll be right over," I said.

"I'm very sorry Lane, but if you wish to keep your job, you will stay right where you are. Despite the recent turn of events, I really think we need to keep playing things cool, am I understood?" asked Jorge, his voice was tight and serious. I sighed, what could I do? He was the producer, and my boss. He was not happy at the moment, I didn't want to do anything to further piss him off.

"Is there anything I can do?" I asked.

"I will deal with Brannon. You will work with Elena today and breathe not a word of this to anyone, comprende?"

"Sure Jorge, whatever you say," I replied coldly, my voice was sad and resigned.

"That's my little angel lips. You're the best

choreographer I've got, I don't want to loose you, you know that, don't you?" crooned Jorge, on the other end of the line. I rolled my eyes miserably.

"Jorge I get it, goodbye," I snapped.

I spent the rest of our time working with Elena exclusively. I wanted to highlight her spins anyway. I decided to give her a little solo with a stunning spin sequence. She was so excited, she was beaming proudly, by the time practice was over.

I had worried what I would say to Elena. I had promised Jorge that I wouldn't breathe a word of this to anyone, I had assumed that would include Elena. What I had forgotten was, how self absorbed Elena was. She never voiced a single concern over Ron's absence, go figure...

After practice, I drove back to my condo, lost in my thoughts of sadness. I brought all my mail in and threw it in a pile on the kitchen counter. I flopped on the couch dejectedly. I tried to keep the sadness from consuming my thoughts, but I couldn't help it. My marriage was over, now it seemed that Ron's marriage was in jeopardy also. I wondered what was wrong with this world. I had always thought that marriages were meant to last forever, till death do us part. In our modern world everything was disposable, including people and relationships.

It was so easy, if you were a man and you wanted a wife that was younger and more beautiful, you could just divorce your old wife, the one that raised your children, and was there for you, before you were successful. The one that had worked full time to help both of you struggle through college.

mean really, what was the incentive for Greg to stay? Our kids were grown, I was already in my forties, and of course, I would only be getting older with every passing year! There would always be someone out there with less lines on their face, more cleavage, no stretch marks...the list went on an on.

I sighed, it was no different for Ron. His retirement had forced his wife to abandon her rich and famous lifestyle, which, it turns out, she wasn't willing to do.

It only made sense to her to go out looking for a man who could support her in the manner she felt like she deserved. I shook my head miserably. I thought about my grandparents and how happy they had been together for more than sixty years. They had been more in love than any couple I had ever seen, right up to the day my grandfather died. When had our world become this shallow, whining, society?

I wandered around the condo aimlessly for a while, then I yawned in boredom. I was suddenly tired. I took off my shoes and went into the bedroom to take a nap. I'm not sure how long I was asleep but I was awakened by the doorbell ringing.

I peeked out the peephole to see Ron standing there. I opened the door, he gave me a sheepish smile.

"Sorry I missed practice this morning," he told me, with a little shrug.

"Yeah, I know," I told him. I was looking down at the floor. I felt so bad for him, I couldn't really look at him.
"May I come in?" he asked.

"I don't think that's a good idea," I told him. He had obviously been upset by his wife's careless antics. But inviting him into the condo, when no one else was around, seemed like a bad idea.

I had been forbidden by Jorge to socialize with Ron at all outside the ice rink. I was stiffened with apprehension, I didn't think it would be a good idea to tempt fate. He was obviously upset, I was already upset over my own divorce being final. Together, Ron and I were about as emotionally stable as Richard Nixon in the final days of his presidency!

"If it makes you feel any better, I checked, I wasn't followed," he told me, flashing me a sly smile.

I rolled my eyes miserably. "How would you know?"

"I think I would know. Besides, I made three different trips around the neighborhood, then I ditched my car down the street. No one will ever suspect a thing," he told me, flashing me a sly smile.

"Are you crazy? This is Hollywood. The reporters here are more covert than the CIA, in fact, I think that might be a prerequisite to get into the CIA, experience being a reporter in Hollywood," I told him rolling my eyes. I was joking with him, trying to blame my apprehension on the media, but it was my own fragile heart that I couldn't trust. Subconsciously, I wanted Ron to make the moves on me. Subconsciously, I knew if he made the moves on me I probably wouldn't stop him, I really just wanted someone to find me desirable!

Ron shook his head and pushed past me into the condo. I sighed in resignation and closed the door behind us. He walked straight into the living room and flopped down on the couch.

"Would you like something to drink?" I asked.

"You got anything hard?" he asked. He was slumped on my couch defeatedly. He looked like a man who had a lot more on his mind then just a really bad hangover.

"The way you look right now, you don't need anything hard," I told him, shaking my head miserably.

"Yeah, I guess I had a rough night last night. I just wanted to apologize to you. I realize how hard you are working on this project and I appreciate everything you do. It was unprofessional of me to get totally shit faced last night and miss our practice this morning," he said, looking at me earnestly.

"Well, sometimes the people we love, drive us to do crazy things," I told him with a shrug.

"You saw the news then?" he asked, eyeing me warily.

"I saw the clip this morning, after I called everyone I could think of who might know what had happened to you," I said.

"I'm sorry Lane. Like I said, it was stupid and unprofessional, it will never happen again," he said, standing up and approaching me till he was standing right in front of me. His face was pained, and he looked completely lost.

"I understand..." I was holding my breath anxiously. I wanted to take an uncomfortable step backwards. I felt like he was standing much too close to me, but he was feeling bad enough about everything, I stood my ground.

"No you don't! I was stupid, everyone tried to tell me, but I wouldn't listen. I was too proud to see she was using me. I should have known this would happen, things have been going sour for a while. I feel like a complete moron, I should have seen it coming," he said, shaking his head miserably.

"I was blind sided too. It's like getting hit by a punch out of nowhere, you never see it coming, but it hurts so bad!"

He nodded his head and gave me a wry smile. "How did you do it? I mean, how did you handle the anger? I gave Jenae the best years of my life, I just..."

"I know..." I still couldn't look at him. I didn't want to feel his pain, when my own pain was still so fresh. I didn't want to cry in front of him. I didn't want to cry over Greg ever again.

"You are so strong, you handled everything with such grace. You're such a class act. If I'd been in your position, I'd want to rip the guy's nuts off!" said Ron.

"I did want to rip his nuts off, but what would that accomplish? I'd end up on the news and everyone would talk about that crazy bitch that ripped her husband's nuts off and I wouldn't get to be here, doing a stupid reality TV show with you," I told him with a smile.

"There's that smile again...you know it's making me crazy," he said, his voice had suddenly changed. It had gone from sad and serious, to silky and sensuous.

"What's making you crazy?" I asked, I was suddenly panicking. I should have never let him come in. The velvety caress of his voice was hypnotizing me, I could feel my resolve slipping away. I tried to steel myself against his charms, Jorge would totally freak out if he knew that the two of us were together...alone.

"Every time you smile, I want to kiss you," he said, taking a cautious step toward me.

"Ron, please, you're upset right now..."

"I wanted to kiss you long before I was upset," he said, reaching out and laying his hand on my cheek. I was completely mesmerized by his eyes, I wanted to stop him, but I couldn't, the very touch of his fingers was electrifying.

"Ron please, I know Jorge will fire me," I pleaded, I could already feel his arm around my waist as he drew me toward him.

"Jorge will never know," he whispered, as his lips gently began to caress mine.

I was mindlessly surrendering to the gentle kiss, which was growing more and more passionate with every moment. The voice of reason in my head had already been extinguished by the fire that was now racing through my veins. At some point I had wrapped my arms around his neck. In moments, we had fallen to the couch, he was on top of me, on the couch, pressing his body against mine seductively. I had completely succumbed to the passion, I hadn't felt excitement like that in years.

It was only then, that the guilt began to wash over me and I finally regained my senses and pushed him away. My entire body was suddenly protesting, and I was panting and fighting to catch my breath. My entire body had been reawakened with sensations I hadn't felt in years. I didn't want it to end, but deep in my heart I knew this was wrong.

"What?" he cried, looking at me as if I were crazy.

"Ron, I can't. I know you are upset about Jenae, and maybe your relationship is over, but not officially," I told him, still struggling to catch my breath.

Ron was struggling to breathe as well. "I'm not upset over Jenae, like I said, I already knew it was over. It's you that I haven't been able to stop thinking about. I've wanted to kiss you, almost from the first moment I met you."

"You are too emotional to make that decision right now. If Jorge were to find out that we were together, he would fire me, he's already eluded to that," I managed to whisper.

"I'm not emotional over Jenae, I just finally feel free to go after what I want. I want you," said Ron, whispering seductively in my ear.

I jumped up from the couch and gave him a very serious look. I needed the space between us. I needed to end this now, or I would never be able to stop.

"If you want me, you'll have to wait. I promised Jorge. If you and I hook up, it's going to be nothing but trouble. Bad publicity for the show, bad publicity for you. Think about it Ron, what if someone saw something..." I breathed, my heart was still pounding, I still felt weak. My head was having a hard time convincing my body that this should not happen.

"Nobody's watching...come on. We both need this," said Ron, holding his hand out to me, his eyes were pleading.

"Somebody's always watching! I hate to always sound paranoid, but do you not realize where we are? We are in Hollywood, and you are the great Ron Brannon, we've already been linked once..." my eyes were flashing, I was completely panicked. If Ron didn't back off, I didn't know how I was going to say no to what my body seemed to think it needed so badly.

"You're afraid...because I'm black," said Ron, looking at me earnestly.

"Ron, you know that's not true. I'm worried about you, and what Jenae might do to you if she found out about us," I cried.

"What could she possibly do? She's already completely destroyed me," he told me with a sigh.

"Believe me, she hasn't even begun to destroy you yet. My guess is, if she could prove you were having an affair, she would keep your girls from you. She would make sure you never saw them again," I snapped.

"Jenae would never do that!" he cried.

"Sure, and she would never cheat on you either...would she?" I seethed. I was being callous, but he needed a wake up call. She was evil.

Ron slumped back down on the couch defeatedly. I sat down next to him, feeling bad that I had hurt him, but he needed this reality check.

"Ron, I'm sorry...we just need to be realistic," I said taking his hand.

He raised my hand to his lips and kissed it tenderly. "I love you Lane. I fell in love with you the first time I saw you. I just couldn't act on my feelings at the time. I didn't want to hurt my wife, I didn't realize she was already out looking. I guess I should have probably realized it would be someone like Roman, someone with a multi million dollar contract," said Ron, his voice broke with emotion.

"Ron, you have to go," I said, gesturing toward the door.

"You want me to wait? Is that what you want?" Ron was inching closer to me, he was so close now, I feared he could hear my heart pounding anxiously in my chest. He looked deeply into my eyes and laid his hand on my cheek once again.

I looked up into his eyes, our bodies were nearly touching and I could feel the heat radiating from his body. "We have to wait, at least till the show is over, I mean otherwise..."

I was struggling to breathe, I reached up and gently removed his hand from my cheek, then I held his hand tightly in mine. I was almost trembling, my body wanted him to stay, of course, the reasonable voice in my head was telling me to get him out of the condo, before I did something I would regret!

"It's not what I want...it's how it has to be. Jorge is worried about negative publicity for the show. If you and I..."

"Yeah, yeah...I know," said Ron, he turned slowly and headed for the door.

"I'm sorry Ron. I feel the same way about you," I whispered, as he opened the door.

"When is your divorce going to be final?" he asked.

"It was final today...I got the papers today," I told him. I still couldn't say the words without them sticking in my throat a little bit. It was still painful.

"I'm sorry...I guess I'm not the only one who's hurting. I'll see you bright and early tomorrow, taping day," he said, giving me a shy smile.

"Yeah, taping day," I said, as I closed the door behind him.

## CHAPTER 15

When I arrived at the rink the next morning, Ron and Elena were already out on the ice working on their program, I was delighted that they had the initiative to go out there and start working without me.

"Hey guys!" I called, as I skated out to them. They were both bursting with excitement.

"Watch this," said Ron, waving to the sound man to start their music.

The music started and I was amazed to watch Elena and Ron get through their entire routine with barely a glitch. Their complex step sequence that I had choreographed for them was nearly perfect and the only element that seemed to require any work was that darn pairs spin. I was smiling broadly as they ended, even though I was sure that they had been practicing without me, which I had forbidden!

"Wow, that was awesome!" I cried, as they both bowed and hammed up their ending.

"Our speen ees steel skanky," said Elena.

"It's shaky," I told her with a little smile. "We'll save the skanky for burlesque night...if there is one,"

Ron was just smiling and shaking his head in amusement. I turned to him.

"You, Mr. Brannon. Have you been practicing without me?" I asked, folding my arms over my chest and peering at him very seriously.

All traces of amusement left his face and he gave me a worried look.

"We wanted to surprise you, you know, get the step sequence down," he said, nervously.

"How are your feet?" I asked. I didn't want to be mad

at him, they'd done such a great job, but Ron was so driven, he was prone to overdo himself. I didn't want him to mess up his feet so badly he wouldn't be able to compete.

"My feet are fine, the blisters I had, are almost all gone. Elena and I have been working both on and off the ice," he said, giving me a little shrug.

"I just worry about you Ron, sometimes, you don't know when to quit," I told him, a small smile was sneaking to my lips. I couldn't stay mad at him.

"I've heard that was one of my better qualities," he said, flashing me a seductive smile.

"It is a very admirable quality, for the most part, but if you mess up your feet so badly that we cannot get skates on them, your entire team will be out of the competition. You understand that, right?" We were a team, I needed him to understand that. He couldn't singlehandedly win this competition, and neither could I.

"I understand, I will not jeopardize the competition by overdoing it. I just want to be the best. I want to win," said Ron.

"Okay, we're all on the same page then. Last week you guys were fabulous, I don't want to loose that momentum. When I first took on this project, I didn't think there was any way we would even make it through the first elimination. You guys have made so much progress, I can actually see us making it to the finals, possibly even winning," I told them with a smile.

Elena and Ron were both smiling broadly and nodding at me. "If it weren't for the pairs spin I'd say we were ready right now, but the spin could use some work."

We worked hard at practice and I felt like we were ready for the taping of the show tonight. As we skated off the ice, I looked up to see Jorge standing there at the gate. I almost rolled my eyes, he gave me a little wave as I approached him.

"I love the program darling, it's so damn cute!" he cried, hugging me as I stepped off the ice. I half heartedly returned his hug. Ron's eyes were narrowed and he was staring Jorge down like a jealous lover, I turned and gave him a bug eyed glare. Ron gave Jorge an arrogant nod of his head, then he snapped his skate guards on and headed toward the changing room.

"How is everything going?" asked Jorge.

"Fine," I told him, dismissively. I was worried, something was up. Why else would Jorge just randomly show up at our practice? He was a busy man, he didn't have time to hang around the rink.

"The program looks fine, how are things with Brannon?" asked Jorge, eyeing me haughtily.

My heart was surging with guilt, surely he couldn't know about my tiny indiscretion yesterday. Could he?

"I had to reprimand him today, he and Elena have been practicing without me. I'm afraid he'll overdo himself and not be able to skate at all," I said, tracing my finger over a patch of chipped paint on the gate. I couldn't look Jorge in the eye, I felt incredibly guilty.

"Have the two of you discussed his wife's indiscretions?" asked Jorge.

"I wouldn't say we discussed it, of course he told me, he apologized for missing practice," I told him, staring him down indignantly.

"I was just worried, that's all. Now he's been wronged, you have also been wronged. Misery loves company, I just thought that he might use that as an excuse to have you hop into bed with him," said Jorge. I resisted the urge to roll my eyes.

"He's perfectly gorgeous, why would I even need an excuse to hop into bed with him?" I asked, nonchalantly. I looked over at Jorge, who was standing there staring at me with his mouth gaping open, he was completely speechless.

"I'm kidding Jorge, I was messing with you," I told him with a giggle.

"God, sometimes you can be such a heartless bitch, you scared the hell out of me," he told me, indignantly.

"Sorry," I told him with a wry smile, even though personally, I thought he deserved it.

That night my team was scheduled to be the second to the last performance of the evening. Seeing all the other teams in their poodle skirts and letter sweaters made me all that much happier that I hadn't chosen a sock hop song. The other performances all looked blandly similar. I thought our quirky, yet sophisticated program would stand out from all the others.

As we sat there in the cast seats and watched all the other teams performing, I was happy to realize that my team was not the only one struggling with the pairs spin, besides that, several of the other teams could barely get by with their lifts and the footwork.

Finally, Ron and Elena skated out to the center of the ice. The lights dimmed and the spotlights shined on them.

"Ladies and Gentleman, skating to the song That's Amore' Elena Denkova and Ron Brannon, choreography by Lane Jensen.

As the music started, things were looking good. The choreography was well suited to the music and Ron and Elena had to play out a couple that was falling in love. I smiled as I watched them performing, they had really gotten into the music. I was so proud of them, they were performing as if they had been doing this their entire lives, they had almost convinced me that they were lovers, even though I knew that the two of them barely tolerated each other.

The cartwheel lift was a bit shaky, but good. The

crowd oohed and aahed, when Elena did her spin sequence.

They had one step sequence under their belt, all they had to do was nail the pairs spin and the last step sequence that led into their finale, and they had it!

I held my breath as they went into the pairs spin, on the second rotation the toe pick of Ron's skate nicked Elena's blade, making a loud metallic squeak. It shouldn't have been enough to ruin the spin, but Elena was jumpy, she was so scared that Ron was going to fall on her and crush her, she stumbled out of the spin early.

This was more than enough to throw both her and Ron off. As result, Ron ended up starting his footwork on the wrong foot, so they ended up being out of synch for the rest of the dance. I sighed in disappointment. I didn't think they had been bad enough to be eliminated, but I was quite certain, we would not be the top team tonight.

Ron and Elena skated back to me dejectedly, I hugged them both, then we sat in the "kiss and cry" area to wait for the judges to comment on our performance and then reveal our scores.

The judges comments were mostly positive. It was hard for them to pick apart our pairs spin, since no other team had mastered it either. Hal Luther smiled and claimed to be "totally in love" with the entire program, he thought that Ron and Elena were both still a bit stiff, he urged them to loosen up a bit.

Finally, our scores were held up, eight, eight and eight. Not too bad, but not what I had anticipated for the night. The last team skated, then all the teams were brought to the ice for the announcement of the elimination.

I was finally able to breathe, when they announced that it was team Maricelle that would be going home tonight. We had ended up third in the standings, behind team Muramsatsu and team Evans.

I was happy enough, we were still near the top of the pack. I was almost glad we hadn't taken first place, if we took the top spot every time, we would have nothing to work toward and of course, every other team would be out to get us!

As the show ended later that evening, everyone was congregating there beside the ice. Everyone was coming over and telling me how well my team had done, including Emi Muramsatsu. When the crowd began dying down, I wasn't surprised to see that Ron had found his way to my side.

"You want to stop by my place for a drink?" he whispered into my ear.

"Is Elena coming?" I asked, turning around and giving him a sly smile.

"Hell no, that bitch hates me," said Ron, giving me a look.

"You know I can't," I told him. He was rolling his eyes disgustedly, I turned and saw that Jorge was pushing his way determinedly through the crowd toward me. I sighed miserably.

"Lane darling, splendid job tonight," he said hugging me, then kissing me on the cheek. "A fine effort tonight Mr. Brannon, with a little work, you might actually end up in the finals." Jorge held out his hand and Ron shook it hesitantly.

"Thank you," said Ron, his face was expressionless. I was almost holding my breath as the two men stared each other down for a moment or two.

"Sweetheart, the crowd is finally dying down, are you ready to go home?" asked Jorge, staring at me expectantly.

"Yes dear," I told him obediently. I gave Ron a haughty nod, then I let Jorge pull me away.

Jorge had taken me by the hand and was pulling me through the crowd in the lobby. He was almost giddy with excitement as he waved and blew kisses to the remaining people he knew that were still hanging around. Then he hauled me unceremoniously out the front entrance, he dragged me out to his limo like a child who had misbehaved in the grocery store.

"Get in!" he demanded curtly. I looked up at him in shock as I slid into the limo as I'd been commanded to do.

"Why are you being such an ass?" I cried, as Jorge slid into the seat next to me.

"If I was not such an ass I would have never got this far in life. I already told you, I am simply protecting my show. I saw you with Brannon," he told me, staring me down determinedly.

"I wasn't going to go with him," I told him, indignantly.

"Good for you. I was not going to give you the opportunity. You are coming home with me. I have decided I cannot have you hanging out at the condo anymore. Whatever will we do if he shows up there?"

"Jorge, don't be ridiculous..."

"Lane please, I know that he was there last night, and I also know that the two of you shared a very passionate kiss. At this point, I think I may be lucky that's all the two of you did," snapped Jorge, staring me down arrogantly.

"You were spying on me!" I cried indignantly. As stunned as I was, I was almost wondering why I hadn't anticipated this.

"I didn't instigate the spying, but I did get the full scoop, and video, of course. In Hollywood you have to be careful, you never know who's watching. It cost me a pretty penny to keep that video out of the wrong hands. Do you not understand the consequences of your actions?" snapped Jorge, angrily.

"Who did this?" I breathed. I was so completely stunned, I couldn't say another word.

"It makes no difference who did it, the point is, you are a celebrity now, you probably have a whole host of stalkers," he told me with a sly smile.

"But how?" I was panicking, worrying that maybe someone had planted secret cameras in my condo. I'm sure stranger things have happened.

I am sorry darling, but it was you, who forgot to close your drapes," said Jorge, giving me a nonchalant shrug.

I sighed brokenly, I kept forgetting, I wasn't in Colorado Springs anymore. When you were in the public eye, everyone always wanted to know what you were up to. There was obviously no such thing as a secret rendezvous, at least not in this day and age. All this modern technology was like a double edged sword, for the stalkers it made life easier, for the stalked, it was a nightmare, the average person could shoot video from their cell phone!

"Tomorrow we will move all your things into my house. That is where you will be staying until the conclusion of the show," snapped Jorge.

"What about Jean Luc?" I asked.

"Jean Luc has decided to take a little holiday in Nice, until the show is over," said Jorge.

I was shaking my head miserably, my entire life was a fiasco. I could see where Jorge was coming from, he needed to protect his show from negative publicity. Ron didn't seem to care, but the media would tear him up if they thought that the two of us were having an affair. I had been afraid that he might show up at my condo again tonight, Jorge had taken care of that little problem.

"Am I under house arrest?" I asked, flashing him a sly smile.

"Essentially. You know we wouldn't have this problem if it wasn't for those big blue eyes and that smile of yours, you even have me completely charmed, and I like men!" cried Jorge.

I rolled my eyes. "Jorge..."

"I'm serious, and I'm not the only one. You're such a flirt Lane, all the guys have been totally eating it up. I doubt you'll be single long."

"My mother was a shameless flirt, I guess I learned it from her," I told him, with a little shrug.

"Your mother...don't even get me started on your mother!" cried Jorge.

Jorge didn't know my mother personally, but he knew of her, of course, lots of people in Hollywood did. My mother was Lydia Gray, back in the day, my mother had been a very a famous dancer. She had been in a lot of movies in the 50's and 60's, even now, years later, she was still kind of notorious. Unfortunately, it hadn't been my mother's dancing that had made her so memorable in Hollywood, it was her hot temper and her numerous male conquests that had made my mother a Hollywood legend.

Maybe that was why I didn't feel all that comfortable in Hollywood. When Jorge first met me, he had been fascinated with the fact that Lydia Gray was my mother. He told me I should feel like Hollywood was my family, not many people could trace their lineage directly back to Hollywood's golden era.

Since my mother was so notorious, Jorge found it to be quite intriguing that I could possibly be the bastard child of some old Hollywood icon. It was a thought I had considered, but never pursued. Since I was a small child, I had my doubts about my lineage, of course, I had heard all the whispered rumors. When I looked in the mirror, it only confirmed all the rumors, I had my mother's eyes, but I didn't look like my dad at all. My nose, my hair, my freckles, they all seemed to come from somewhere else, they were things I didn't share with my parents or either of my siblings.

Of course, my own father claimed me, but even he, had heard the rumors, I imagine. It was not something my family had ever spoke about, but I had heard the whispers when I was just a child. My parents were both so busy, my grandparents had essentially raised me, they tried to shelter me from all the speculation, but people are cruel. The gossiping eventually filtered down from the adults to my classmates. I pretended not to care, when the kids made fun of me and my family.

Who knows what had been speculation and what had been true? I did know that my mother had a series of affairs, she had apparently not been very discrete about them. Apparently my mother had set her sights on Hollywood idol, Troy Donahue, and that is who our neighbors seemed to believe I had been fathered by. Of course, I did have blonde hair and blue eyes, while my own father had green eyes and stunning auburn hair.

Jorge had also pointed out to me that I had Troy Donahue's nose, I had shrugged that off, at this point I didn't even care. I certainly didn't have my mother's or my father's nose. It didn't really matter anyway, I was still not comfortable in Hollywood!

I yawned as the limo cruised through the streets of Hollywood, I knew I was resigned to stay at Jorge's home in the Hollywood Hills until this media circus was over.

"What about my car? Are we going to stop off and get my car?" I asked, suddenly wondering how I would get to the rink in the morning.

"You'll ride with me," snapped Jorge.

"Holy shit, I really am under house arrest, aren't I?" I asked, staring at him in shock.

"Yes darling, and it is for your own good," he replied as he watched the streets of Hollywood slip by in the night.

# CHAPTER 16

When I arrived at the house that night, Jorge set me up in his guest room, then he sent his assistant Ed over to the condo to get some of my things. I didn't really feel comfortable staying at Jorge's house, but I was sure it was for the best.

When Ed arrived later that evening with my laptop, I took it out by the pool so that I could do a little research. Our next music choice had to be from a Broadway musical. Once again, I wanted something different. I had guessed that everyone would be using music from "Phantom of the Opera" and "Cats" and all the more recent, popular musicals. I wanted something different, something quirky, that Elena and Ron could make into a memorable routine that would stand out from all the others.

Ron was essentially still a beginner, so of course, he didn't know a lot of moves. On the up side, Ron had quite a personality, and he knew how to project that out on the ice, so I had to make that work for us, as much as possible. If I could play up his showmanship and personality, maybe it would deflect criticism from his basic skating skills.

"Can I get you anything to drink? A glass of wine, perhaps?" asked Ed, as he approached me on the patio later that evening.

I was stunned. "Um sure, a glass of wine would be nice," I told him.

"Red or white?"

"White please," I told him. I smiled as he walked away. Maybe I could get used to this, living the life of the rich and famous.

I began searching through the thousands of songs I had loaded on my i-tunes library. Greg and I had well over 500 cd's that we'd loaded onto i-tunes, not to mention all the other music we'd bought.

I'd pretty much grown up in the theater so I already knew most of the music from all the Broadway shows. I clicked down my list, listening to clips as I went along. After a while, I was beginning to get overwhelmed, there was just too much to choose from. Besides, I still wasn't sure what I was looking for. I was waiting for a fun, quirky, song to just jump out at me.

Jorge walked out on the patio and gave me a wry smile.

"How's it going?" he asked.

"Terrible, I'm completely overwhelmed. I have no idea what Ron and Elena will be skating to next week," I told him, sighing heavily.

"This week should be easy for you, it's Broadway week, you should be right at home. I can only guess that you grew up listening to all that music," said Jorge.

"I know it should be easy, I'm just overwhelmed, there are just too many choices," I told him.

"What is your favorite musical?" he asked, sitting down next to me.

"That's just it, I could never pick just one. I have tons of favorites," I told him with a shrug.

"What are they?"

"I don't know, I like West Side Story, Gypsy, Hello Dolly, My Fair Lady, there's so many.

"Why don't you just listen to some of the music from those shows and see which ones strike you as something that will work," said Jorge.

"I already know all the music, I just can't see them..."

"Listen to the music Lane, you have to feel it. Then you will get an idea of what your team can skate to." he said, standing to leave.

Jorge bent over and gave me a peck on the cheek, then he walked back into the house. I sighed, I still wasn't inspired, my brain was completely overloaded. I stared distractedly at the pool in front of me, as the surface of the water was illuminated by constantly changing colors of the fiber optic lights. The shimmering light danced across the glass-like surface of the water that was barely ruffled by the filter jets. The light kept changing from blue to green to yellow, then pink.

I put my ear buds in and got to work listening to clips, but soon I was bored. This was impossible, none of these songs would have the effect I wanted them to have. I wanted the audience to remember my team, therefore, I needed them to stand out. Elena and Ron seemed to do best when they had actual characters to portray, and they both enjoyed acting a little bit silly. Suddenly I had a fabulous idea!

I began paging down my huge list of songs until I finally found what I was looking for. I played the clip and smiled serenely as I listened to it. This song was exactly what I had been looking for. In moments I was almost bursting with excitement. I could see the costumes, and the program in my mind, almost as if I had already completely pulled it together. I was going to make Ron into a English gentleman, and Elena would be Eliza Doolittle.

# CHAPTER 17

I showed up at the ice arena the next morning, accompanied by Jorge, of course. It wasn't often that the producer would show up for a mere practice, but these were special circumstances and Jorge was determined to play it all out! I was getting the uneasy feeling that Jorge was going to become a permanent fixture at all of our practices, if for no other reason than to convince everyone that he and I were a couple.

I thought that the portraying the idea that Jorge and I were lovers was completely ridiculous, at first, I thought no one would buy it. I guess just had no idea how strong the power of suggestion could be. I had never expected that people would actually believe that Jorge and I were truly a couple.

I had known almost from the first moment I met him, that Jorge was obviously gay. He wasn't really one of those guys that you silently wondered about, he was kind of flaming! Now that Jorge and I were "dating", apparently, everyone thought he was straight, but a bit odd. That's the power of suggestion.

I was excited about our new program. I had told Jorge about it and he thought the idea was fabulous, though Jorge seemed to think everything I did was fabulous!

My excitement faded quickly that morning at practice as I realized that Ron was not himself. He was more than a little distant, it was obvious he had been stewing all night about something. I wasn't sure if he was mad at me, or what? I couldn't imagine what I could have done to hack him off.

I played the music for them and explained my ideas. Elena clapped excitedly, but Ron shrugged half heartedly.

"If that's what you want," he said, the tone of his voice confirmed it, Ron was angry about something.

"You don't like it?" I asked.

"What difference does it make. I'm the puppet, you're the puppet master, just pull my strings, I'll do whatever you want!" he snapped, in a strange, fake voice.

"Did I do something to hack you off?" I asked, my voice dripping with sarcasm. He was being a child, and now I was getting hacked off as well.

"Don't worry about me, I thought that the two of us were friends, but you're just as fake as everyone else in Hollywood," he snapped, rolling his eyes miserably.

I gave him a stunned look, I couldn't believe he had just said that. "How about you stop blaming me for all your problems and you focus on what you were brought here to do, which is skate," I told him, I forced my voice to sound as cold as possible.

I'd been stupid, I slipped up. I should have never let my feelings for Ron jeopardize the show. We needed to separate our private lives from our work. I sighed miserably. Jorge was smart to forbid me to get involved with Ron for the time being, he was riding an emotional roller coaster right now!

"Fine, like I said, you're the puppet master," snapped Ron.

I gave him a haughty glare and skated away from him. I wanted to clear my head, so I did a couple of laps around the ice while Ron and Elena stood there staring at me, slightly confused.

I felt discouraged, it seemed like it was impossible to make it through an entire practice without someone acting like a child. I had originally thought that my six figure salary was ridiculously excessive, now I was beginning to see that working with "stars" was harder than I had anticipated.

I returned to Ron and Elena feeling energized, I ignored Ron's attitude and began working on teaching them the new routine. The newest required element was side by side spins. It had been my least favorite element back when I had skated, it was a timing thing, the spins were supposed to look identical, a very hard task. Fortunately, the network had made things relatively easy for us. The pair could do any spin, even the most basic of spins, and they only had to complete two revolutions, a piece of cake, as far as I was concerned.

At least, now I would have a bit more to work with for our programs. We would have a lift, a pair spin and a side by side spin, maybe even the death spiral, if I wanted to throw that in. We had a good practice and Ron even seemed to be enjoying himself. At some point during our practice Jorge had wandered off to the wardrobe department to get them started on my costume designs.

When practice was over, I skated over to the edge of the ice and picked up my water bottle. Elena waved goodbye as she slipped her skate guards on. Ron skated up to me and eyed me arrogantly as I gulped down my water.

"Where were you last night?" he asked.

"What do you mean, where was I last night?" I asked.

"I called you a bunch of times, then I finally stopped by your condo, but you weren't there," he said, I could hear the hurt in his voice.

"The condo is officially no longer my home," I told him nonchalantly.

"What do you mean?"

"I mean, Jorge is so worried about "us" he's moved me into his house, he's very serious about this," I told him.

"He can't do that!" cried Ron.

"Ron, Jorge knows what happened the other night. Someone videotaped you at the condo with me, Jorge saw everything, and he's pretty hot about it," I whispered.

"You're kidding me right?" cried Ron, completely shocked that our seemingly private moment had been stolen from us.

"I'm not kidding. Listen Ron, this is all for the best. You have so much going on in your life right now, you're upset about your wife, now is not the time..."

"I am not upset about my wife. Jenae uses men, I can finally see that, she used me until I no longer suited her purposes, now she's found another man to manipulate!" he cried.

"That is why I think it would be best if we kept our relationship professional, at least until we're done with the show," I told him.

"Is that what you really want, or is that what Jorge told you to say?" he asked, his voice was laced with sarcasm.

"Don't act like a child Ron, Jorge does not tell me what to say," I told him, rolling my eyes miserably.

"Fine, you are my boss and I will obey you, just like you obey Jorge," he said, his tone was mocking.

"Fine," I said, raising my eyebrows at him. He shook his head miserably before he slipped his skate guards on and walked away.

I sighed as I watched him walk away. I felt bad that I had to be so hard on him, but I couldn't lead him on, that wouldn't be fair.

I snapped my skate guards on, and in moments Jorge had appeared there at my side.

"Trouble in paradise?" asked Jorge, his tone was slightly sarcastic.

"No trouble," I snapped.

"Listen Lane, I'm sorry, but Ron Brannon will be free and clear soon. I am quite certain his wife will divorce him for the more lucrative Roman Fleming and then two of you can hook up, after the show is done!"

I gave him a rueful smile. I didn't really know what to say to him, suddenly I felt like crying. I was an emotional mess!

"Personally, I think Mrs. Brannon may be shooting herself in the foot. Ron is quite a personality, you seem to bring it out in him. I think he may have quite a future in Hollywood," said Jorge, giving me a sly smile.

"Hmmm, then count me out. When I'm done with this show I'm going back to Colorado Springs," I told him.

"Why would you possibly do that? You can't fool me Lane, Hollywood is in your blood, this is where you belong," said Jorge.

"No, I don't think so," I told him, shaking my head.

"Oh come on Lane, what's in Colorado Springs that you feel the need to go back to. You have nothing to go back to but an empty house. Baylee is closer to you here, at Stanford, Ramsey is at school far away in Boston," said Jorge.

"I don't really need to be reminded how much my life sucks, " I told him ruefully.

"Nonsense, your life doesn't have to suck. You're finally getting your chance to be somebody. Don't let it pass you by," said Jorge.

"You're right, I have a real future as the fake girlfriend of a gay Hollywood producer," I told him, rolling my eyes miserably.

"Ouch! You don't have to be so harsh about it," cried Jorge, giving me a hurt look.

"Look Jorge, I'm playing the game. I totally get it. But when this is all over, I'm done. I'm going home, I'll be happy to leave Hollywood behind me."

"Okay, we'll see," said Jorge taking my hand and giving me a dubious smile.

# CHAPTER 18

The rest of the week went by, essentially without incident. I was pretty excited about our program, it was truly turning into something spectacular. Ron and Elena had both thrown themselves into the music and were playing out the characters like a couple of professionals! Our lift, side by side spins, and even our pairs spin were all coming along nicely and I was excited. Before I knew it, it was Wednesday once again and we were back at the rink to tape, yet another episode.

My team was performing third in the line up tonight and the song they were skating to was "The Rain in Spain", from the musical <u>My Fair Lady</u>. Wardrobe had pulled all the stops out and made Ron a navy blue, crushed velvet smoking jacket, complete with an ascot. Elena was dressed in a prim and proper high necked dress, with her hair piled elegantly on top of her head.

The original song had been approximately two minutes and twenty six seconds, so it had been cut a bit to make it fit into the two minute routine, but the sound guy had done a fabulous job. It still had exactly the drama I wanted.

I watched the first two performances of the night from the edge of the ice. The first two teams did a fine job, they made a few mistakes that were barely noticeable, but their programs were hardly memorable, they had no personality. I was nearly bursting with excitement as the stage crew hauled the props for our number, out onto the darkened ice.

True to the movie, Ron was going to begin the number seated in a high backed, leather desk chair, with his feet up on a big wooden desk. Elena would start out perched in a smaller chair. The furniture was placed at the far corner of the rink. I had designed the routine to stay far from the furniture after the opening, to avoid any accidents.

When the music started, the magic began. Ron and Elena played out their characters like true professionals.

From the opening they went straight into my footwork sequence. They gave a stunning performance, every element was executed cleanly, including my ambitious set of two side by side spins. I was ecstatic! At the end of the program they both skated over to me and I hugged them both excitedly. Then we went to the "kiss and cry" area to wait for our scores.

The comments from the judges were all positive, even Hal Luther, who was known for his nit picking, could barely find anything in their performance to pick apart. Moments later, when the scores were revealed we'd received two nines and a ten!

I could barely contain myself I was so excited! I tried to calm myself and watch the rest of the performances, but I could barely sit still. I can't say I could remember any details of any of the performances that followed ours.

At the end of the show, the couples were all brought out to the ice for the announcement of who was going home. Not only were we not going home, we were the top scoring team of the week once again!

Elena and Ron were elated. When they skated back to me Elena hugged me hard, then Ron picked me up and spun me around. I was laughing joyfully, so I was almost caught off guard when Ron tried to plant a kiss on my mouth. As much as I wanted to kiss him, I couldn't let him ruin, what I had worked so hard to create. We were top contenders now, I couldn't let all that come crashing down. I turned my head just in time and he ended up kissing me on the cheek, then I pulled myself out of his arms uncomfortably.

I sighed guiltily and looked away, whatever feelings I felt for Ron, had to wait, that's just how it had to be. No matter how much I wanted him to kiss me, I knew that the cameras were always watching, one small slip up, could be magnified to look like a torrid affair. I just couldn't let Ron do that to himself, he was married, even if that marriage was slowly falling apart.

Ron was giving me a hurt look as I made the rounds on the now crowed ice, hugging everyone who wanted to congratulate me. In moments, Jorge had pushed his way through the crowd to me and had his arm possessively around my shoulder. It was a struggle to keep from rolling my eyes. I wasn't a complete idiot and I didn't need a babysitter.

I left on Jorge's arm once again that night, and our little scam dragged on. I wondered what Elena thought of all this. Did she truly believe that Jorge and I were a couple? Did she ever notice the barely disguised sexual tension between Ron and I? Elena never said a word about any of it, so I wondered if she was completely oblivious, or if she just didn't care.

Later that night I was already busy working on our next week's routine. The problem with having a wonderful program like the one we'd done tonight meant that I always felt the need to top it with something even more spectacular. It wasn't going to be easy, my team had their limits, and I was afraid we would be reaching those limits soon.

Ron's body was designed for football, not figure skating, and as the show progressed, the producers were adding more technical difficulty each week. It was really only a matter of time before we were in over our head.

I was frustrated in my search for music this week, but not because I was overwhelmed by choices as I had been last week, but rather because I felt limited to bad choices by the week's awful theme. This next week the teams were to skate to TV show theme music. I was cringing when I heard that announcement. How could I ever make a decent program out of TV theme music?

Of course, I didn't have any TV theme music loaded on my computer, so I had to surf the internet for ideas. As I sifted through the hundreds of titles I found, I sighed miserably. This was going to be impossible! I was out by the pool, completely stressing out as I tried, without success, to find a song that I thought I could actually work with. Jorge ambled out on the patio with his glass of wine and sat down next to me.

"How's it going, love?" he asked, flashing me a bit of a smile.

"I hope that TV theme night wasn't your idea, because it's a horrible idea. There is absolutely not one TV theme song out there that I care to make into a skating program," I told him, whining miserably.

"Oh come on Lane, have fun with it. You're creative, you can think outside the box and make this work. I think it's going to be a blast!" said Jorge, flashing me a sly smile.

"It's going to be completely hideous," I told him with a frown. "What is the next week going to be, TV commercial jingles?"

"A very amusing thought, though if anyone could pull it off, I trust it would be you," said Jorge.

"Please Jorge, save your bogus compliments for when we are in public," I told him rolling my eyes.

"Are you implying that my admiration of you is not genuine? Lane, you cut me to the quick, I truly believe that you are my best choreographer by far. If your team doesn't win, it will be by no fault of yours," he cried, giving me a hurt look.

"Thank you for that sincere vote of confidence, and a completely hideous repertory of music to choose from," I sighed.

I paced restlessly back and forth across the pool deck. A cool breeze was rippling the pool water, and the lights of Hollywood twinkled in the valley below me. I was anxious and I couldn't sit still, but I needed to focus and concentrate on finding music for our next program. My team couldn't very well start working on a new program tomorrow, if I hadn't picked out the music yet. I sighed miserably, I wanted something fun and upbeat, like my team. None of the music I was finding online was doing anything for me.

Suddenly I had an idea. Jorge was right, I needed to think outside the box. Originally, I had been thinking of the music from all the sit coms I remembered from my childhood, but I had forgotten. There was a whole host of really cool westerns on TV, that aired before I could even remember. I sat back down with my computer and started a new search.

I pulled up the theme song for the TV show "Bonanza" on You Tube, and listened to it. I chewed on my lower lip as I considered it. The song was kind of what I wanted, but that particular song had been overused.

Now that I had an idea, this was going to be easy. I typed in "TV Western theme songs" in my search engine and scrolled down through the results, listening to a few clips here and there, soon I found what I had been searching for. Next week Ron and Elena were going to skate to the theme song from the show "Wild, Wild West".

I was finally excited about TV theme show night! Ron was going to make the cutest cowboy ever. I could already see the entire program in my mind, including the costumes, this was actually going to be fun!

# CHAPTER 19

I was back on the ice bright and early Thursday morning. Elena and Ron were excited to hear my ideas for the new program, for once, both members of my team seemed to be excited about the music and the theme. I was happy, though they were still riding high from our victory last night. I hoped that we could keep up the momentum and push through to the finals.

Ron was a bit distant to me, I was sure he was not too thrilled by my thwarting his kiss last night. I guess in the grand scheme of things, most people would have missed it, amongst all the other excitement, but I couldn't help but be wary, it seemed as if there were always cameras recording our every move.

My little run in with Maurice had set me on edge, to this day, I still worried that his "incriminating footage" would show up someplace it shouldn't. It would be particularly shameful to be kicked off the cast of the show mid season. I had no doubts that Jorge would have me removed from the show, if he were angry enough.

That evening after the show aired, I relaxed on the sofa with a glass of wine. I was tired, but I was much too keyed up to go to bed. Jorge was relaxing in the hot tub, since he was not really my lover, I didn't feel all that comfortable climbing in there with him. I flipped through the channels on the huge flat screen TV, finally settling on the local evening news. I hated to watch the news, but I was beginning to feel like a hermit. I had been living in my own little world, as of late, and I felt totally out of touch with reality. Hollywood was a bit like a world of it's own, seeing the rest of the world would be a good idea, I thought.

I was still a bit lost in my own thoughts, and I had mainly tuned it out, until my attention was grabbed by a familiar name. I snapped to attention as the reporter announced that Jenae Brannon had officially announced today that she was divorcing her husband Ron. I was staring at the television completely stunned. The reporter went on to say that Jenae had admitted she was pretty serious about Roman Fleming and the two of them would probably marry once her divorce was final.

I was suddenly panicking as I reached for my phone. I knew that Ron would be upset, he knew their marriage was over, but of course, it would still hurt. I wanted to call him, but I wasn't sure if that was a good idea.

I walked out to the patio and approached Jorge. He gave me a smile and raised his glass to me, in a mock toast.

"Hello darling, are you coming in?" he asked, flashing me a seductive smile.

"You can cut the crap Jorge, there are no witnesses," I told him shaking my head in amusement.

"I'm finding this rather fun. I can't really remember the last time I had a girlfriend," he said, giggling.

"I hate to be the bearer of bad news, but you really don't have a girlfriend now," I told him, rolling my eyes.

"Oh Lane, have you not realized how the mere illusion of a girlfriend has changed my entire life? The network "Big Whigs" think I must be a total stud, to have a hot girlfriend like Lane Jensen," said Jorge, flashing me a sly smile.

"I'm glad my presence here is working out so well for you, because my entire life is totally screwed," I snapped.

"Don't despair my dear. The show will be over before you know it, and you and Ron can hump like a couple of rabbits. What's going on? You seem upset."

"I need to call Ron, but I don't want you to be angry with me," I told him.

"Will you be calling him as a coach, or as a lover?" asked Jorge, giving me a sly smile. I frowned at him. I was getting the impression he was a bit buzzed.

"I want to call him as a friend. It was just announced on the news that Jenae has filed for divorce. No matter how evident it was, that this was coming, he's going to be hurt," I told him.

"And you just want to be his shoulder to cry on," said Jorge, his voice was laced with sarcasm.

"He will be very upset, we can't miss another day of practice. We have a new element to learn this week, things are getting down to the wire," I told him.

"You can call him, but you can't go to him," said Jorge.

I nodded. I could only hope that Ron would be able to pull it together after this harsh announcement. I was worried about his two little girls. Custody battles were always nasty and he loved his girls so much and was so proud of them. I couldn't bare it, if he were cut out of their lives.

I called Ron at his condo and on his cell, but I got no answer. I was worried about him. He took things personally, he could finally see how Jenae was using him, but he would still blame himself for the destruction of their marriage.

"There's no answer, what should we do?" I asked Jorge.

"I'll take you over there, hopefully he hasn't done anything stupid, like swallowed a handful of pills," snapped Jorge, who's patience was obviously wearing thin with the whole situation. He hauled himself out of the hot tub and wrapped himself in a towel and walked away to the master bedroom to get dressed.

We drove to Ron's condo in Jorge's car, but when we arrived the condo was dark and unoccupied, Ron's shiny black Escalade was not in it's spot.

"Good lord, I hope he hasn't run off somewhere to drink away his sorrows, we might never find him," said

Jorge.

I tried his cell phone again, but still, there was no answer. I was beginning to panic. Ron had been riding an emotional roller coaster lately. I worried about him, but where else could I look? I didn't have a clue.

"We should just go home, if he doesn't show up for practice, we'll worry about it then," said Jorge.

I sighed, I didn't know what else I could possibly do. I had no idea where he might have gone. We went back to the house and I went to bed, but I didn't sleep well. I woke up dozens of times until finally, it was time for me to get up and go to the rink.

I was consumed with a feeling of impending doom as Jorge drove us to the rink. I couldn't help but worry about Ron and his already messed up emotional status. This announcement would either hurt him badly, or be the closure that he needed. I could only wait and see how he handled the news.

I worried how this announcement would effect our team and our upcoming performance. Ron was a very caring person and his heartless wife Jenae had publicly left him for another man. It would be bad enough if he were not a celebrity, but unfortunately Ron's divorce was about to become a very public ordeal.

I was afraid that a lack of inspiration on Ron's part would ruin us, we had a lot to accomplish this week, a new program and a new element. Luckily, this week's new element wasn't really new to my team, it was the death spiral, an element Ron and Elena had mastered way back in week one. Still, even missing one practice this late in the game would be bad.

I was relieved when I arrived at the rink and realized that Ron was already there. Elena was sitting on a bench near the ice, tightening her laces, Ron was standing near the ice talking on his cell phone. I couldn't tell from where I was standing, what Ron's mood was like.

I wasn't sure if I should approach him to talk about it, or if I should just wait until he brought it up. He had his cell phone, so obviously he would know that I had called him last night. My chest was tight with indecision.

I hadn't realized I had been clinging to Jorge's arm tightly as I obsessed over what to do. Jorge kissed me on the cheek and told me he had some business to attend to. Then he gave me a meaningful smile. I gave him a weak smile as I realized what he was doing for me. He was giving me space so that I could talk to Ron alone. I waved to him as he left the ice arena. I sighed wondering what, exactly, I was going to say to Ron.

"Good morning," said Elena, slipping off her skate guards and stepping onto the ice to warm up.

"Good morning," I told her with a little nod.

I stood there uncomfortably as Ron finished his conversation and slipped his phone into his skate bag.

He stood up and assessed me carefully. "Hi," he said, his voice was hesitant. He was wondering what I knew.

"Hi," I said. I was biting my lower lip. I didn't know what to say to him. I wanted him to bring it up first.

"I saw that you called, sorry I never returned your calls last night. I guess you know," said Ron, looking at me defeatedly.

"I know," I said, nodding my head grimly. I was watching him carefully. I couldn't tell if he was sad or mad, he just seemed defeated. I knew he was hurting, he had done everything he could, to please Jenae.

"Well if you're worried about this messing things up for you, don't. I'll be okay," said Ron, shaking his head miserably.

"Ron I'm so sorry. I wasn't worried about this messing things up for me. I was worried about this messing things up for you. I know she hurt you, I was worried that she might try to keep your girls from you and I knew that would be very hard on you," I told him, looking into his eyes earnestly.

Ron was scanning the room nervously. "Where's your boyfriend?"

"Jorge left, he is giving us some space, so I could talk to you," I told him.

"What's there to talk about? She wants out. She wants a guy who's not washed up, who makes millions. I'm forty, I have a bad hip and I don't make millions," said Ron, shaking his head sadly.

"If you truly love somebody, it shouldn't make any difference," I told him.

"I loved her, I thought she loved me no matter what. Now I see, it wasn't the real me she loved. She loved Ron Brannon the star quarterback," said Ron, shaking his head miserably.

"I'm sorry," I said, taking his hand gently. He snatched it away angrily.

"Don't you dare pretend you care about me! You're a fake too! You show up at all these big Hollywood parties hanging on Jorge Broussard's arm, kissing him, like the two of you are lovers. Do you know how that feels for me? When I want you so badly?" cried Ron.

"Ron I'm sorry. I was trying to protect you. Jorge was trying to protect his show..."

"You're just as fake as Jenae," snapped Ron.

"I had no choice," I seethed.

"I thought you were different, I thought that you cared about me," snapped Ron, looking away disgustedly.

"Ron I'm sorry. I do care about you. Please understand, I had to do something, everyone could see what was going on! Did you ever wonder what happened to Maurice? He tried to blackmail me, he made the moves on me and tried to..." I couldn't speak anymore, the tears were already falling down my cheeks, I turned away completely embarrassed. I loved Ron and I was tired of playing these games.

Ron grabbed my shoulders and turned me to look into his eyes. "Are you trying to tell me that Maurice tried to rape you?" cried Ron, looking completely shocked.

I was biting my lower lip, trying to stem the tears that seemed to be coursing down my cheeks without my permission. "He tried to use his influence, he said he had incriminating video of us together," I sniffed.

"What incriminating video?" cried Ron, his anger seemed to be growing.

"I don't know, I never saw it. I only knew it was impossible for me to hide my true feelings. My guilt was overwhelming me and I didn't want to ruin your marriage," I cried.

"Lane, my marriage was already ruined, I was just too proud to realize it. Maybe it would have been better if Maurice would have just ratted us out, then I wouldn't look like such a schmuck," said Ron, ruefully.

"I think Jenae is vengeful Ron, she would have kept the girls from you and ruined you financially, believe me. It's better this way," I told him.

"I'm sorry you were worried about me. Jenae came to town to talk to me in person. I was at her hotel most of the night, trying to work things out. I thought I was going to have to fight her for partial custody of the girls. The ironic part is that she doesn't even want them. She's giving me full custody. She wants them on Christmas and spring break. That's all. I'm happy, but can you believe a mother can give up her daughters so easily, all so that she can start over with another man?" asked Ron, his face was a mask of disgust.

"No I can't believe it," I told him. I had my theories about Jenae, but I kept my mouth shut, it wasn't what Ron needed to hear right now.

"You're right, it really hurts. Even though I saw it coming, it hurts," he said, his eyes were glassy, like he might start crying.

I was torn, should I hug him, because he needed the support right now, or would that be a bad thing? I was standing there chewing on my lower lip nervously. I had no idea how to comfort him.

"Ron...I'm sorry..." I said, my voice quivered with emotion. I could feel his pain. I could still feel the pain of my own divorce, though I would never let anyone see that pain, this late in the game. I had cried enough tears over Greg.

"Don't be sorry. I only wish I could be as strong as you were over your own divorce," he said.

"I wasn't strong, just because I don't let people see my pain doesn't mean that it didn't hurt me, it hurt, it still hurts," I told him.

"Thank you for caring," said Ron, he kissed my hand and then he skated out onto the ice. I sighed, I knew that he couldn't talk about it anymore. Maybe it would be good for us to get to work, and maybe that would help him to keep his mind off of his pain.

I put my skates on and in a few minutes I had joined Ron and Elena on the ice. This week would be hard, we had to squeeze in all the required elements, a lift, a pairs spin, side by side spins and now the death spiral. We also had to bring out the personality of the TV show theme I had selected. That was the beauty of this show, my team got to play different characters every week, and they were actually good at it!

Our practice went well, but I could tell Ron was somewhere else, he wasn't focused, and his drive in life seemed to be completely gone.

We worked hard all week. Technically, the program looked fine, artistically, our team had lost our spark. The fire that Ron usually infused into our program was gone.

Wednesday finally rolled around, and I was worried. Our last practice had went well, but the program seemed lifeless. I had just created the most stunning program of my career, but my lethargic team couldn't do it justice.

I wasn't sure what I could do to save my team from spiraling into Ron's depression, but I felt like I needed to do something. This program had everything we needed to take first place this week, except for Ron's personality. It was gone!

Jorge had arrived to pick me up at the rink, he was standing on the side of the ice frowning as I skated over to him.

"Lane, I hate to see you slip from the top spot to the last, but your team kind of blows right now, they are completely lifeless," said Jorge as I approached him.

"Ron's depressed, what can I do?" I asked shrugging.

"Hmmm, desperate times call for desperate measures. Do you think it would it help, if you had sex with him?" asked Jorge, he was struggling to hide the smile that was creeping across his lips. I fought the urge to roll my eyes, Jorge was messing with me.

"It might make his mood better, though he'd be so completely spent, he'd be unable to perform on the ice tonight," I joked, stifling a little giggle.

"Yes, you're right. I seriously doubt he'd be able to walk, let alone skate," said Jorge, giving me a sly smile.

I cracked up. He started laughing too.

"Why is it that men seem to think that having sex will solve all their problems?" I laughed.

"It's not that we feel it will solve all our problems, but it sure as hell makes us forget about them for a little while. You know, the brain becomes completely useless when all the blood in your body heads straight to the wanker," laughed Jorge.

"Well, that explains a lot. I'm glad we had this conversation," I told him blandly.

"Anything for you my dear," said Jorge, flashing me a sly smile.

# CHAPTER 20

That evening was the taping of the week's show. I was nervous. Our practice today had been fair, but my team was lacking the personality I knew we needed to stay in this competition. We were slated to skate last, which could be good, or it could be bad, at this point, I wasn't sure which.

I hoped that maybe if my team was forced to watch all the performances before theirs, they would be a bit more inspired to put their heart and soul into this performance.

First up was team Evans, they did a cute routine to the music from "I Dream of Jeannie". They nailed all the elements and the female counterpart at least, completely blew me away.

The night seemed to drag on with all sorts of tiresome theme songs, I personally, would have never picked for my team to skate to. Team Muramsatsu put in a good performance with their song from "Hawaii 5-0". Finally our team was up, I was so nervous I could barely breathe.

My team was announced and they skated to the center of the ice. Ron looked incredibly handsome in his chaps and gun belt. The wardrobe department had done a fabulous job with Elena's costume. She was dressed in a red saloon girl dress, with feathers in her hair, they had even given her fish net stockings and they had covered her skates with black boot covers that looked like old fashioned button up shoes. Elena was loving her character this week and she was totally into playing up her role. Ron had flashed the cameras a fake smile when he arrived on the ice, but his face had been expressionless ever since.

The music started and I was nearly holding my breath in anticipation. Elena was doing fabulous as she hammed her way through the program, Ron, on the other hand, looked like a zombie. He was doing all the moves, but his body was void of any emotion, it was completely obvious, he was merely going through the motions. I sighed miserably as I watched, I had built all kinds of fun dance steps into the routine so that they could have fun with it, but Ron seemed to be a million miles away.

Technically, the only glitch came right before our lift. I had went all out this week and taught them a real pairs lift. Pairs lifts are harder than ice dance lifts as the man needs to be strong enough to lift the woman over his head. Ron was getting so much better on skates and Elena was so tiny, I figured it would be no problem for my team. They had done quite well with the advanced lift in practice, but still, I was anxious, any misstep on the ice could be dangerous for Elena!

Ron was supposed to reach down and pull Elena through his legs, then there were a few connecting steps and they would do a lasso lift, which would lift Elena high above the ice, above Ron's head.

Ron pulled Elena through his legs, but then it seemed as if he had forgotten the connecting steps, he fumbled across the ice for a few seconds, then he did manage to get Elena up into the lasso lift, but Ron brought her down so quickly, I feared the lift hadn't lasted the required two seconds that would actually give us credit for the move.

Finally, the program was over and Ron and Elena were taking their bows. They skated over to me and I hugged them both half heartedly. I was trying hard to conceal my disappointment, but I was sure there was a good possibility that my team was going home tonight.

The three of us huddled in the "kiss and cry" area waiting for our scores. Elena was mumbling harsh words in Russian. Luckily, neither Ron nor I knew exactly what she was saying, but her displeasure with the performance was evident!

The judges made a few positive comments about the technical difficulty of our routine and the choreography, what they all seemed to agree on, was that our program lacked the fire and personality that we had shown in all our other performances. We received a disappointing score of one eight and two sevens. I was much too nervous to remember the other teams scores, so I wasn't sure if we were doomed, or not.

Moments later, all the couples were brought to the ice for the judge's decision. I could barely breathe, I was so nervous. The announcement was made and I was so stunned I couldn't even absorb which team had been eliminated, I only knew that it hadn't been my team, we had been spared!

I watched numbly as team Biermann returned to the ice to take their final bows. When I saw the male counterpart of the team skate out in his white Captain's uniform I suddenly remembered. This was the team that had done a really lame program to the theme from "The Love Boat".

I sighed in relief, as the house lights came back up and everyone seemed to be scattering for the night. We had made it through one more week, but if we gave another performance like that one, I seriously doubted we'd be able to hang on for another week.

I socialized with a few people I knew as I wound my way through the crowd. I finally found myself in a quiet corner of the arena, where I could just hang back and watch everyone else as they interacted. Elena and Ron were still on the ice socializing with the other remaining couples. Jorge was standing near the judges box, having a very animated conversation with a few of the judges and some network executives.

I had to smile to myself. I loved to watch how people interacted. Hollywood was never short on interesting interactions. Everyone had an angle, it seemed.

Before I knew it, our camera man Javier had found me. He was training his camera on me, and giving me a sly smile.

"What did you think about your team's performance

tonight? I believe that Hal Luther called it lackluster," said Javier.

"That's exactly what I would call it. Luckily we were not eliminated tonight and we will have a chance to redeem ourselves. I'm hoping to reclaim the top spot next week," I told him with an enthusiasm that wasn't quite genuine. My face didn't betray what my heart feared deep inside. Ron had been hurt deeply, his heart was broken. I wasn't sure that Ron could be snapped out of his funk by next week, let alone by the end of the season. I was sincerely hoping that my team wasn't done in this competition.

# CHAPTER 21

I had been anticipating that the ride home in the limo with Jorge would be tense, he was disappointed with my team's performance and he was displeased with me, as if I had any control over the emotional health of my team members.

"Your teams' program was very frustrating to watch tonight. I've seen what they can do, but tonight's performance was just pallid and lifeless. I know that Brannon is upset over his wife's shenanigans, but you need to reel him in and get him back on track, or you are going to lose this competition," snapped Jorge, shaking his head miserably.

"Thank you for telling me that Jorge, I truly had no idea," I told him, my voice was laced with sarcasm. I wish I could control people's emotions, but unfortunately I could not.

"I am sorry Lane, but you have a talent, a talent that could take your team all the way to the finals. Your programs are so magical and they always blow everyone away, when performed properly, that is."

"I don't know what to do Jorge, I'm not sure that Ron can get over this. He's in pain, I'm getting the feeling he's going to be worthless for the rest of this competition. Jenae really hurt him, the only reason he even came on the show is because his soon to be, ex-wife coerced him. He was doing it for Jenae and the girls, now he has no motivation to perform, he's only here because of the contract he signed," I told Jorge, shaking my head miserably.

"You're going to have to give him that motivation. Isn't that what coaches do, inspire and motivate? I'm beginning to think that maybe I was wrong to forbid you to hook up with him, maybe..."

"No Jorge, under the circumstances, I think it's a bad idea," I told him.

"No, it's a fabulous idea, think about it, he's been attracted to you since day one. I mean really, what raises a guy's spirit more than..."

"Jorge please, I may be your employee, but I'm not some sort of trollop you can call up and use for favors at your discretion!" I cried.

"Lane, a trollop or a whore would pay favors to many men, but I am only asking you to do something I well know you already want to do. You forget...I saw the video. Believe me, I am well aware that the two of you were merely seconds away from it becoming pornography, thus making the video footage way out of my price range.

I know you're attracted to him, what's the big deal? I know I forbid you to see him, but under the circumstances, waiting to consummate your relationship could possibly ruin your chances to win this competition. I mean why wait, to do what you're going to do in seven weeks anyway? I am quite certain if we could do this discreetly enough, maybe no one would even catch on."

"If **we** could do this?" I cried.

"Well I wouldn't be physically involved, of course, but I could help in the planning. It would have to be very discreet, Hollywood seems to notice everything. Maybe if I had him over to the house for dinner one evening. You could just bang him there, no one would even know."

"I could just bang him there? No one would even know?" I cried, glaring at Jorge, as if he were insane. "Have you lost your flipping mind? First of all, I am not a prostitute, I will not be plotting any seduction of Ron with you, the man who all of Hollywood is convinced is my lover.

Secondly, this is Hollywood, you're fooling yourself if you don't realize that everyone is going to know the actual moment anything happens between the two of us! The big deal is that he is not divorced yet, and I am.

Besides the obvious scandal, which would be bad enough. I refuse to give Jenae any fuel for her lawyers to use against Ron," I snapped.

"Lane, I just think..."

"No Jorge, just let it go. Let me handle this," I snapped.

"That's the problem, you're not handling it. Last week you were at the top, but your team is teetering on the edge now. This week could be your last week, if you don't do something!"

"Jorge, I want to win, but I cannot jeopardize his reputation and his entire life, just to win this competition. I'm afraid of the repercussions, he has his daughters. He loves them. I don't know what he would do if Jenae tried to keep them from him."

"Here's an idea, maybe if we had him over here for dinner tomorrow night, I could..."

"I swear to God Jorge, I'm going to..." I made a fist and gave him a threatening glare.

"Sorry, sorry, I'll shut up," said Jorge when he saw that I was finally losing my cool.

I rolled my eyes. I was beginning to hate my life here in Hollywood. I hated how everyone knew everyone else's business. I really hated how I had become nothing but a pawn in the business! I sighed and shook my head miserably, I didn't know why I was here, I didn't belong in Hollywood.

# CHAPTER 22

The next morning I arrived on the ice before anyone else. I was working on some new footwork and I wanted to skate alone for a while. I loved being on the ice in the morning before anyone else got there, it was quiet in the chilly, echoing rink and the ice was still smooth and unmarred. There was no music, no voices, no one else there to intrude on my thoughts, no producers, no cameramen. It was exquisite!

I was worried about my team, especially Ron. I hoped that Ron could pull himself out of this depression and make a comeback. It wouldn't be so bad if my team just totally sucked anyway, then at least, I knew there wasn't even a chance. But Ron had it in him, I knew he did. He was a champion on the football field, and I knew now, that he had the drive to be a champion in anything he put his mind to. Unfortunately, his own wife had damaged him, his heart was broken. I didn't know if Ron would recover himself in time to save our team in this competition. Broken hearts just didn't heal overnight.

I hoped to completely blow the judges out of the water with this week's routine. This week we would be adding the final required element, a throw jump, which made me glad that I had a female professional skater on my team, someone who had a bit of experience with jumps in general. It would be hard to take someone with basically no skating experience and tell them that their partner was going to throw them across the ice.

I'd had a difficult time selecting the music for 80's week. I graduated from high school in the 80's so I was emotionally attached to a lot of the music. It brought back a lot of good, and a lot of bad memories for me. Finally, I chose a song that I loved for a lot of different reasons. The song was, "In a Big Country" by the band, Big Country.

I was drawn to the song because it was fast moving, it was unique, and the band was Scottish. So of course, the music had a unique Scottish flavor to it. My father was Scottish, which would supposedly make me half

Scottish, that is, if you didn't listen to the whispers that I was most likely the bastard child of some Hollywood actor. Still, I felt a bit of a connection to the music and I felt like I could make the music work for us.

My idea for the costumes was to dress Ron and Elena in black, 80's style spandex outfits that were trimmed in black watch plaid. I was excited about this program, if I could just get Ron to perform in the caliber I knew he was capable of, we might just walk away with first place this week!

I skated alone in the vast, echoing rink for about an hour, soon Ron and Elena arrived on the ice. I explained my plans for our program. Ron seemed okay with everything, but Elena was frowning and rolling her eyes.

"I want to skate to Michael Jackson," she whined.

"Everyone will be skating to Michael Jackson and Madonna, and stuff like that! I want us to stand out. We need to do something unexpected and memorable," I told her.

"Oooh, what about Cyndi Lauper?" cried Elena excitedly.

"No!" I told her, now I was rolling my eyes.

Elena pouted for a little while, but after a while it seemed as if she was finally getting into our program. Ron seemed to be doing a little better, though I was still a bit worried. Our big element, the throw jump was very important, I hoped he could focus enough to get it down. I really didn't want Elena to get injured.

I planned to have them do a throw toe loop, but Elena had her heart set on a throw double axel. I shook my head dismissively. Elena was getting caught up in the big illusion here.

I almost broke out in hysterical laughter, when she brought it up. Elena and Ron were not really pairs skaters. They were two athletes, from two very different sports that were brought together for a reality TV series. I thought that trying anything too advanced was an accident waiting to happen, Elena was not a pairs skater, so she had no experience with throw jumps. I just thought it would be best if we didn't try to overdo it!

The week seemed to fly by quickly and my team was doing much better than I had expected. Ron was still not one hundred percent, but at least, he was not the zombie he had been last week.

I had taught Ron and Elena the throw toe loop and it looked as if they would have it perfected before we taped on Wednesday.

When I arrived on the ice Monday morning, Ron and Elena were already busily running through their program. Elena had really gotten into the music and was pouring her heart and soul into this program.

I smiled as I watched them, as a team, they had come so far, it was truly amazing to watch them skate together and realize that Ron had never ice skated at all, before he came on this show.

The big throw jump was coming up and I held my breath as they skated around the ice gaining speed. My eyes were wide as Elena got herself in position to do an axel and before I knew it, Ron had flung her into the air and she was spinning above the ice in a double axel. I stood there with my mouth gaping open in shock, in an instant, she landed it gracefully and they both skated gracefully to their ending.

"Holy crap!" I cried, completely oblivious to the fact that Javier was right there with his camera trained on me, in an effort to get my reaction to their jump.

Ron and Elena were both breathing heavily and smiling broadly at me as I skated out to them on the ice.

"I can't believe it, that was incredible!" I cried throwing my arms around Elena.

"You are surprised?" she asked, beaming up at me.

"Hell yes, I'm surprised," I cried, going to Ron and hugging him briefly. He squeezed me hard, but I pulled myself from his arms uncomfortably, then I stood there staring at them both in shock.

"You two did this on your own?" I asked.

"Elena wanted to try it, she said we could win with this jump," said Ron.

"Well I seriously doubt any other team has a throw double axel. I can't believe you guys got it down so fast!" I was still completely in shock. If Elena had been a pairs skater previously, I could believe it, but this was something completely out of her comfort zone. I was so proud of both of them!

We trained hard for the rest of our practice and I left that morning more confident that we wouldn't be going home this week.

I spent the afternoon out by the pool, Jorge was in meetings all day, so I had the whole house to myself, it was very relaxing.

Jorge arrived home at five thirty and announced that we would be having guests for dinner. I rolled my eyes and grimaced painfully, so much for having a nice, relaxing evening.

"Don't worry, no need to dress up, it's a pool party, it's just casual," said Jorge, giving me a sly smile.

I frowned, I wasn't sure who would be coming, but I was certain I would much rather go to bed early. Instead, I would be trying to entertain whatever tiresome guests Jorge had invited over for the evening.

At almost seven on the dot, the doorbell rang and Ed stepped into the foyer to answer it. I was wearing a casual sundress and was standing behind him as he answered the door.

"Good evening Mr. Brannon," said Ed, gesturing for him to come in.

I could only stand there and stare at him in shock. Ron had brought a bottle of wine, which he handed to me, but I was still too stunned to say anything as I took the bottle from his hands.

"Wow, this place is great. I really appreciate the invite," said Ron casually, as he followed Ed into the main part of the house, while I trailed along behind them numbly.

"Mr. Brannon, welcome," said Jorge, greeting him cordially and shaking his hand.

"Please, call me Ron," said Ron.

"Okay, please call me Jorge," said Jorge, flashing him a cordial smile. I was just staring at them both numbly. I struggled to draw in a deep breath, as my mind raced crazily. I couldn't believe Jorge had done this, I was aghast.

My heart was racing nervously and I was suddenly feeling very dizzy. I was shaking my head, completely bewildered, Jorge had set me up. He had told me that he felt his house was a safe place for Ron and I to hook up. How stupid was I? I had never believed he would actually pursue it.

"May I have a word with you Jorge?" I asked, when I had finally recovered my voice. I was giving him a fake smile, trying to disguise how horrified I was by the entire situation.

"Certainly, please excuse us Ron," said Jorge, giving him a gracious smile. I fought the urge to roll my eyes. Jorge led me into the study and carefully closed the doors behind us.

"Is there a problem my love?" he asked, flashing me a fake smile.

"What do you think you are doing?" I cried.

"My darling Lane. I am not doing anything. I am waiting for you to do it yourself. You see, I am a scientist, a chemist, if you will. I am simply bringing the volatile ingredients together, to see how they interact, when they are not being subjected to the mundane pressures of taking part in a reality TV series," said Jorge, giving me a sly smile.

"I'm not going to sleep with him Jorge, you're wasting your time!" I cried, shaking my head miserably.

"Why not?" he asked, assessing me haughtily.

"It's not the right time," I snapped.

"And you believe the right time will be after you lose the competition?" he asked, a sly smile lingered on his lips.

"I believe the right time would be after his divorce is final," I said.

"Good God Lane, why wait? You want him, he wants you. I can't see any reason to put it off. No one will ever know. Believe me, it will do wonders for his attitude, which in turn, will do wonders for my show," said Jorge.

"Prostitution is illegal in the state of California," I snapped angrily.

"Well, don't let him slip any money into your thong and I believe all is well," said Jorge, almost giggling.

"It's a bad idea Jorge," I told him shaking my head miserably.

"It is not a bad idea, it's a fabulous idea! If you could only see how splendid the two of you are together. There is so much restrained passion between the two of you. I only wish I could have the two of you skate together on an episode of the show, that would be hot. In fact, I get the impression that performance would be so steamy, the entire audience might have an orgasm," said Jorge, giving me a sly smile.

"Oh Jorge," I cried shaking my head miserably.

The doorbell rang, and I was momentarily diverted.

"Oh good, that's Elena. See, you've got me all wrong darling. I simply invited your team over for a little team bonding," said Jorge, flashing me an evil smile.

I sighed. I felt like this was part of the reality show, because I had definitely been outwitted!

Elena was obviously very excited to be there at Jorge's house. Of course, Elena had big Hollywood aspirations and unfortunately, she thought that by sleeping with Jorge, she could attain those aspirations. Of course, she didn't realize that Jorge was gay.

It was not a big dinner party, Elena and Ron were our only guests. We had a nice, Hawaiian themed dinner on the patio. Elena and Jorge dominated most of the conversation, though I did talk a little bit about our upcoming performance.

After dinner, we lounged around on the patio until Jorge suggested that he give Elena a tour of his house. She was very excited as she strolled away with him. I almost giggled aloud. I was certain that Jorge was giving me space, he was so sure that Ron needed to get laid. Though, I was afraid that Jorge was the only one in danger of getting laid tonight.

An uncomfortable silence had fallen over Ron and I. He knew how I felt about the situation and the alone time was making us both uncomfortable. The air in the hills was very still tonight, and a smothering mugginess was enveloping the patio area. It was very uncomfortable just sitting there with Ron, not really knowing what to say to him.

I stood up and walked over to the edge of the pool and sat on the edge and let my legs hang over the edge into the pool. The water was warm, not at all refreshing, but I could look out over the twinkling lights of the city and not have to look at Ron. What do you say to someone you've already fallen in love with, when you know you just can't pursue that love?

Ron was probably sorry that he had come here. I was not being a very good hostess. In a moment Ron had stood up and was striping down to his swim trunks.

"Watch this," he said, trotting over to the diving board.

He climbed up on the diving board and proceeded to do a flip into the water, making a huge splash.

I screamed when the water hit me, then I applauded as he smiled and pretended to bow over his performance. I was laughing as he swam toward me, but his face was totally serious.

He swam up to me and placed his body right between my legs and casually draped his arms around my waist. My heart was suddenly pounding out of control as he pressed his body against mine.

Water was dripping off of him and soaking my sundress, but I didn't care. It took every ounce of self restraint to just sit there and not wrap my arms around him, like I really wanted to. I was still getting the feeling that we were not really alone. Granted, Jorge was with Elena, but I assumed that Ed was somewhere nearby, most likely watching us, to see what happened when we were left unattended.

"I think we were left alone on purpose," said Ron, gazing deeply into my eyes and giving me a sly smile.

I fought to take in a deep breath. My heart was thundering loudly in my chest. "It was a bit obvious, wasn't it," I managed to choke out. I was trying to scoot away from his body. The way his body was pressing against me was making me feel shaky and completely turned on for some reason.

"So Jorge has had a change of heart, I'm guessing," said Ron, looking into my eyes, very seductively.

"Yes," I could barely even say the word, it was an effort to breathe. The water was coursing down his body in little rivers, dripping onto my legs. I could feel the heat radiating off of his body. I had all sorts of scenarios running through my head, and they were all naughty. He had to know what he was doing to me.

"Why did the two of you ask me here tonight?" he asked, his tone had changed and I was suddenly alarmed.

"I was surprised when you showed up. I knew that we were having dinner guests. I never asked who," my voice was breaking with emotion. I could hardly stand to have his body pressed against me like that, my heart was pounding with excitement.

"It was my poor performance last week wasn't it? Jorge changed his mind because of my poor performance. Do you not realize how he's using you?" asked Ron, staring deeply into my eyes.

I could barely concentrate on the words that were coming out of his mouth. My brain was completely focused on the sensation of his body pressed against mine, as the water ran off of his body, soaking through my thin cotton sundress. I wondered if he could hear my heart thundering in my chest right now? The sound was almost deafening to me.

"Every man could use a performance enhancing drug, right? I can see what is going on. Jorge is offering you up as a performance enhancing drug for me. He wants you to sleep with me, so I won't totally fuck everything up this week," said Ron, his voice was suddenly dripping with sarcasm. He had pulled himself up on the edge of the pool and was leaning over me now, still pressing his body into mine. I could barely think or breathe.

"What?" I was so confused I could barely follow.

"I know what you've been instructed to do. I can see right through your little plan," seethed Ron.

"No, I told you...I didn't even know who was coming here tonight."

"Listen to me Lane, you may be nothing but a pawn in Jorge Broussard's little game, but I will not be used. I do what I want, I will not let the two of you use me to your liking," he spat, then he swam to the other side of the pool and hauled himself out of the water. He gave me a disgusted glare and then stalked away. I was too shocked to even utter a word.

I stood up on shaky legs and followed him back into the house, I wanted to tell him that he had it all wrong. I heard the front door slam, I arrived in the foyer just in time to see Ron squeal angrily down the driveway. My heart was pounding with shame. I realized what this must look like to him and I knew he was furious.

I went into my room and flopped down on my bed and cried. I felt like, not only did I destroy any chance of Ron and I ever getting together, but now I feared he would quit the show. Jorge had ruined everything!

I took a hot shower then I pulled my robe around me and relaxed on my bed with my laptop. Soon there was a tentative knock on the door.

"Come in."

Jorge opened the door and stepped in. "What happened? Ron was gone much sooner than I expected," said Jorge.

"There was a small problem with your master plan. Ron realized that you were whoring me out," I told him distastefully.

"Damn, it seemed like everything was going so well. Ed told me he went to his room and left the two of you alone on the patio because he was certain that the two of you were about to do it in the pool. What the hell happened?" cried Jorge.

"See! That's exactly why no one can have a real relationship in Hollywood. There's always someone watching. What would you have done, if we did do it in the pool. Videotape it and sell it?" I cried angrily.

"I beg your pardon! I wasn't going to video tape anything. Actually, I would have thought that you'd have the good sense to take the gentleman back to your room. You've heard of Google Earth haven't you? Google Earth photographs everything! Doing it in the pool would not be exactly private!" he cried.

"Well now he's angry, he feels set up. I think he probably hates me, he thinks I was just playing a part, using him," I sighed.

"Oh Christ, I'll talk to him," said Jorge, shaking his head miserably. He turned abruptly and headed for the door.

"How did it go with Elena?" I asked, giving him a sly smile.

"Oh my God!" he cried, closing the door again quickly. "I was merely trying to give the two of you a little space, so I gave her the house tour. I thought it was all perfectly innocent, she's always a bit flirty with me, but I never flirt back."

"When we arrived in the master bedroom, I was a bit taken aback. I had never seen anyone, man or woman strip down so quickly, and before I knew it, she was attacking my penis with an appreciation I have never seen before," said Jorge, almost distastefully.

I was suddenly laughing uncontrollably. I could only imagine the look on Jorge's face.

"Did you stop her?" I asked, giggling.

"I couldn't, I was already...interested," said Jorge uncomfortably.

I was nearly rolling laughing, thinking of Jorge in such a compromising position.

"Then what happened?" I cried, completely delighted by his amusing story.

"Oh, this is quite uncomfortable to talk about. Well, I... ummm...finished. And she wanted to...you know, do everything. I just told her that I couldn't. I love you and I could never cheat on you like that."

I was giggling uncontrollably. "Then what did she say?"

"She told me I was an eeediot. She told me that you were probably screwing Ron, and I was so stupid I could not see that the two of you were attracted to each other."

I frowned, Elena was not as oblivious as I'd thought she was. I had been right about how ambitious she was, poor Jorge had never seen that coming!

"Well I feel as if I've made a terrible mess of things now, I'm going to pay a visit to Ron," said Jorge, waving to me. I sighed miserably. I wasn't sure if Jorge paying a visit to Ron was a good thing, or not.

# CHAPTER 23

I arrived at the ice rink early the next morning. I was worried about how our practice would go. I had gone to bed before Jorge had arrived back at the house last night, so I hadn't had a chance to ask him how his little talk with Ron had gone. He'd left early for a meeting this morning and I had driven myself to the rink, so I had no clue what would be in store for me this morning.

Ron was the first one to show up on the ice with me.

"I'm sorry I acted like an ass last night. Jorge told me that he set you up too. I had assumed that you were in on his little plot," said Ron.

"I stand by his original decision. I like you Ron, but with everything that is going on, I think it's best if we wait. I know you've not been yourself, but jumping into bed with me is not going to help matters at all," I told him, shaking my head miserably.

"Well, I might beg to differ on that point," he said, giving me a sly smile. "But I see where you're coming from, it does seem as if there's always somebody watching," said Ron.

"So are we okay then, you're not mad at me?" I asked.

"I couldn't be mad at you long. In fact, I've been falling in love with you since the day I met you," he said, looking down into my eyes.

"Remember when I kissed you, at your condo?" he asked, his deep velvety voice seemed to caress the words.

"Of course I remember," I managed to whisper, even though I could barely breathe at the moment.

"I haven't been able to stop thinking about it...about the taste of your lips. I just want to kiss you again...this is killing me."

I looked up into his eyes and was suddenly mesmerized. I didn't even realize that he had reached out and was caressing my cheek softly. He gathered me into a hug and I pretty much melted into his arms. I wanted him to kiss me, but of course someone was always watching, it was too dangerous!

"Good morning!" called Javier as he skated toward us, his camera rolling.

I gasped and pulled myself from Ron's arms abruptly, hoping that Javier hadn't captured that entire emotional moment on video tape. I gave Javier a guilty smile, he just raised his eyebrows and gave me a sly smile. I sighed miserably.

In moments, Elena arrived on the ice and she seemed to be assessing me carefully. I was anxiously trying to pull myself together and at least, appear professional. My heart was still pounding with guilt over my emotional encounter with Ron. Elena was eyeing me haughtily as she skated up to us.

"Good morning," I managed to mumble, self consciously.

"Good morning," she said, flashing me a sly smile. I almost cringed, I wasn't sure if that meant she had witnessed my emotional moment with Ron, or if that was the smug smile of a woman who thinks she took liberties with my man. I almost giggled at that thought. I hated to tell her that what she actually did, was violate a gay man.

Our practice went well, once we were all able to settle down and concentrate on the actual program. It was hard, I really was falling for Ron, and it was getting harder and harder for me to ignore those feelings and keep pushing him away.

Wednesday night arrived and we were back in the rink taping yet another episode. Our practice this morning had went well and I was ready to wow everyone with our stunning program.

There were just six teams left and all of them were doing quite well. The competition just kept getting harder.

My team would be performing second tonight. The first team skated out onto the ice all decked out in their eighties glam. I had to smile when I saw them, all spiked and teased hair and sequins. I shot Elena a satisfied smile as the music started, they were skating to Michael Jackson's "Wanna be Starting Something".

The program as a whole was okay, the concept and the choreography was good. Technically, their program was a train wreck, their throw jump barely got off the ground and the lift they did, could only be described as lame. I was feeling a bit more confident about my own team, after seeing this one skate, though after we performed, there would still be four more teams left to skate their programs.

Finally, my team was announced and they skated to the center of the ice. I smiled proudly as they took their positions on the ice, their costumes were very cute and Elena had her hair up in a high ponytail that was all teased up Cyndi Lauper style. The program was fast paced and showy, and neither Ron or Elena missed a beat.

I was beaming proudly as I watched them, they had come back in high style and I was so proud, I was ready to burst! The entire arena gasped when they finally did their throw double axel. When Ron and Elena finally took their bows, the entire arena got to it's feet in a standing ovation. The response of the crowd was overwhelming. I was nearly moved to tears.

Ron and Elena both skated back to me at the edge of the ice, while the judges were called upon to comment on their performance. All in all, the judges were completely blown away by the entire program, not to mention the fact that they had nailed a throw double axel!

I was hugging them both excitedly as the judges

revealed their scores. Three tens! I was completely beside myself with excitement, we had scored a perfect thirty! We were all three jumping around excitedly like a bunch of school children. We were definitely not going home this week!

When the show was over and the next team had said their goodbyes I was still at the edge of the ice socializing with everyone. I was talking to two of the producers and Elena was there hanging on our every word as Jorge approached us with a huge smile on his face.

Elena gave him a shy smile, as he approached. I think she was expecting Jorge to say something to her. I was smiling at him happily until he did something completely unexpected. Jorge told Elena hello briefly, then he gathered me into his arms and gave me a passionate kiss on the lips. I was completely caught off guard, it took all the restraint I had, to keep from slugging him.

"Darling, your program blew me away, it was completely incredible," he gushed, he was still holding me in his arms, looking deeply into my eyes, a proud smile on his lips.

I was staring at him, completely stunned, unable to utter a word. The passionate kiss had totally thrown me off, I really wanted to grimace and make faces, but of course everyone thought that Jorge and I were lovers, so I refrained from making a scene. I knew that Jorge was acting, possibly for Elena's benefit, and I was obliged to go along with it, despite the fact that I really didn't possess good acting skills.

Luckily, Ron was across the ice talking to another group of people and he hadn't noticed the scene that was playing out over here. Thank goodness, he already gave Jorge jealous glances. I was afraid if Ron had witnessed the kiss, maybe **he** would have slugged Jorge!
I wasn't sure if Jorge's little show was for Elena's benefit, or for the benefit of all the cameras that were always there rolling in an effort to catch every single moment of the "reality".

"Thanks babe," I crooned as I tried, almost uselessly, to disguise my disgust with the kiss.

Jorge had draped his arm around my shoulders possessively and was animatedly conversing with everyone in our little group. Soon the crowd began dying down and we told everyone good night. I gave Ron a wry smile and a little wave as Jorge pulled me past him and out to our waiting limo.

"What was that all about?" I cried, when we were safely inside the limo. "Are you afraid Elena's going to grab hold of your dinkus again?"

"No, I'm almost afraid to admit, I actually enjoyed that. I've never had anyone attack me with such...hunger. I thought that she was going to gobble me right up," said Jorge, giving me a sly smile.

"Oh god," I cried, cringing and shaking my head distastefully.

"That's exactly what I said! All I could really do was surrender and let her have her way with me. It's impossible to run away when there might be teeth involved."

I rolled my eyes. "Jorge why did you kiss me like that?"

"People were talking, I was trying to squash the rumors! Unfortunately, I think it may be too late. Everyone can see right through your little act. It's perfectly obvious that you and Ron are attracted to each other!" said Jorge.

I sighed. "But I didn't do anything!"

"Lane you don't have to do anything, I've been able to read you like a book since day one. I don't know what it is, but the two of you have chemistry, if only I could bottle it and sell it, I would be a very rich man!" said Jorge.

I sighed, hopefully the the clips that aired on TV wouldn't be too revealing. I had to admit, it was hard for me to hide my feelings anymore, the more I was with Ron, the more I knew I was meant to be with him. Everyone could see that we were a perfect match. I could only hope it wasn't going to ruin things for Ron, if his soon to be ex-wife figured it out.

# CHAPTER 24

Five teams were gone, five were left. It seemed completely incredible that my team had made it this far, considering what I had to work with when I began this competition.

I had to admit, it was beginning to become quite obvious when you watched the entire show, Ron and I were becoming closer and closer. It was almost impossible not to notice it, the lingering glances, the emotional hugs.

Unfortunately, every little emotional moment had all been captured by the camera and like any good reality show, the editors felt the need to play up any little bit of drama for all it was worth, though I'm sure the show's editors thought I was a terrible cheater. Nearly everyone at the network was convinced that Jorge and I were lovers. We lived together, and of course, Jorge was always there at my side, they all assumed that we would be engaged soon. That thought always made me giggle! It was a reality show and the camera was always rolling, and it was getting very stressful for me. I had never been good at hiding my feelings. Ron had told me that he was falling in love with me and I already knew that I was falling in love with him, but there was still more than a month left till the end of the show, when we could safely do anything about it. I was tired of living this lie as Jorge's girlfriend.

This week we were working with music from original movie scores. This was when my need to be different and all my creativity seemed to go right out the window. The only movie score I could even consider for this program was the music from "Pirates of the Caribbean". It was my all time favorite movie and Klaus Badelt was one of my favorite composers.

Ron was loving the idea of dressing up as a pirate and wearing dreadlocks. I thought that the program was going to be awesome even though Jorge had rolled his eyes miserably and said. "Oh my God, are you kidding me? Lane Jensen is going mainstream? Couldn't you find anything remotely austere?"

I know, mainstream is not really my style. As a rule, I usually tried to stay away from the popular stuff, but I couldn't help it, I was a sucker for a sword fight! Of course the best part about the show was the costumes and the props, and I was like a kid getting ready for halloween. I was so excited, I was almost giddy. The disappointing part was that Elena actually got to do the program, not me.

I would be transforming Ron into Jack Sparrow and Elena into Elizabeth Swan, and they were going to play out a "love, hate relationship" which shouldn't be too hard, they already had the "hate" part down.

This was the last week before, what the show considered to be, the finals. There would be four teams in the finals. Next week would be a recap week. I was happy about that, if we made it through, we would have a bit of a break as the show would air clips from all the final four teams programs and clips of their practices showing their progress. There would be no new program to learn next week.

Then the last four teams would face off in the finals and each week during the finals things would progressively get harder.

I was certain everyone would be pulling the stops out from here on out, so each routine had to be a little bit better than the one prior.

his pirates program was probably our most ambitious yet. The music was very dramatic and I wanted every second of that drama conveyed to the audience through our program.

Our last practice before taping was stressful. I had so much I wanted to focus on, yet it was hard for me to focus on anything, as obtrusive as Javier had become.

When he had first started working with us, Javier had been polite, and he had tried not to get into the way.

Now he was seriously cruising for bruising, as he felt the need to be in the midst of everything all the time! I guess it wasn't completely his fault, he was only following orders. Each week the drama was increasing and the producers were pushing the cameramen to make sure they didn't miss a beat.

That evening, I sat in the ice arena waiting for my team's turn to perform, we were to perform third out of five, right in the middle. That was fine with me. The studio had stepped up the drama by giving everyone assigned seats for the show from now on. Of course, the network wanted to make sure that all the teams were at the side of the ice so that we wouldn't miss a moment of the action, except for the performance prior to ours when the skaters were allowed to leave the area for their warm up.

Of course, my assigned seat was right there between Ron and Elena. It was an evil plan, implemented by the network to ensure that the camera men could catch our every expression as the show was taped. The shock, the tears...it was all about the drama. What drama we didn't provide to them, I was certain they would edit in later. I had been practicing my poker face, as a result, I wasn't getting a lot of camera time whenever the shows aired...whoo, hooo!

The first couple to perform, skated to music from the movie "Braveheart". It was a fine performance, but it was almost the finals. Technically, this team had done nothing to step up their performance.

After that performance, I headed down to the warm up area with Ron and Elena. They were both stretching and warming up as I gave them a few last minute pointers. As the second couple skated off the ice from their performance to the music from the movie "Twilight" I hugged Ron and Elena hard and they skated out onto the ice for their warm up.

After the other teams scores were announced, Ron and Elena skated out to the center of the ice and the announcer's voice rang out across the arena.

"Skating to music from Pirates of the Caribbean, Elena Denkova and Ron Brannon!"

The music began and I watched as Ron and Elena performed to the crowd. The music was fast paced, and so was the program, but Ron and Elena seemed to do better with that type of music anyway. They nailed every single element, including our most ambitious lift, which required Ron to complete two full rotations, while supporting Elena off the ice. When it was over, it almost seemed like it was much too soon. Like a dream that you woke up in the middle of. I wasn't ready for it to be over.

Ron and Elena bowed to the crowd as they received a standing ovation. The crowd was overwhelmingly loud! They skated over to me and I hugged them both excitedly. Then we all walked, hand in hand to the "kiss and cry" area.

The judges had nothing but good things to say about the performance. Even Hal, who was notoriously harsh on everyone, had nothing but praise for the program. I was pretty excited. When the scores were revealed, we had two tens and a nine. We had almost certainly earned a place in the finals.

We returned to our assigned seats. Both Ron and Elena were flying high. I doubted anything could bring them down at this point. We only had to watch the last two performances and see who was eliminated tonight.

The fourth couple was on the ice skating to music from "The Lord of the Rings". I was surprised when I felt Ron reach out and take my hand and hold it in his. I almost giggled, I felt like I was back in junior high. Of course, it was all we could get away with at this point, everyone was watching us constantly anymore. The arena was relatively dark, except where the spotlights illuminated the skaters. No one would even notice that Ron and I were holding hands. I wrapped my fingers around his tightly.

Finally, the elimination portion of the show had

arrived, all five couples skated out to stand in front of the judges and await their fate.

I breathed a silent sigh of relief when the team was announced. The team that had skated to "Braveheart" was going home. My team was once again safe. Elena and Ron skated back to me excitedly and they both hugged me. Ron actually lifted me up and spun me around planting a kiss on my neck. I pulled away nervously. Hopefully Javier hadn't got that on film.

# CHAPTER 25

The next several weeks flew by. There wasn't much we needed to do for the recap show, we were scheduled to do a few interviews, but fortunately, I had no program to throw together that week. I was quite relieved to have a little bit of a break. Plus, it gave me more time to work on our next program.

I was not relaxing and taking it easy by any means, there was no time to rest on our laurels. We had been the top team at week six with our "In a Big Country" program and we had tied for first with team Muramatsu, in week seven with our "Pirates" routine.

The theme for week nine was music of the sixties. I loved sixties music, though not all of it was good to skate to. When I was growing up, my own skating coach Hans, had loved sixties music, so I had already skated to a lot of it. I tried to avoid those songs, I felt like it would be hard for me to develop a program to music I had skated to years ago. It was a bit like reheating your dinner, it was never as good the second time around.

I had finally decided on the song "Hit the Road Jack", by Ray Charles. It was an upbeat song and I felt like it was something my team could work with.

As the weeks passed, Ron was growing into a real performer, so I had choreographed a series of complicated dance steps to bridge the gaps between all of the required elements. It was an ambitious program, but I knew my team could do it.

I tried to keep our practices as light and professional as possible, but Ron and I were attracted to each other, unfortunately it was becoming harder and harder with each passing week to disguise that fact. I was feeling scrutinized by Elena and Javier. Every look, every touch, between Ron and I was being recorded by the cameras.

I knew now that Jorge was no longer worried about the negative publicity, I mostly worried about Ron. He was not officially divorced yet and I didn't want the media to make a big thing out of our relationship.

I had been feeling especially tense today. Ron had been very flirty and not at all discrete. I was losing the will to keep this whole thing under wraps.

I went back to Jorge's house that afternoon feeling blue. I did feel a bit like a pawn on a chessboard. My life had never been my own. Here I was, waiting for the show to end, or Ron's divorce to end, just so that we could pursue our relationship.

It reminded me of my teenage years. When I was just fifteen years old, Justin and I had been offered a contract skating with the European Theater Company. Of course, it was a lucrative offer of fame and fortune my parents didn't want to miss out on. Unfortunately, I was a minor, and unable to tour Europe without a parent or guardian.

My father was the one that came up with the brilliant idea to arrange my marriage to Justin. We were best friends, he reasoned, who else would I possibly marry?

So that was it, at the age of fifteen, my own father had me married off to my best friend and skating partner. It seemed fine at first, we went away to tour Europe and endured nearly three years of marriage until the unthinkable happened. I fell in love...

The taping of the first installment of finals was on Wednesday. After our morning practice, I was sure we were ready. That night we were back in our assigned seats next to the ice. Of course, the cameras were there to catch our every comment and expression on our faces. We were slated to perform last, which was fine, we would watch the first two performances, then we would do our warmup, while the third team performed.

I watched the other performances as expressionless as possible, as I secretly clung to Ron's hand. It was the most contact we allowed ourselves anymore since every touch, every glance while we were together, could possibly end up on TV.

Finally, I was back beside the ice watching Ron and Elena skate out onto the darkened ice. Their program was announced and the music was soon playing. I smiled as I watched them, they were perfect! Ron and Elena did the dance steps in perfect harmony and their throw toe loop was stunning! We had a different cartwheel lift this week, I almost gasped as the landing came off a bit uncontrolled. Elena managed to recover from the uncontrolled landing, but I was staring at them blankly, trying to figure out what had happened. The program was nearly over, but Ron was suddenly moving in slow motion, and I cringed when I finally realized that he was hurt.

The program finally came to and end, I was happy that Ron had managed to finish the program, but inside I was worried, I could tell by the look on his face, he was in serious pain.

The program had not been perfect, but it had still been good. I guess it was up to the judges now, to decide if it was good enough to take us through to next week. Ron and Elena were smiling and waving to the crowd. I could tell by the way that Ron was carrying himself that something was not quite right, he was injured, but I had no idea what had happened. When they finally turned and skated off the ice to me, I bit my lower lip nervously, it was obvious that Ron had been hurt, there was no disguising the pain on his face.

"What's the matter?" I cried, as Elena skated into my arms, I hugged her briefly, then pushed her away.

"I felt something pop in my back," said Ron, he was obviously in a lot of pain.

"Oh crap," I sighed, hugging him carefully.

I helped Ron to the "kiss and cry" area. He was lumbering slowly, obviously in a lot of pain.

Before I knew it, the show's host, Zach Reid, had caught on that something big was up, and soon he was there with us, in the "kiss and cry".

"Ron, you suddenly look like you are in a lot of pain. Did you get hurt out there?" asked Zach, coming over and sticking his microphone in Ron's face.

"I hurt my back," said Ron. I cringed painfully, his face was completely distressed. I was biting my lower lip, fighting tears. I felt like it was my fault for pushing him so hard.

"Wow, that could really put a damper on things, do you think you can continue in the competition?"

"I can continue," said Ron, waving him away disgustedly.

I was so worried about Ron, I was clinging to his hand nervously as we sat there, completely unaware that everyone was watching us, not that I even cared at this point. My concern was for Ron. I was feeling guilty that maybe I had pushed him too hard!

"Lane, in recent weeks, your team has been one of the most promising teams on the show. Do you feel like you're going to have to withdraw from the competition?" asked Zach, turning and hoisting his microphone into my face. He glanced down at my fingers wrapped tightly around Ron's, but he didn't say anything.

"It's too soon to tell. Of course we don't want to withdraw, but if circumstances are beyond our control..." I was suddenly close to breaking down in tears, I felt like I personally, was responsible for Ron's pain.

"We won't be withdrawing from the competition. I'm a football player, I'm used to pushing through the pain. I'm not a quitter," snapped Ron, snatching the microphone from the host angrily.

"Okay then," said the Zach, raising his eyebrows at the camera. "Let's see what our judges have to say about their performance."

All three judges were mostly positive, they worried that Ron wouldn't be able to recover from his injury by next week, to give a stunning performance.

Finally the scores were announced. Three nines, not bad, but would it be enough to take us through to next week?

All the couples were brought to the ice for the announcement, I held my breath nervously as the decision was read. I finally sighed in relief, when I realized that we had nearly been eliminated, but we had made it to perform again next week!

I was hugging Elena and Ron excitedly. As things were winding down the team doctor approached Ron and took him to the back office so he could check him out.

I chewed on my lower lip nervously, I was worried, I hoped that Ron had just pulled something and that he would be fine to skate again next week. I wasn't so sure. He was forty, not a kid any more, besides, football had abused his body for years, of course, there was a serious chance that he had injured himself badly and wouldn't be able to skate next week.

# CHAPTER 26

After a trip to the ER and an MRI, Ron was diagnosed with an acute lumbar strain. I was glad that it was nothing more serious, but still, I wondered if Ron would be up to skating. We didn't have the luxury of giving him time off to heal. We had a new program to learn. I was worried, muscular strains could take weeks to heal.

In the morning, Ron was back on the ice, he wasn't himself, but he was determined to go as far as his body would take him. As I watched him struggle through our practice, I had the sneaky feeling that this would be our last week on the show. Unfortunately, the will to succeed can only take you so far!

I had just begun my campaign to convince myself that getting eliminated next week, might be for the best. I was getting tired of playing this game, not to mention that the constant scrutiny of my private life was about to drive me bonkers. It hadn't seemed all that bad at first, but as the number of couples in the competition dropped, that only meant that the show could spend more time hovering over and picking apart the few remaining couples.

Each week, as the number of couples dwindled, speculation about my relationship with Ron seemed to be the big topic. Of course, the sneaky camera men had captured every emotional moment between Ron and I and paraded it across the TV screen for everyone to gawk at and speculate about.

I had worried that Jenae would watch the show and use my relationship with Ron as a weapon against him, but it turns out that she wasn't taking any chances of loosing her new beau, Roman. She was done with Ron, and she was working hard to expedite her uncontested divorce before Roman could get away. She was salivating in anticipation of his multi million dollar contract, and she expected to have her divorce finalized before the end of the month.

It was now week ten in the grand scheme of things. It was time to go big, or go home. I knew I needed to step up our program, but I was worried about Ron. I wasn't sure what his back could handle. I was already feeling guilty about his injury, I felt I was to blame, maybe I had pushed him too hard, though the only one who pushed Ron harder than I did, was Ron himself!

The theme for this week's show was disappointing to me, it was Elvis week. Once again, I was not happy about the theme that the show's writers had come up with. I know it sounds un-American, but I had never been a big Elvis fan. I could never really put my finger on why.

My mother had completely worshipped Elvis, which could possibly be why I loathed the very idea. I guess maybe I had been overloaded with Elvis-mania as a child. Anyway, at least this week my decision for the music would be easy. There was really only one song I would consider in the first place, it was "Jailhouse Rock".

I had my ideas, what I wanted to do with our program, unfortunately, I would just have to wait and see how Ron's back held out, so far he wasn't moving very well.

That night I sat by the pool as a light breeze barely rippled the surface of the water. I was deep in thought, trying to devise a program that would minimize the strain on Ron's back, yet still blow everyone away. Ron's pain seemed worst anytime he was forced to twist, so minimizing the amount of twisting he was required to do in our program, was foremost in my mind. The throw jump and the pairs spin were going to be the hardest things for him to execute, at least that is what I had decided.

Suddenly, I had an idea. My partner Justin had suffered through a lumbar strain right before we had to perform in the world championships, he would know what to do. I called him on his cell, since I was never really sure where he would be at any given time.

"Hello?"

"Justin, it's me, Lane."

"Hey Lane, how's life in Hollywood?" he asked playfully. Justin still loved me and he knew me well, and he knew that Hollywood was definitely not my style.

"It's definitely Hollywood," I told him, I could barely disguise the disgust in my voice.

"I've been pretty busy, but I've been watching the show whenever I can. You've been doing a great job. I was worried for you when I saw the first episode, it didn't seem like they gave you a lot to work with," he said.

"Thanks, my team was a little bit raw when I first got a hold of them!" I told him with a little laugh. It seemed like that first episode had been a long time ago, but it also seemed like time had flown by.

"All right, now tell me the truth. Are you really getting involved with Ron Brannon, or is that just a bunch of reality TV hype?" asked Justin. I sighed miserably, of course, he would ask me that, why wouldn't he?

"Officially the word is no, unofficially, the whole ordeal has been awful. The moment our producer saw that the two of us had the tiniest attraction to each other, he freaked out! I'm not even sure what I feel right now. I have basically been forbidden to have any contact with him, except on the ice. He's still married, and you know...my luck with the media. It just seemed like it would be best for us to wait until the show was over to see where things led." I sighed, in that respect, time seemed to be moving in slow motion.

"So are things going to work out between the two of you? Is he a nice guy?" asked Justin, he was always concerned about my welfare.

"He's a great guy. Whether things will work out or not, it's hard to say. I mean, I'm hoping that once the show is over, Ron and I will be free to live our lives however we see fit. It's been hard, having a camera in my face almost every moment of the day. It's not something you can ever get used to," I told him, shaking my head miserably.

"If anyone can do it, it's you. You are the most amazing woman I know. Besides, I've heard the network is already planning a sequel," said Justin, with a little laugh.

I laughed too, I missed having Justin around. He was my best friend and I hardly ever got to see him anymore.

"Where are you?" I asked. He kept himself busy traveling the world, he claimed to not have time for romance. I worried about him being alone.

"London...Lane are you doing okay?" he asked, his voice was quiet, serious.

"Sure, I'm fine, why?" I asked.

"You never called me, when the divorce was final, I was worried about you. I mean you and Greg, you were together more than twenty years, I know he hurt you. I just thought you might want to talk about it," said Justin, he almost sounded hurt. Justin always felt the need to share my pain, he had been there for nearly every tear I had shed since I was twelve years old.

Justin had always been my best friend, from the day I met him, and I had never kept anything from him in my life, even when we had been married and I had inadvertently fallen in love with our mutual acquaintance, Andre' Dumonde, I had told Justin.

I had never planned for my marriage to Justin to end, even though I'd had no say in the marriage in the first place. I was committed to stay, it was like a contract I felt I couldn't violate. My life as Justin's young bride, was much better than the life I would have endured, if I had stayed with my parents.

It had been pure chance that I had been seated

next to Andre' Dumonde at dinner that evening. How was I to know that our seemingly innocent conversation would cause my entire world to come crashing down?

Though I felt an undeniable attraction to Andre', I had never planned to pursue my feelings for him, I was happy enough with Justin. Andre' had fallen in love with me, and he had been appalled when he realized what my own parents had done to me. An arranged marriage in this day and age was hardly heard of. Andre', of course, felt the need to "save me" from the arranged marriage I had been entered into.

Andre' was only doing what he felt was right, of course there was a lack of passion in my marriage to Justin, it was a marriage of convenience. Justin and I had always loved each other, but marrying Justin had come at a price. I entered into the marriage knowing that he could never give me children. It was a condition I was not quite certain about. I had dreamed about being a mom since I was old enough to have my own doll. It was a dream that didn't fade away easily for me.

It was the media, that had taken my affection for Andre' and paraded it across newspapers and TV screens all across the world. It had hurt Justin terribly, and to this very day, I still felt incredibly guilty about it. It was that guilt that caused me to abandon whatever feelings I had for Andre' and send him away, even though my arranged marriage was clearly over.

It was only later, after my entire life was in shambles, that I returned to the states and met Greg. Greg was perfect for me, it seemed. He knew nothing of the scandal I had endured in Europe, he didn't follow figure skating at all, so he'd never even heard of me!

Maybe that was why I had kept my pain over my divorce with Greg to myself. Maybe I felt that I had hurt Justin enough, maybe I was still in denial? I only knew that I really couldn't talk about it. I had given Greg the best years of my life and he had cruelly cut my heart out and stomped on it!

"Sorry Justin, I guess I really had no desire to talk about it. I've been so busy with the show, it was just easier for me to immerse myself in my work," I told him.

"I get the feeling you're not calling to talk to me about it now," he said, still sounding hurt.

"Justin I'm sorry. You know I love you, but I can't share this pain with you. It hurts too bad. Maybe I deserved it, after what I did to you, maybe it was just karma, giving me a little kick in the ass," I told him.

"You know I've never faulted you for our breakup. We were both young, we were doing as we were told. Think how bored you would be with me right now, if we had stayed married," said Justin, with a laugh.

I smiled. He was right, he never faulted me, never tried to hurt me, he was the best friend ever! "I probably would have never cried all these tears, if I had stayed married to you," I told him ruefully. I had hurt him and he had taken it, he had never tried to retaliate, we had stayed just as close as ever.

"You wouldn't have those two gorgeous kids if we had stayed married," said Justin.

"I know, but I do miss you," I told him.

"But that's not the main reason you called me, is it?" he asked.

"Actually, I have a technical question, I hope you don't mind. Ron has strained his back and I need your advice on what we can use in our program, variations on the required elements that will be easier on his back."

Justin still seemed hurt that I refused to pour my heart out to him, but I just couldn't. Luckily, he had a whole host of ideas for me to help Ron through this week's program. All I needed to do was get busy and implement them into our routine.

I now had a modified pairs spin, a balanced lift, that

would use Ron's thighs, more than his back and pointers to help him with the throw jump.

Ron was loading up on anti inflamatories, so he seemed to be doing a bit better. We worked hard all week and before I knew it, it was Wednesday again. Ron was doing better, but he was obviously still not one hundred percent.

We were now down to the last three teams, all three teams had been consistently at the top, we would be slated against team Muramsatsu and team Evans.

Our final practice had gone well and I felt like our "Jailhouse Rock" program was definitely good enough to put us in the top two, if only Ron's back could hold out.

That evening we were back in the ice arena. Ron and Elena were to perform first tonight. A lot of the program was going to revolve around Elena's spinning and jumping abilities, Ron was a bit limited on what he could do.

The lights dimmed and Ron and Elena skated out onto the darkened ice. When the music started, the spotlights illuminated them as they skated one of the most perfect routines I had seen. Elena's spin sequence solo was sheer perfection, but I was hard pressed to find any sort of fault with either of their performances. They had poured their hearts and souls into this performance and it was completely obvious. When the music ended they bowed to a standing ovation from the crowd. I was completely blown away!

After the bows, Elena skated to me and pretty much dove into my arms, nearly knocking me over. Then Ron wrapped me in a huge bear hug and I pretty much melted into his arms. The cameras were panning in close, but I didn't even care at this point. The speculation over our "relationship" was already there, let the audience drool in anticipation for two more weeks, I thought.

I was trying to talk to Ron and Elena and tell them

how wonderful they had done and how proud I was of them, but it was useless. Standing there in the echoing arena, we were essentially deaf, the crowd was still roaring loudly in our ears!

I was clinging to Ron and Elena's hands as we headed to the "kiss and cry". Everyone was still screaming and calling out to us from the audience. When the crowd had finally settled down enough that they could be heard, I was happy to hear that the judges were completely wowed by the performance, they had nothing but positive comments about the performance.

When our scores were finally announced we had received three tens, once again, a perfect score! I was completely elated as I squeezed Elena and Ron again excitedly. I nearly had tears in my eyes, we had made it to the finals, I was sure of it!

We settled into our seats, to watch the rest of the performances. I clung to Ron's hand the entire time. I watched the performances, but didn't really see much of either of them, I was in my own little world. I doubted either of these teams could beat a perfect score.

At the end of the performances, all three teams congregated on the ice to await the announcement. I was almost coming unglued, I was so nervous. Finally Zach made the announcement, team Evans was going home, we had made it to the top two!

I was hugging Ron and Elena excitedly. Jorge was soon there hugging all of us. The entire arena was in an uproar! The crowd had emerged from their seats and the entire arena was teaming with bodies. Someone had opened champagne and was passing out glasses of champagne to the group of us that was standing there on the ice.

If someone had told me weeks ago that my team was going to be in the final two, I would have told them they were crazy. Who would have thought that a big clumsy football player, who had never skated before and a tiny little Russian skater would have made such a good team?

I had wondered about their motivation at the start, but they had both had the drive to take us to the very end!

The rest of the night was essentially a blur to me, there were dozens of interviews, everyone wanted to talk to me, or my skaters, or me with my skaters to get our point of view.

It was after midnight when I finally fell into Jorge's limo, completely exhausted.

"I'm so tired! I still can't believe we're in the final two," I said, smiling at Jorge as he slid into the seat next to me.

"You my darling, are the most popular woman on the planet," said Jorge, returning my smile.

"I wouldn't say most popular woman on the planet."

"I actually had to stand in line to hug you...my own girlfriend!" he cried, feigning disgust.

I giggled, I'd had a bit too much champagne so everything was exceedingly funny to me right now. "Thank you for asking me to come on the show. It's had it's ups and downs, but I've had a wonderful time," I said, hugging him warmly.

"Don't you dare make me cry! I'm actually going to miss having a girlfriend, I'm going to miss having you at the house," said Jorge, his voice was emotional.

"Oh Jorge, Jean Luc will come back from Nice and your life will be back to normal," I told him.

"What is normal exactly? I really don't want the show to end, I've been so happy. Don't take this the wrong way, but I love you Lane, I don't want you to go back to Colorado Springs," said Jorge, tears suddenly coming to his eyes.

"Jorge really! How much champagne did you have? I admit, I'm feeling a bit tipsy myself, but I can't stay here forever and pretend to be your girlfriend!"

"I'm not drunk. You're a rare talent Lane, you're wasting your talent in Colorado Springs. I want you to stay here, and work for me," said Jorge.

"Doing what?" I was completely in shock.

"I don't know yet, but I don't want you to go back to Colorado Springs and vegetate. And I don't want you to run off to New York with Brannon!"

My head was spinning and I was starting to feel a bit ill. "Jorge, can we discuss this another time, when the limo isn't spinning," I asked.

He laughed and put his arm around me. "Yes, of course, darling."

# CHAPTER 27

I woke up the next morning still in shock, it seemed like a dream that my team was now actually in the top two. As hard as they had been pushing themselves lately, I was glad that my skaters would get to have a little bit of a break, even if it was just for one week.

In an effort to draw the competition out a twelve full weeks, for episode eleven, the producers were putting together a recap of all of our performances and all the performances of team Muramsatsu. They were marketing it as an emotional journey, from day one, to the final two. That was all fine with me, I was happy I would have an extra week to hone our program for the grand finale!

I was having a hard time believing that in just two weeks, the show was finally going to be over. It was going to be quite an adjustment for me, going back to Colorado Springs after everything I had been through. I wondered what I would do now. Would I go back to Colorado Springs and my adolescent skaters, to the house Greg and I had been so happy in at one time? The life I had led back in Colorado now seemed like a hollow existence, like it had never really happened, I wasn't sure I could even return there.

There had been a time when I couldn't wait to leave Hollywood. Now it seemed as if it would be much harder for me to leave all this behind. Now that it was almost time for me to leave, I felt like I had finally made the adjustment to Hollywood. Maybe Jorge had been right, maybe I belonged in Hollywood. I feared I would be lonely when I returned to Colorado Springs, there was really nothing left for me there. Now, everyone on the show was my family...they were the only family I seemed to have any more. I kept in touch with my kids, but it just wasn't the same as having them at home.

As the days passed by, I grew more and more excited about the show's upcoming finale. The show's executives were bringing both of my kids to Hollywood to sit in the guest audience for the taping of the finale. I was excited to get to see them, and to have them meet Ron.

They both watched the show faithfully and they had been following all the drama. We talked on the phone quite a bit, but they never asked me about the rumors, though I was almost certain, that they had heard the murmurings about Ron and I.

I worried what my own kids thought about the misguided drama. Sometimes when I watched the show on TV, it was so carefully edited, I felt like the characters were totally different there on the screen, than they were in real life. I hoped that my own kids didn't have a skewed view of who I was, or what my life had been like over the past several months.

The show itself, had changed so much over the past several weeks, there were just two teams remaining, which meant we were now allowed more practice time on the ice, which was good. My team had been skating a lot and they could now tolerate more time on the ice.

The bad part was that now, each person on my team had one camera person assigned to them, it was quite annoying, as if having a cameraman that followed my entire team wasn't bad enough. My personal cameraman Brandon, was so obtrusive, I was quite certain the two of us were going to get into a fist fight at some point, before the season was over!

I had been very busy working on our new program for the finale. I was happy to be enjoying complete creative control for this last episode. I had been delighted to find out that for the last show there was no theme, and most requirements and restrictions for our music were removed. I was free to pick any song I wanted to use, and the programs were no longer limited to just two minutes, they could last anywhere from 2-4 minutes and they must include all the required elements. Also, for this last episode, a new element had been introduced, it was showmanship. We could use up to 45 seconds of our music for showmanship, which would be a "setting of the scene" with props and scenery, and my team did not necessarily have to be on the ice, skating during those 45 seconds.

I was excited, this was my chance to do something really creative and completely blow everyone away! I wanted the program to be memorable, not only through the skating but by the entire mood I was setting. I had skated for the European Theater Company for five years and setting the mood was definitely their specialty. Every production I had been in with the company had been colossal.

It wasn't hard for me to select a song for the finale. I knew I wanted something that I could set a grand mood with. The song I had selected for our program was "Kashmir" by Led Zeppelin. The song, itself, was more than eight minutes long, so it needed to be extensively edited. Fortunately, our music editor, Kevin, knew what I liked. He could listen to a song one time and pick out the parts I considered to have the most effect and drama, and he almost always edited the songs to my liking without much tweaking.

I loved "Kashmir", it had always been one of my favorite songs and I thought the middle eastern flavor of the song would be a good theme for my team to run with. When I excitedly told my team what song I had selected, Elena shrugged half heartedly, she told me she had never heard of it.

I gave her a blank stare, unable to believe that she had never even heard of the song. Come on! People told me I was abnormal because I didn't worship Elvis Presley!

I was much happier with Ron's reaction to my announcement. He told me there would be no better way to end the season than to win it, skating to one of his favorite songs!

Of course, Jorge was beside himself with excitement. Like me, he had a vision for the program when he listened to the music. He was equally inspired and his vision for the costumes was so overpowering, he had already run to the wardrobe department to get the staff there started on them.

One really fun thing about the show, as compared to a regular skating competition is that we were allowed and encouraged to use props of any type. Of course, this was Hollywood.

I wasn't an experienced TV choreographer, so thus far, I hadn't used a lot of props in my programs, but I had decided that since this was the season finale, I should give it a try.

My motto for the finale was, go big, or go home. My ultimate plan was to go big and win! The network was hyping up the finale, so the entire show was going to be a huge production anyway. Since we only had to get through two teams programs at the taping, the network had removed all previous restrictions and pretty much given the choreographers full creative control.

I didn't want to take away from the actual skating, but I felt that playing up the mood of my song would be fun. I had originally arranged for huge potted palm trees to be brought in and placed at the entrance of the ice, and another clump of small palm trees was going to be set in the center of the ice to give the illusion of a desert oasis.

Then, after doing a bit of research, I realized that most of the Kashmir region of India was not really desert, as I had envisioned that it was, but Jorge didn't want me to change a thing. He told me that the words of the song set the scene as a desert and he wanted to go with the original plan. He liked the idea, and told me that America, as a whole, had no clue where Kashmir even was anyway, so all my worries were for nothing.

The most exciting part of my Kashmir theme, though, was my biggest idea. My idea was, to have my skaters ride into the arena on a live elephant at the very beginning of the program.

Jorge was completely beside himself with excitement! He thought it was the greatest idea ever! I was pretty excited myself, but I hadn't told Elena yet. She was pretty much scared of any animal larger than a chihuahua. It was going to take a lot of convincing to get her to ride in on a live elephant.

I was also getting wardrobe on the task of making some sort of authentic looking saddle, or pad for the elephant. It needed to be showy looking, but functional. I didn't want the elephant to get cut by my a team member's skates, even though I knew it was a small risk, elephants had very thick skin.

We would also need to find a elephant handler, though hopefully, that would come with the elephant. I wasn't quite sure, I'd never rented a elephant before!

I was glad to have a week with no new program hanging over our heads. Ron was still recovering from his lumbar strain and I didn't want to overdo him. Hopefully, by the night of the finale, he would be completely recovered.

We were working hard on all our elements, before the finals we had usually spent two hours on the ice in the morning. Now that the finals were approaching, we had two hours in the morning and two late in the afternoon.

We also tried to spend time in the gym, Ron liked to blow off steam by lifting weights. I was enjoying my time in the gym, though I guess I must admit, the best part about going to the gym was the outstanding view. Seeing Ron's muscular legs in shorts everyday was definitely worth it!

Unfortunately, lately, we were obligated to spend a great deal of time going to interviews and photo shoots as the final two teams in the competition.

The producers were gearing up for the finale of the show and they were going all out with the promotions! It was the rumors of romance between Ron and I, that seemed to be getting the most attention. Neither Ron or I had confirmed anything, so of course, rumors were running rampant.

It seemed as if everyone had their own theory. Some people thought that the entire romance had been created by the producers of the show, as some sort of a lame attempt to grab ratings from a rival network.

Some people, of course, thought that we were having a secret romance, but were laying low, because Ron's divorce was not yet final.

The most hilarious view, brought up one evening on late night TV, was, that Ron and I had been having an affair, but it ended, but the network was still using it as a ploy to grab ratings. The late night TV host was predicting that Ron and I would have a lover's quarrel on the night of the finale, and it would be the most spectacular fight on TV. I was almost surprised that they weren't placing wagers. I could only roll my eyes when I heard the speculation. Didn't these people have anything better to do with their lives?

Unfortunately, as the finale grew closer, things weren't getting much better. I was relaxing on the couch one evening, I was nearly asleep as I listened to music on my I-pod, suddenly I was jolted awake by a shrill scream. I sat up abruptly.

"Jorge, what the hell?" I cried, pulling my earbuds out and staring at him in shock.

"Look, he said, pointing at the TV screen in horror.

I looked up at the TV, the late night TV host was introducing his next guest, it was Maurice Dubois!

"Tonight our first guest is Maurice Dubois from the reality TV show "Fire on Ice". Maurice was the cameraman assigned to team Jensen at the very beginning of the season. He got to see his team in all kinds of situations, on and off the ice. Welcome Maurice," said the host.

"Thank you for having me," said Maurice, smiling for the camera, I cringed disgustedly, I could barely stand to look at him, he was such a slime ball!

"I'm sure all our viewers have heard all the speculation about the possibility of a blossoming romance between ex football star Ron Brannon and his current coach and choreographer on the show, Lane Jensen. We were wondering what you noticed as an insider. I mean you were there on the ice with them every day. Do you think it's true, that Lane and Ron might be having a bit of a romance, or is it just a bunch of hype invented by the network to grab ratings?" asked the host, leaning toward Maurice smiling, his eyes wide in anticipation.

"It's definitely not hype, it's all true. In fact, I can assure you there were sparks between them on the very first day. They've been trying to hide it since the very beginning, when the show first began. I know that they had been trying to hide it at first, since Ron was supposedly happily married, but Lane and Ron had something going on, even before his wife started the divorce proceedings. It was all very secretive, but I could see what was going on," said Maurice.

"Now I just want to let all our viewers know, we have interviewed several promoters for the show and the official word coming from the network is that Lane Jensen is living with Jorge Broussard, who is the chief producer of the show. Our reporter, Shannon Bright, spoke to Jorge today and he told her that he and Lane have been in a relationship for quite some time, it began just weeks after the show began. He told Shannon that all the speculation about a relationship between Lane and Ron is nothing but a bunch of garbage," said the host.

"Oh don't get me wrong, I don't dispute that Lane is living there with Jorge Broussard. But that, much like their relationship, is nothing but a scam, the real attraction is between Ron and Lane. The relationship between Jorge and Lane was created as a buffer to keep the heat off of Ron Brannon, since he wasn't officially divorced, at the time. Besides, Jorge Broussard is gay, everyone knows it," said Maurice.

"Oh my God!" cried Jorge, shaking his fist at the

television screen. I cringed, I couldn't help but feel for Jorge, but I was afraid the worst was yet to come. Maurice was going to embarrass me publicly, since I had denied his advances. My heart was racing in fear.

"As far as I know, he's still not officially divorced, yet his soon to be ex-wife is running wild with football superstar Roman Fleming. I guess I wouldn't blame Ron if he did hook up with Lane Jensen, I mean she's beautiful and quite talented. Anybody that watches the show regularly will know what I'm talking about. When I saw the practice clips during the first episode, I thought her team would be the first to be eliminated, Ron Brannon couldn't skate at all! The fact that her team is now one the two finalists is just a testament to her talents," exclaimed the host.

"I will not deny that Lane Jensen has her talents. When she set her sights on Brannon, the poor bastard didn't have a chance. Even I, have found myself a victim of her seductions," said Maurice, raising his eyebrows at the camera.

"So you do not believe for a moment that Jorge Broussard and Lane Jensen are a couple?" asked the host, who was, thankfully, ignoring Maurice's claim that I had seduced him.

"I know Jorge Broussard well. He is a brilliant producer, I had worked for him for years, we were quite close. It was no secret to me that his tastes run more to the buff, muscular men, than to women. Of course, he adores women, but Jorge is a creative genius, he has a knack for finding talent and bringing all the elements together to create a masterpiece," said Maurice.

"It sounds like you have a great deal of respect for Mr. Broussard, and a long career with him, I might add. What happened to end your partnership with him and the network?" asked the talk show host.

"Well I hate to kiss and tell, but unfortunately, I was fired as a result of an evening I spent with Ms. Jensen. I guess it is easier for Mr. Broussard to overlook it when she turns her attentions to one of his stars, but not so much when she is involved with a mere cameraman," said Maurice, as he smiled slyly at the cameras.

"You made the moves on his girlfriend, and he fired you?" asked the host, staring at him in shock.

"I didn't have to make the moves on her, she wanted me! It was only one night, but believe me, it was worth it. Loosing my job with the network wasn't all that bad. I was able to sell some of my secret footage from the show, I believe what I captured speaks for itself," said Maurice. I was seething, I was horrified that Maurice had implied to everyone on National TV that we spent a night together, the man was a total sleeze bag!

"America, we have some of that secret footage to show you tonight. First we will show you the footage of Lane and Jorge together, which was provided to us by the network, this footage has been taken over the past, nearly four months. Take a look at some of these images and decide for yourself if you believe Jorge and Lane are truly a couple," said the host, smiling for the camera.

The footage provided by the network began rolling. It was a series of clips from parties, practices and performances. The first clip was obviously from the end of a show taping, I was kissing Jorge on the cheek, and the two of us were chatting with other cast members. The next clip showed the two of us standing there with our arms around each other at a party. Then there was a clip of Jorge helping me out of the limo at the premier party. Then a clip of Jorge with his arm possessively around my shoulders as I oversaw a practice session. I smiled serenely, I was actually a better actor than I thought, the clips certainly looked convincing, anyone would believe that Jorge and I were a happy couple.

"I think you will find my revealing clips a little more convincing," said Maurice, smugly.

"Can we run Mr. Dubois' clips please?" asked the host, then Maurice's clips began flashing across the screen.

There was a covert looking shot of my wine toast with Ron, taken on the first day we met. A very disturbing clip of Ron staring into my eyes and touching my cheek, yeah, that was definitely a "busted" moment. Then there were several clips of us skating together, which were hardly convincing. All in all, it made Maurice's claims seem kind of lame. I had to smile a bit to myself, maybe the viewers would realize he was full of hot air and not believe a word he said.

Maurice was smiling smugly when the cameras panned back on him, but the host was not so easily convinced.

"I don't know, I'm not seeing any evidence of a torrid affair in these clips. I mean, sure, they obviously don't hate each other, but to me, what I see here is, two people who are close friends. Two people, who have had to work closely together and have become quite close because of their working relationship," said the host, dismissively.

"Lane and Ron are the real lovers, there is nothing between Lane and Jorge," spat Maurice.

"Can we roll the clips from the network again," said the host, indicating they should run the clips of me with Jorge again. As they flashed up on the screen the host began speaking again.

"I think they look very happy together. They seem to have a genuine affection for each other."

I smiled, that much was true. I may not be Jorge's lover, but I really had grown to love him.

"Jorge is not her type. He stepped in when the media caught them together, he was worried about his ratings. Ron and his wife were still, supposedly happily married at the time. It was later that she announced that she wanted a divorce," said Maurice, his lip curling with displeasure.

I rolled my eyes miserably, what did Maurice stand to

gain from rating me out?

"Well next week is the grand finale, maybe we will find out then. Will Lane Jensen take her team all the way to the top? Will Lane and Ron find true love as a couple when the show is over? Tune in next Thursday at seven and find out. I know I'll be watching," said the host.

I sighed miserably as they cut to a commercial. I looked over at Jorge who was now about to burst with excitement. "This is completely amazing, it's like everyone is doing a commercial for our show. I love it! There's nothing better than free advertising!"

I was glad that Jorge was excited, I was beginning to wonder if anyone realized that there was actually going to be skating on the show next week. It seemed as if everyone thought it was some sort of soap opera, and all the loose ends were going to be tied up next week.

"Are you going to sue Maurice for slander?" I asked Jorge. I was sure he was upset that Maurice had told the world that he was gay, and I was completely pissed that he had implied to everyone that we had slept together.

"I had thought about it at first, with that whole gay thing, but in the end he ended up doing me a favor. I'm guessing that even people who don't watch the show regularly will now be watching the finale, just to see what all the hype is about! Maurice was trying to kill us, but I think he just put our ratings over the top!" cried Jorge, giggling excitedly.

"Well I'm glad you're excited because the jerk just implied to the entire world that the two of us slept together," I snapped angrily.

"That's what men do, it's an ego thing. Do you actually think anyone is going to believe that crap? I mean you're gorgeous and he's well...not," said Jorge.

"I'm glad that you're happy, since all you care about is your precious ratings," I told him, glaring at him angrily.

"Oh Lane, just enjoy all the speculation. America loves fast women who know how to wield their power over these poor besotted men, you're like Joan Collins, or Elizabeth Taylor, ggrrrrr!" growled Jorge.

"I'm going to bed," I snapped, standing up.

"Good night my little ratings enhancer, sleep tight.

I rolled my eyes and gave him a little amused smile. Then I leaned over and kissed Jorge on the cheek. "Good night love."

## CHAPTER 28

Before I realized what had happened, nearly two weeks had passed and the taping of the finale show on Wednesday was approaching quickly. The best part, was that Ron was feeling completely recovered from his lumbar strain, and I had a very ambitious program put together.

I couldn't wait to see the entire performance, complete with the costumes, lighting, and of course, the elephant. The costumes were jewel colored satin, trimmed and embroidered in gold, I thought they were completely incredible. I giggled excitedly as Jorge and I swooned over them in the wardrobe department, they were perfect! Ron's costume was a deep sapphire blue, embroidered with gold. Elena's satiny, chiffon embellished sari dress was a deep, rich purple. I knew they were going to look gorgeous!

Our program included a brand new pairs spin, side by side camel spins, a star lift, a throw double lutz, a death spiral and a stunning new spiral sequence. Kevin, our sound guy had edited my song down to just under 4 minutes, which would be the equivalent of a competitive skater's long program, which would be pushing my team's endurance a little bit. Luckily, the first thirty seconds of the music would be devoted to my team's ride in on the elephant, so the actual skating part of the program would be about three minutes and thirty seconds, not too shabby, if I do say so myself.

Of course, all our practices had been off limits, to everyone except to a select few people. Jorge had been spying on the other team a bit. He couldn't tell me any details of what the other team was doing, of course, but he seen both of our teams in their practices and he told me in confidence that we had team Miramsatsu beat by a landslide!

As taping day approached, I became more and more anxious and excited. I was usually pretty laid back, but for some reason this competition had me completely turned upside down. I wasn't sure if it was one hundred percent all about the competition, or if much of my anxiety revolved around my secret romance with Ron. When the show was over, I guessed I would be free to live my life without any repercussions from Jorge or the network, but would Ron still want me then?

Tuesday night I was out by the pool at Jorge's house, I was trying to relax, but so far I hadn't had much luck. I was hopelessly keyed up. I had a glass of wine and I was listening to music on my i-pod, trying to calm my frazzled nerves. The taping of the finale was tomorrow night and my stomach was all in knots. I was like a kid on Christmas eve, I was so excited, I could hardly stand it.

Jorge had finally left to go have drinks with friends. I was practically bouncing off the walls and he couldn't take it anymore, he just wanted to get out of the house, and away from me.

I was excited that my kids were both flying in for the finale in the morning. I couldn't wait to see them, I missed them so much! I was startled when my cell phone started ringing. I looked absently at the caller ID and was stunned to see it was Greg. I stared at my phone for a moment completely stunned, what could Greg possibly want?

"Hello?" I wanted to ignore his call, but I was curious. I wasn't sure why he would be calling me, though I thought that perhaps he had grown up a little bit, and wanted to wish me luck tomorrow night.

"Hi Lane, it's me Greg," said the voice on the other end of the line.

"I know, caller ID," I snapped. Why was he calling me now, when I was finally over him? Up to this point he hadn't found the need to stay in touch with me, he had never even called to say good bye when our divorce was final. The only confirmation I got from him, was his signature on a piece of paper, from his lawyer. More than twenty years of marriage, and that was all he could offer me.

"I guess you're wondering why I'm calling now, after all this time," said Greg, he didn't sound at all like himself, but I hadn't heard from him in almost six months. In fact, I was surprised to be hearing from him now.

"I was wondering, why you would call me up out of the blue, more than six months later, after you tore my heart out and stomped all over it," I told him.

"I guess we didn't part on the best of terms," his voice was soft, and gravely sounding, I was suddenly acutely aware that he was upset about something.

"No we did not."

"How have you been?" he asked, I frowned, he was beating around the bush. Greg didn't like small talk, and he never did anything without proper motivation. Something was up.

"Right now I am on top of the world, but I am getting the sneaky feeling, my euphoric mood is about to change. Why are you calling me now Greg?"

"Well...um..."

"You know the best thing to do is just spit it out," I was mocking him, I had already cried away all the affection I had for him. He had hurt me badly, my feelings for Greg were gone.

"Jill kicked me out," he sighed.

"What? I thought that the two of you were in love," I cried, my voice was dripping with sarcasm.

"Lane, I'm sorry for what I did, it was stupid," said Greg.

"You're right, it was stupid, but what's the point of apologizing now, it's too late now, you've already ruined everything," I told him very matter of factly.

"So that's it, you're going to just forget what the two of us had, after more than twenty years together?" he asked. I almost burst into hysterical laughter, he was loosing his mind.

"Have you forgotten Greg? It was you who divorced me! It was you, who was already gone. It was already done and over with by the time I got home from China. You never even gave me a chance to try and work things out! Now that your nubile little girlfriend has suddenly wizened up and realized what a putz you are, you have no place to go. I'm sorry Greg, but I'm not a complete moron. I didn't want our marriage to end, but it did. What we had is over!"

"Yeah I know, I watch TV. I guess you're going to hook up with that football player, Ron Brannon. Everyone has been talking about it, they've all been talking about how you've been practically throwing yourself at him, even though he's still married," said Greg, his voice was laced with disgust.

"Yes that's right, I'm a terrible slut. Think whatever you want Greg, as long as it makes you feel better. Just remember it was you, who ditched me. Besides, Ron is a much bigger man than you...in a lot of ways!" I almost giggled, I was being kind of catty now, but I couldn't help it, how dare he act like this. He was being a child!

"I just think you need to have a little more discretion, you're making a huge spectacle of yourself in Hollywood. It's kind of embarrassing...think about our children," he said. I rolled my eyes. He was the one that divorced me after more than twenty years of marriage, for a twenty seven year old, and he hadn't been discrete about it at all!

"Well since we're no longer married, I guess that's no longer your business," I snapped, fully prepared to hang up on him. He was trying to turn the tables on me, but that wasn't going to work. I wouldn't accept the guilt he was piling on me for the end of our marriage.

He had destroyed our marriage, I had never even seen it coming!

"Lane wait, I'm sorry. I have nowhere to go, and I was wondering if I could stay at the house, until I find an apartment or something," he was on the verge of tears, at least it sounded like it. I rolled my eyes, Greg wouldn't hear any of my pleas back when we were breaking up. I could be just as cold hearted. I was done, he was not using me anymore!

"Sorry Greg, I've already sold the house. In case you haven't heard, your slutty ex-wife is not only throwing herself at Ron Brannon, but she is living with a Hollywood producer! I didn't need the house in Colorado Springs," I told him. It was a lie, the house in Colorado Springs was exactly as I had left it. I had planned to go back there, and back to what was left of my life there, but now I wasn't so sure. Regardless, I wasn't about to let Greg hang out there. He'd wanted out of the marriage so bad, he gave it all up, now he'd ruined another relationship. I wondered if he even realized what a pig he was!

"Oh," he said, he seemed to be at a loss for words.

"If you find a place to live you should watch the show Thursday night, it's going to be awesome," I told him.

When I finally hung up the phone, I was shaking nervously. It took a lot of resolve for me to be mean to Greg, and not give in to him. He had hurt me at every possible opportunity, I had already decided that this was Karma, turning around and kicking him in the butt, finally. As far as I was concerned, he could go back to Chicago and live with his mother, she'd take him in, in a second!

Finally, Wednesday arrived. I was nervous, but our dress rehearsal had gone so well, I knew my team would do fine. Elena was even fine with riding in on the elephant, and I actually think she was excited about it.

Baylee and Ramsey had arrived in town and I took

them out to lunch at one of my favorite restaurants. We had a lot of catching up to do, I hadn't seen either of them in months. They were both excited to be in Hollywood for the finale of the show. They were being treated like stars themselves, the network had taken care of everything for them and they were both completely blown away, they were were being so spoiled.

"So what song is your team skating to tonight?" asked Baylee, she was smiling at me broadly, her face was flushed with excitement.

"I can't tell you, it's a surprise, but you're going to love it. The entire program is going to blow everyone away," I told them.

"I can't believe how far they've come, when I saw the first episode, I felt so bad for you. They were so awful, I thought your team would be the first one eliminated," said Ramsey, taking a sip of his soda.

"You really are amazing Mom, I mean the past several weeks your team has been fabulous, even with Ron being injured," said Baylee.

Yeah, speaking of Ron, what's the deal? I've heard all the rumors over the past several weeks, that there is something going on between you and Ron, but I have also heard that you are living with Jorge Broussard, and the two of you are lovers," said Ramsey, shrugging in confusion.

I bit my lower lip nervously. Even though my kids were grown, it was hard for me to talk to them about things like lovers. It had been hard enough for me to talk to them about Greg's affair with Jill. I didn't want them to think their own mother had been playing it fast and loose in Hollywood, even though if one listened to the rumors, they might believe that I had been sleeping with at least three different guys, when in reality, I hadn't slept with anyone!

"I have been living with Jorge, but we are not a couple. The truth is Ron and I have feelings for each other, but under the circumstances, we haven't been able to act on those feelings," I told them. They were both nodding at me in understanding.

"He has two young girls, and even though his wife is divorcing him, I worried that she might use our relationship against him, to keep him from his girls. Jorge had been worried about negative publicity, we have pretty much been waiting for the show to be over, or his divorce to be final, whichever comes first, I guess," I told them.

Baylee and Ramsey were both very understanding and supportive of my semi-secret romance with Ron. They really just wanted me to be happy. They knew that the divorce had nearly destroyed me. I was very close to both my kids and I didn't keep things like that from them, we'd always had a mutual respect for each other.

That night at the taping, the format turned out to be a little different than we were used to. The host brought both teams out to the main stage before we began so he could interview us. The skaters had their costumes on already, so we got to assess the other team for the first time.

Team Muramsatsu was dressed all in white, I wasn't quite sure what their theme was, or if they even had one. It was very obvious what our theme was, when you saw my team in their brightly colored costumes trimmed in gold. To keep with our team's theme, tonight even I, was in costume. I was wearing a red dress, that was trimmed in gold, and it was modeled to look a bit like an Indian sari.

After the interviews, it was time to get down to business. Both teams had a three minute warm up, then team Muramsatsu would perform first.

After the warm up, my team joined me in our assigned seats, next to the ice. As soon as the house lights dimmed, Ron took my hand, just like he always did. He looked over and gave me a sly smile. I squeezed his hand excitedly and smiled back.

The spotlights came on and team Muramsatsu began their program. They were skating to the song "Hey Ya" by Outkast. Their program was energetic and fun and it had a little bit of a hip hop, type influence. I enjoyed it and thought it had good entertainment value, but it was not nearly as technically difficult as our program and I found I was smiling to myself.

Team Muramsatsu had done a fine program, but it was not what I would consider finale caliber material. They had gone the safe route, and they were going to loose because of it. I hated to be overly confident, but if my team nailed all their elements, we would win by a landslide!

Team Muramsatsu stood before the crowd taking their bows. The crowd had enjoyed their program, it was fun and it had been nearly flawless. The crowd rewarded them with a standing ovation, I imagine to the general public, the program had seemed like a winner. I did consider myself to be overly critical at times.

The team headed to the "kiss and cry" area to await the judges comments and their final scores of the season. I was still clinging desperately to Ron's hand in anticipation of our own performance that would be coming up in only moments.

The judges were very polite, they all liked the routine, except for Hal Luther, who was British and a very tough critic. He deserved to be, of course, he was one of the greatest skaters of all time! He said exactly what I had been thinking. He told team Muramsatu that their performance had been fine, except for the fact that they hadn't raised the bar for themselves in weeks. This performance had been entertaining, but it didn't stand out over their past performances and he felt like they had stagnated.

I bit my lower lip hard, so I wouldn't burst out laughing, at his comment. That wouldn't be professional at all. It was quite a struggle to contain myself and not flash Emi a smug smile. I was almost bursting with pride, I couldn't wait for her to see our routine!

The judges gave them two nines and a ten, then they returned to their seats beside the ice dejectedly. In all those weeks they had given many good performances, but they had never attained a perfect score.

Elena, Ron and I headed for the ice. I took their jackets and their skate guards from them as the stage crew was busily setting up our props on the ice.

I was excited to see my daughter Baylee and my son Ramsey sitting in the front row of guest seats. They both waved to me excitedly. Jorge gave me two thumbs up from where he was standing and I gave him an excited smile.

Elena and Ron had gone offstage to climb onto the elephant. A hush had fallen over the darkened ice arena. I was standing there beside the ice, shivering with excitement. In moments, the stage assistant came out and gave the thumbs up to the sound manager, indicating that Elena and Ron were in position, on the elephant.

I knew that the crowd and the judges would be a little thrown off by my team's entrance, the skaters almost always started near the center of the ice. Instead, there were blue spotlights illuminating a group of palm trees arranged near the garage door that housed the Zamboni, the door slowly began to raise as the announcer introduced my team. I giggled in anticipation, the entire crowd was awestruck, they had no idea what was going on. Of course, the elephant wouldn't fit through the regular gate, so we'd improvised.

"Ladies and gentlemen, let's hear it for team Jensen, skating to the song "Kashmir" in their final performance on Fire on Ice, Elena Denkova and Ron Brannon."

In seconds, the music cued up and the spotlights turned to white as they illuminated the palm palm trees at the Zamboni entrance of the ice as a man in Indian garb lead the huge elephant to the edge of the ice.

The crowd gasped as the elephant lumbered slowly onto the ice carrying my team on it's back. Ron and Elena were all smiles as they waved to the crowd from their perch, high atop the elephant.

On his musical cue, Ron leapt down from the elephant's back. He then bowed to Elena and caught her above his head as she jumped from the elephant's back. Ron held Elena above his head in a platter lift, spun around twice and lowered Elena gently and gracefully to the ice. The crowd roared appreciatively! My heart was pounding anxiously as they began their routine, the entire arena was suddenly charged with a positive energy.

Ron and Elena began skating their program with all the fire and charisma I had hoped for. Elena had become especially good at interpreting the middle eastern mood of the music. She had even went above and beyond and taken a few lessons from some Indian dancers so that she would be more convincing in her interpretation of the music.

I watched as they nailed every single element, including the difficult ones they had essentially, just learned. I was so proud of them, they had come such a long way.

When they finished, I had tears rolling down my cheeks. The program was even more than I had hoped for and I was certain that Ron and Elena had won.

They took their bows to a standing ovation, both looking completely elated. Then they skated to me. Elena threw her arms around me and hugged me. I squeezed her hard. Then Ron threw his arms around me and picked me up in his arms. I was laughing elatedly as he squeezed me, then he pulled me tighter in his arms and kissed me.

I was surprised, it was not a friendly kiss by any means, it was a passionate kiss. I had wrapped my arms around him and was kissing him back urgently. It was what I had been waiting for, for so long, I could barely help myself. I figured the show was over now, what the heck?

I'm not sure how long the kiss lasted, but when I finally returned to reality, the crowd was roaring and the show's host, Zach Reid, had showed up at our side with his microphone.

"Well Ron, that was quite a kiss. Was that a congratulatory kiss, or what?" asked Zach.

"That was a, I've been waiting a very long time to do this, kiss," said Ron, he still had his arms around me and he was gazing down into my eyes.

"So all the rumors are true, you and Lane have been a couple the whole time?" asked Zach.

"I wouldn't say that we've been a couple the whole time. Lane and I have had feelings for each other for a long time. When you're in Hollywood, especially on a reality TV show everyone is watching you, it's hard to have any sort of a relationship without the whole world knowing about it."

"Lane and I both decided it would be best to wait until my divorce was final, and I am happy to announce that I got the final papers yesterday morning...I am a free man! Even Lane didn't know until just now. I wanted to surprise her tonight," said Ron, smiling at me.

Ron wrapped his arms around me and kissed me again, causing the entire audience to start screaming and clapping. The host started laughing.

"Okay, that was a spectacular end, to a spectacular performance. How about that America, that is why this is called reality TV, did anyone expect that to happen?" cried Zach, as the crowd continued to scream and clap wildly. "Well let's head over to the "kiss and cry" and see what the judges had to say about your performance," said the host.

We headed to our seats in the Kiss and Cry area, I was

clinging to both Ron and Elena's hands as we waited for the verdict. The first two judges told us they loved our performance, they thought the team did a great job going above and beyond all their previous performances. Hal Luther was up next to comment, of course he was the harshest of the judges, I was almost holding my breath I was so anxious.

"This was one of the most incredible performances I have ever seen, amateur or professional. If someone had told me weeks ago that Lane Jensen could make this big clumsy football player into a world class caliber skater, I would have thought they were daft," he cried.

"Like everyone else, I was completely blown away when the two of you came riding out on an elephant, but I have to say my favorite part was the end, when Ron kissed Lane. I was moved to tears," said Hal, dabbing his eyes with a handkerchief.

I was sitting there giving Hal an embarrassed smile. Ron had his arm around me and he squeezed me and kissed the top of my head.

"As a team, you all have an unbelievable magical together. I wish you the most happiness," said Hal, giving two thumbs up.

"Wow, can you believe it? Hal Luther can be a nice guy," said the announcer.

"Hey, I've gotten a bum wrap all these years. When I have something nice to say, I say it. Unfortunately I don't often have something nice to say," said Hal.

"Okay ladies and gentleman, the moment you've been waiting for. Elena Denkova and Ron Brannon get their scores, right after this," said the announcer.

I rolled my eyes, this was a taping, it wasn't being filmed live. I hated all this putzing around. I knew they did it all for the drama, but I was sweating it, we weren't filming live here!

"Ladies and gentlemen, welcome back. Before we left, the judges were preparing to reveal their scores for team Jensen, retired professional football player Ron Brannon and his partner, professional skater Elena Denkova. Judges, please reveal your scores."

I watched as each judge revealed their score, ten, ten and ten. I was beside myself with joy, we had won! Ron, Elena and I were all attempting to hug each other, but we were too excited so we were essentially bouncing off of each other's chests. I finally hugged and kissed Elena, then Ron caught me in a tight embrace and kissed me passionately while the audience howled in delight.

Zach Reid came over and put his arm around me. "Now that the show is officially over, America wants to know the truth. For the past several months, everyone here has been under the impression that you and our producer Jorge Broussard were an item, but it is becoming evident to me now, that might be a false assumption," said Zach, flashing me a sly smile.

"I love Jorge so much, I love working with Jorge, but we are only friends," I told him.

Jorge smiled at me and waved at me from across the room.

"Well Lane Jensen, your team has scored a perfect thirty points, and you have blown the entire world away by bringing a 9,000 pound Indian elephant onto the ice. I am pleased to announce that team Jensen is our winner!" said Zach, beaming proudly.

With that, the immense crowd began surging toward us and suddenly everyone was crowding around us, hugging us and congratulating us. The crowd was completely engulfing us and soon security showed up to try and usher all the excess people from the judging area. The producers were trying to get the rest of the taping done, but it was almost impossible with the huge, surging crowd.

Soon the area was mostly cleared and the announcer approached us again with his microphone. He explained to us that they were merely going to do some closing comments on the show and a few other miscellaneous type things.

Zach was approaching us and he had his arm around Jorge.

"I have just been speaking with our executive producer Jorge Broussard and he has just told me that our show has been approved by the network to run for another season," said Zach.

The crowd erupted into a roar of shouts and applause. I was straining to hear what was being said, the arena was so loud and echoing.

"Unfortunately, when the next season airs, I will be quite busy working on a show I have already been contracted for, in New Zealand," said Zach. I was staring at him blankly, wondering where he was going with this.

"Our executive producer Jorge Broussard, has come up with a fabulous idea. He would like it very much if we had a team, a host and hostess next season. One would be a professional athlete, of course, and the other would be a professional skater. That way, the audience could get a perspective, from both sides.

The network already has two very popular personalities in mind already. Jorge wanted me to ask this question on the air tonight. Ron Brannon and Lane Jensen, will you host the next season of "Fire on Ice"? asked the host.

I was staring at him blankly, I wasn't sure that he was serious. Then I saw Jorge's face, he was beaming at me, and I knew it was true, he didn't want me to leave, and he was offering the job to Ron and I.

Suddenly Ron had his arms around me and was gazing down into my eyes.

"What do you say, do you want to co host this show with me next season?" asked Ron, his sly smile was infectious.

"Do you want to do it?" I asked, I wasn't sure that hosting this show was quite his style, or mine for that matter.

"Here's my only condition. I'll only do it, if you do it," said Ron.

"Okay, I'll do it," I said, nodding at him.

"Hey all right! cried Zach, excitedly. I now pronounce the two of you co hosts, you may kiss the co host," he told us with a smile.

Ron lifted me up in his arms and kissed me again. I was so happy, I had waited so long for the show to be over so I could let him kiss me. It was even better, now that he had word that his divorce was final.

In moments the crowd was surging around us again. Usually being in a crowd like that totally freaked me out. I would get claustrophobic and have a bit of a meltdown, but for some reason just having Ron's arm around me was strangely comforting, I felt like I was safe for the first time in my life. I plunged into the crowd and our sea of admirers fearlessly. I'd been welcomed home to Hollywood with open arms!

## ABOUT THE AUTHOR

Jean Stanberry lives in the Rocky Mountains of northwest Montana with her husband of twenty three years, Gary and their two children, Ryan and Lauren. Jean is an avid figure skater who began her career skating for Europe's "Holiday on Ice" with her pairs partner Jack Adams. Since that time, Jean has kept active as a coach, choreographer and production consultant. She has also been a contributor on several international figure skating blog sites and has written articles for "Fire and Ice" magazine. She works full time as a surgical nurse and she enjoys, ice skating, hiking, kayaking and cross country skiing in her free time.

Made in the USA
Lexington, KY
26 April 2013